THE WORD HAS GOTTEN OUT—
SHOT, AND THE ENTIRE STANLEY
HASTINGS MYSTERY SERIES, ARE
"VERY FUNNY, VERY SMART"   —*Booklist*

"Hall uses a smooth narrative style to make
Hastings seem extraordinarily ordinary and the
secondary characters believable."
—*Chicago Tribune*

"Mr. Hall wins our respect for Stanley's
intelligence and perseverance—qualities that give
him the edge over his bolder and brawnier
competition. And the last laugh too."
—*New York Times Book Review*

"For mystery fans, there is plenty to ponder. For
action fans, Stanley gets into enough fixes to suit
the most rabid reader. For folks who want a good
book to sit down with of an evening, they will do
well with this edition, and this series."
—*Lincoln Journal-Star*

"Hall's observations of life in New York are
interesting enough that a novel with Hastings at the
center would be worth reading even if there were
no mystery."   —*The Drood Review of Mystery*

"The charm of Stanley Hastings lies in his
chummy, loquacious, self-deprecating
commentary."   —*Washington Post*

P9-DVY-430

SHOT

by Parnell Hall

AN ONYX BOOK

ONYX
Published by the Penguin Group
Penguin Books USA Inc., 375 Hudson Street,
New York, New York 10014, U.S.A.
Penguin Books Ltd, 27 Wrights Lane, London W8 5TZ, England
Penguin Books Australia Ltd, Ringwood, Victoria, Australia
Penguin Books Canada Ltd, 10 Alcorn Avenue,
Toronto, Ontario, Canada M4V 3B2
Penguin Books (N.Z.) Ltd, 182–190 Wairau Road, Auckland 10, New
Zealand

Penguin Books Ltd, Registered Offices:
Harmondsworth, Middlesex, England

Published by Onyx, an imprint of New American Library, a division
of Penguin Books USA Inc. This is an authorized reprint of a hard-
cover edition published by Donald I. Fine, Inc.

First Onyx Printing, February, 1993
10 9 8 7 6 5 4 3 2 1

PUBLISHER'S NOTE
This novel is a work of fiction. Names, characters, places and inci-
dents are either the product of the author's imagination or are used
fictitiously. Any resemblance to actual events, locales, organizations
or persons, living or dead, and beyond the intent of either the author
or publisher is entirely coincidental.

Books are available at quantity discounts when used to promote products
or services. For information please write to Premium Marketing Division,
Penguin Books USA Inc., 375 Hudson Street, New York, New York 10014.

For Jim and Franny

1

I GOT A CLIENT.

I do that now—take on clients, I mean. I don't even try to talk 'em out of it anymore. I don't tell 'em I'm not a real detective, or at least what people think of as a real detective, which is the kind you see on TV. I don't point out that I'm basically nonaggressive, never had a fist fight in my life, and don't even carry a gun.

Nor do I point out that the majority of my work as a private eye consists of chasing ambulances for the law firm of Rosenberg and Stone, which involves mainly interviewing accident victims and photographing cracks in the sidewalk. While this is real private eye work, it's not the kind you see on TV and I doubt if anyone would be particularly impressed. So I don't bother to mention it.

And I don't sweat my obligation to Rosenberg and Stone anymore, either. When a client comes along with a case I wanna handle, I just call Richard Rosenberg and tell him I won't be available for a while. I've finally learned that while Richard may squawk a bit—make that one hell of a lot—he's not about to fire me. After all, I'm his senior investigator. And by a wide margin. Aside from me, he's never had one last as long as six months. I've been there for more years than I want to think of, especially since the detective work was supposed to be a temporary job to tide me over during the lean years in my writing career. It tided me over all right. Now I'm on the wrong side of forty, going on senile, with no immediate career prospects in sight.

At any rate, over the years Richard and I have more or less come to an understanding. I understand he's never gonna give me a raise over the ten bucks an hour and thirty cents a mile the cheap son of a bitch pays me, and he understands I got a wife and kid to feed and when other work comes along I'm gonna take it. Not that he won't piss and moan and give me a hard time about it. It's just that when he does I let it roll off my back. Just like he lets it roll off his back every time I bring up the unobtainable raise.

At any rate, Stanley Hastings Detective Agency is taking on clients now. Which means I am, since my agency's a one man show. And like I said, I don't do anything to discourage 'em anymore. I just listen to the story, take down the information, nod my head and say, "Two hundred bucks a day plus expenses."

I been thinkin' about saying two-fifty.

2

HER NAME WAS MELISSA FORD. No relation to the past president. At least, I assume no relation—actually I didn't ask her. But if she were, I imagine she'd have brought it up.

But maybe not. Melissa Ford was a shy and timid person, perhaps even more than me. Which made me fairly comfortable during the interview. Made me feel like I was actually in charge.

She met me at my office on West 47th Street, the one room, hole in the wall affair that used to house my father-in-law's plastic bag company, and which he still carried on the company books but allowed me to use for my detective work—which was the only reason I had an office at all, otherwise the rent would have been prohibitive. She was standing there when I showed up at nine o'clock to pick up the mail. Any other time she would have missed me. I don't hang out in the office much. I'm out most of the day, chasing down accident cases.

Melissa Ford was one of the mousiest women I'd

ever met. She was small and frail, but that wasn't just it—I've know many women her size who were tigers. Not her. She had short-clipped hair, curled under, forming a lopsided, brown halo around her head. She wore narrow-lensed glasses with pointy corners, slightly down on her nose, and she kept her chin down and her head tucked in, and peered up over her glasses, birdlike, when she looked at me, which wasn't often.

As to how she was dressed, well, I'm about as good at describing women's clothes as I am at discussing German opera, which is to say, not at all. At any rate, she was wearing a print dress of some sort, which might have been gingham or calico or something like that, if I had any idea what those things meant. Whatever it was, it was faded and unbecoming, and did nothing to enhance a figure that, to the best I could determine, was flat as a board. Despite that, she was wearing a white bra, the shoulder straps of which occasionally showed through the neck hole of the gingham or calico or whatever print dress she was wearing, which seemed to cause her no end of embarrassment, 'cause she was constantly fiddling with the shoulders of the dress and adjusting it over the straps.

We were seated in my office. I had determined that she was indeed waiting for me, opened the door, uncluttered a chair for her, seated her down and begun the interview, which, I realized early on, I was going to have to carry myself.

"Now, Miss Ford," I said, once I'd gotten the matter of identity squared away. "What can I do for you?"

The question seemed to terrify her. She dropped her gaze to the ground, then glanced around the office, looking anywhere but at me. "It's my boyfriend," she said.

Her voice was so soft I had to lean in to catch it. Even then, I wasn't sure I'd heard her right. Somehow I couldn't imagine Melissa Ford with a boyfriend.

"Boyfriend?" I said.

"Yes," she said, again not meeting my eyes, giving the impression that having a boyfriend was some great sin of which she ought to be ashamed.

I waited for more but it didn't come. Instead, she reached up and tugged the left shoulder of her dress over her bra strap, then hunched her shoulders together and hugged herself, as if as a gesture of modesty after the damning admission of having a boyfriend.

"What about him?" I said. "Is he in trouble?"

That startled her. She put up her hands, and even raised her eyes. "No, no," she said. "Nothing like that. David wouldn't do anything like that."

"David?"

"Yes."

She looked down at the floor again.

Good lord. This was like pulling teeth. I summarized, trying to prompt her. "All right," I said. "You came to see me about your boyfriend, David. What is it that you want?"

Her thin lips had been set in a straight line. Now they curved down at the corners, like a cartoon drawing of an unhappy person.

"I feel so guilty," she said.

"Guilty?"

"Yes. For being here."

The situation became clear. Her boyfriend, David, was stepping out on her, and she wanted to hire me to verify the fact.

I must say, my sympathies were all with David. Why

he would be stepping out on this woman was not one of the great mysteries of the modern world. Why he'd ever hooked up with her to begin with, was.

"Let me get this straight," I said. "You think David's seeing another woman?"

Her eyes widened and her jaw dropped open. "Why do you say that?"

"Well, I—"

"You don't even know David. Do you?"

"No. Of course not."

"Then why would you say that?"

"Well—"

"That's a horrible thing to say."

"I'm sorry," I said. "I shouldn't have jumped to that conclusion. But when a woman consults me about her boyfriend, that's usually the case."

That was pretty ballsy of me to say, since I couldn't recall a time a woman had *ever* consulted me about her boyfriend.

But Melissa Ford didn't know that. She took my statement at face value. She also took it as a personal rebuke. She looked down, fidgeted, and then hurried to cover her right bra strap, which had become visible in the heat of the moment.

"I'm sorry," she said. "I'm nervous. I've never done this before."

I wasn't sure if she meant consult a private detective, or have a boyfriend.

"No problem," I told her. "Take your time, and then tell me what you want."

She did. She took a few moments to compose herself, then raised her eyes and spoke. She didn't raise 'em as far as eye level, and she seemed to address a corner of my desk, but at least she got on with it.

"My boyfriend, David. David Melrose. I've been seeing him for two months now. I like him very much. That's why I feel so bad about being here. But I need to know."

"Know what?" I prompted.

"If he's serious."

Once again the situation became clear, only this time I was right about it. It was something I'd read about somewhere, probably, I must confess, in the *New York Post*. Whether it was fear of AIDS, whether it was natural prudence, or whether it was just another yuppie trend like VCRs, CDs and fax machines, more and more women were hiring private detectives to check out their sexual partners before making a commitment.

I can't say I thoroughly approved of the practice. On the other hand, I can't say I thoroughly approve of a good deal of the ambulance chasing I do either. At any rate, the bottom line was I needed the work.

And in Melissa Ford's case, there actually seemed to be a point to it. I hate saying that, but there you are. You see, it turned out she happened to have some money. Not multi-million, hold-the-phone, bug-your-eyes-out-of-your-head money, but a comfortable enough nest egg to assure her she would never have to worry about working again. Naturally, she needed to know if her ardent young suitor was interested in her or the cash.

Which is what I hate to say, particularly the "naturally." But that's the way I saw it. In mousy, plain Melissa Ford's case, it didn't seem a bad bet that Davey-baby was after the loot.

Now I know that's a horribly sexist thing to say— the woman's unattractive, how could anyone like her for herself? Couldn't this guy just like her for her mind?

Yes, he could. And maybe she likes him for his. And maybe they get on great together. Maybe they converse freely. And maybe when they do, she even looks in his eyes instead of at the doorknob. And maybe this was a match made in heaven, and the best thing I could possibly do for Melissa Ford and David Melrose would be butt out and let 'em get on with it.

Yeah, maybe.

And maybe some day I'll actually write the great American novel and it will get published and I'll be able to quit the private detective business altogether and get by on just my writing.

But I wouldn't bet on it.

3

You mustn't judge me too harshly.

No, not about the sexist stuff—go ahead and blast me for that, I got it coming. No, I mean for my greed.

See, I took the Melissa Ford case. With a five hundred dollar advance—two hundred bucks a day for a two day minimum, plus a hundred for expenses. All straightforward and aboveboard. No problem with that.

The greedy part, the not entirely kosher part, the part where you mustn't judge me too harshly is, having taken Melissa Ford's money for two days' work, I didn't feel it had to be exclusive. I mean, checking out this guy's background wasn't gonna be a rough job. There was no reason to get all excited about it, go rushing around like a lunatic and turn down other work.

What I'm trying to tell you is, even though I'd worked it out with Richard Rosenberg that if something came up I could call him and tell him I wouldn't be available for a while, just because I was *able* to do that, didn't mean I *had* to. And the thing was, I already had an assignment from Rosenberg and Stone to go see a potential client in the Bronx at eleven o'clock that morning. I saw no reason to give it back.

Now, I know that's excessive greed. I already had two hundred bucks from Melissa Ford, so did I really need another thirty from Rosenberg and Stone for a three hour signup the same day? Was it morally and ethically right for me to take it?

Well, probably not. But you gotta understand. Living in New York City isn't cheap. And I got a wife and kid to feed. And my work for Rosenberg and Stone isn't steady, I usually average about thirty hours a week. And a client like Melissa Ford doesn't come along every day, or even every week. And I'm always behind on the rent, the telephone, my son Tommie's tuition or Con Ed. So every little bit is needed and every little bit helps. So I wasn't *really* giving Melissa Ford short shrift, and what I was doing wasn't *really* that bad.

At least, that's what I told myself as I drove up to the Bronx to interview Joe Oliver, who had fallen on a cracked sidewalk and broken his arm.

Joe Oliver lived in one of those neighborhoods in the South Bronx that you would never go to but always see on TV, usually under the heading DRUG BUST or COP SHOT or often a combination of the two, an undercover cop shot as the result of a drug bust gone bad. Oliver's street looked like a war zone. Half the buildings torn down, leaving rubble-filled empty lots. Some of the buildings gutted but still standing. Nestled in among these, a few buildings still occupied. Not that the gutted buildings weren't—junkies and winos hung out on the steps of several of them. It was the type of neighborhood that used to terrify me when

I started my job. Actually it still does. It's just that I've gotten used to it, that this is my cross to bear, to go into places like this and be scared out of my mind. And I know rationally that I'm pretty safe doing it, that no one's gonna mess with me. 'Cause scared as I am of the junkies hanging out, they're even more scared of me. Because without meaning to be, I am a symbol of authority. I am a white man in a suit and tie. And in neighborhoods like that, a white man in a suit and tie is a cop. And in buildings like Joe Oliver's, junkies part before me like the Red Sea. When that happens, I know I've been taken for The Man, and unless I accidentally walk in on a drug deal, I'm relatively safe. This knowledge does not stop me from having a nervous breakdown every time it happens.

Aside from where he lived, the Joe Oliver case was a piece of cake. He'd fallen on the sidewalk outside his building and broken his arm, and now he wanted to sue the city of New York. I had him sign retainer forms, employing Rosenberg and Stone to act in his behalf in the suit, which cost him nothing unless he got a settlement, in which case Rosenberg would get a third, which the city of New York would pay. Which was fine with him, as it was with all of Rosenberg's clients. Filing an accident claim was a no-risk gamble—if they won they made out, and if they lost they didn't pay. It was no wonder the city's courts were clogged with civil suits, I, of course, being a prime contributor to the problem.

I filled out a fact sheet on Joe Oliver, had him sign all the necessary forms, took a picture of the cast on his arm, and then went outside with him to shoot pictures of the broken sidewalk. He was happy to go out with me, saying he felt safe having me along. I didn't express the opinion, but I felt the same about him. Whipping out my camera in front of a bunch of junkies is never my idea of a good time. I figure they might see it as half a gram. I also figure when they see I'm packin' a camera instead of a gun, they might reevaluate that cop determination.

At any rate, Joe and I stuck together for moral support, no junkies hassled us, and I fired off a whole roll of shots of the sidewalk outside his building, which was in bad enough repair to have felled a whole army of Joe Olivers. I finished the assignment, shook hands with Joe, and made for my trusty Toyota, which was parked right out front, and which had never been stolen in neighborhoods like this thanks to the two hundred and fifty dollar code alarm I'd had installed in it. I opened the door, punched in the code for the alarm, started the motor.

And my beeper went off.

Damn.

The office was beeping me with another case. Ordinarily that would have been great. But I had Melissa Ford to take care of.

Here's where you have to bear with me. I was gonna turn the case down. Honest.

I cruised around the Bronx, found a pay phone that hadn't been gutted and called the office with every intention of turning the assignment down.

But Richard wasn't there. He was in court. The only one there was Wendy or Janet, Richard's two switchboard girls who happened to have identical voices, so you never knew who you were dealing with. And whichever it was, Wendy or Janet, she wasn't about to listen. Richard hadn't told her I was taking time off, Richard hadn't told her I was turning down cases, if she was gonna let me do that, she was gonna have to hear it from Richard. Which, of course, couldn't happen with him in court. And, Wendy/Janet pointed out, the case was in Harlem, I was just across the bridge in the South Bronx, and what was the big deal?

Now, I know all that's no excuse, but it was easier to do it than argue, and the long and the short of it was I took the case. And, I must admit, it did occur to me, I knock this off real quick, put two hours on my pay sheet and wind up with a two-hundred-and-fifty-dollar day.

I hopped in the car, went over the Willis/Third Avenue Bridge, and drove to the address on Adam Clayton Powell.

It was another combat zone. The building I wanted was no worse than Joe Oliver's, but certainly no better. There was a bunch of teenage kids hanging out in front, which boded ill—it was late September, and by rights, they should have been in school. Plus there was the usual number of disreputable types hanging out in front of the building and prowling the street.

None of this was enough to dissuade the fearless investigator. I parked my car in front of the building, set the code alarm, grabbed my briefcase, put my heart in my mouth and marched determinedly up to the door.

They gave way, but not like at Joe Oliver's. Teenagers don't fear the law the way that junkies do. They figure being underage gives them a certain immunity, and in a way they figure right. And they're unpredictable on the one hand, and stupid on the other, like the teenaged girls who terrorized the Upper West Side for a while by sticking pins in white women. Or like the pack that attacked the Central Park jogger. Wilding, a new word, a new concept, what a great idea.

Anyway, they made me nervous, and I went inside watching my back and hotfooted it up the stairs looking for Apartment Four. None of the apartments had numbers, natch, but by counting I located the most likely door and knocked on it. After a few moments, it was opened by a young black woman, attractive and thirtysomething. She looked tense and anxious, but not surprised to see me, and I figured I'd hit paydirt.

"Raheem Webb live here?" I said. "I'm from the lawyer's office.'

She nodded. "Yes, yes. Come in."

She ushered me into a clean but modestly furnished living room. Actually, "modestly furnished" was a charitable assessment. The couch and chairs appeared to have been gathered off the street. I sat down on the couch, opened my briefcase.

"Shall I get Raheem?" she said.

"Why don't we get the paperwork out of the way first?" I said. (Wendy/Janet had told me Raheem Webb was ten years old—in such cases, the less the client had to be involved the better.) "I take it you're Raheem's mother."

"Yes. I'm sorry. I'm Sheila Webb."

"I'm Mr. Hastings from the lawyer's office. Let's go over the background information, then we'll get Raheem."

I pulled out a fact sheet and, with her help, filled in Raheem's name, address, birth date and Social Security number, then filled in Sheila Webb's birth date, Social Security number and telephone number as mother.

"Does his father live with you?" I asked.

It was a question I used to find terribly rude. But it was actually one that saved embarrassment. When I started the job, I used to just ask the mother for the kid's father. I soon found with poor people, in many cases I was dealing with single mothers, and by asking for details on the father I was getting half-remembered addresses and phone numbers and never-remembered birth dates and Social Security numbers for some long-since departed individual who obviously had nothing to do with the current family structure. Compared to that, the simple, direct question was painless. Particularly since I had perfected the rap that followed the negative response. When Sheila Webb said, "No," I came in smoothly with, "Then *you* will be responsible for signing all of the forms in this case. You understand your son Raheem is actually the client, but since he is underage, you are filing suit in his behalf."

She nodded. "I understand."

"Fine," I said. "Now, I'll need to hear it from Raheem, but why don't you give me the background of his accident?"

Her eyes shifted slightly and she said, "He fell."

That was strange. She hadn't been fazed at all by the father-live-with-you question. But the question about the accident bothered her.

Which bothered me. I'd had cases before where the parent had sued in the child's behalf, and everything had not looked entirely kosher. Sometimes, what a parent claimed was a trip and fall could actually turn out to be child abuse.

In this case, I couldn't see it. I couldn't imagine this nice, intelligent woman sitting opposite me abusing her child. But it was always possible she had some boyfriend or other who thought it was macho to keep the kid in line.

It was none of my business, and there was nothing I could do about it, but I caught it and I didn't like it.

"I see," I said. "And where did he fall?"

"On the street. Outside. You'll have to ask Raheem about it."

"You weren't there?"

"No."

"When was this?"

"Yesterday."

"What time?"

"Yesterday afternoon. About three-thirty. I was here. He came upstairs. Told me he fell down. His face was all bloody."

"You take him to the hospital?"

"Yes."

"What hospital?"

"Harlem Hospital."

"Ambulance come for him?"

"No. Car service."

"There were no police on the scene?"

"No."

"Any witnesses?"

"I don't think so. You'll have to ask Raheem."

"What were his injuries?"

"His forehead was cut." She indicated with her finger. "From here to here."

"Were there stitches?"

"Yes."

"How many?"

"Forty-four."

"Forty-four stitches?"

"Yes."

"They keep him overnight in the hospital?"

"No. They sent him home."

I nodded, but I wasn't happy. Forty-four stitches was a hell of a result from a trip and fall. This was looking more and more like child abuse.

"All right," I said. "I guess I'd better talk to Raheem."

She nodded, got up and went through a door into the back of the apartment. After a few moments I could hear her talking, though I couldn't make out the words. Then her voice was joined by another—high pitched, whiny, reluctant. I envisioned the scene without seeing it—the kid lying in bed, the mother prodding him to get up, the kid protesting.

She was back moments later, looking somewhat apologetic. "He'll be right here. He's getting his pants on."

"I understand. I got a kid of my own. I'm always waiting on him."

Her smile looked somewhat forced. She was plainly nervous.

Or was she? I mean, come on. Maybe I was imagining it. Wasn't it natural to be nervous with a stranger in your house and an unpredictable ten-year-old who was keeping him waiting? This is none of your business, just get the job done so you can concentrate on Melissa Ford.

There were footsteps and we both looked up.

Raheem Webb stood in the doorway. He was a skinny kid, who appeared to be in that awkward phase where his limbs were growing faster than he could learn to control them. He was maybe five foot six goin' on seven feet. His skin was coal black and smooth. He had nice features, like his mom. What I could see of them, anyway. His head was wrapped round and round with white bandages. It covered his entire forehead and his left eye. The white gauze made a sharp contrast against the black skin, made the bandage seem even more extensive than it was.

I smiled. "Hi, Raheem. I'm Mr. Hastings, from the lawyer's office." I shifted over on the couch. "You look like you've had quite a fall. Come here. Tell me about it."

He hesitated in the doorway.

"Raheem," his mother said, impatiently. "Go sit with the man."

He gave her a look, rolled his one visible eye, then shambled over and flopped down on the couch.

"Now," I said, "what can you tell me about the accident?"

He shrugged his shoulders. "Fell down."

"Where'd you fall down?"

He jerked his thumb. "Outside."

Just like Joe Oliver.

Maybe.

"In the street?"

"Yeah."

"The street or the sidewalk?"

A pause. "Sidewalk."

"Where? Right out front here?"

"Yeah."

"Why'd you fall down?"

He frowned. At least I think he frowned—I couldn't see his forehead with the bandage. The corners of his mouth turned down. He gave me a one-eyed squint, but said nothing.

"Raheem," his mother prompted, "answer the man."

He shrugged again. "I jus' fell."

"Yeah, but did you trip on something? Slip on something? Was the sidewalk broken?"

"Yeah," he said. "The sidewalk."

"It was broken?"

"Yeah."

"Yeah," I said. "That's what I thought. So the sidewalk was broken. Can you show me where that was?"

"Why?"

I reached in my briefcase and pulled out my camera. "I have to take pictures of it. For your case."

"Oh."

"So can you show me where it was?"

Shrug. "Guess so."

His mother let out a breath in exasperation. "Raheem. The man wants you to go show him. Now get your shoes on."

"Aw, mom."

She pointed at the bedroom. "Raheem. Go."

He got up and shuffled into the bedroom.

She looked at me. "Really," she said. "He's a good boy. Just lazy."

Yeah, I thought. And mighty reluctant to show me the crack that tripped him.

Raheem came back with a pair of worn tennis sneakers. He flopped back down on the couch next to me and began pulling them on over his bare feet.

A high-pitched "beep, beep, beep" filled the room.

Damn. The office. Of all the luck. I was having a hard enough time dealing with Raheem Webb without being interrupted. And the last thing I needed was Wendy/Janet giving me yet another case I didn't have time to handle.

I reached on my belt and pushed the button to shut my beeper off.

But nothing happened.

The damn thing kept beeping.

I'm a slow take, and I actually pushed the button again before I realized it wasn't my beeper.

Before I saw the sick look on Sheila Webb's face.

Before I saw Raheem Webb fumbling under his T-shirt and suddenly the noise stopped.

That's when it hit me.

Shit.

Raheem Webb was wearing a beeper. And it seemed unlikely that ten-year-old Raheem Webb was a doctor or lawyer or private detective like me, a professional man who needed to wear a beeper for his job. No, the beeper meant he was one of those heartbreaking kids you read about in the *Post*—a crack runner, a mule, a kid carrying dope for a pusher.

I felt sick. But it was none of my business, and there was nothing I could do. Hell, even a cop couldn't do anything. There was no law against wearing a beeper. Kids can walk right by cops with beepers hanging off their belts in plain view and the cops can't do a damn thing about it. Not unless they catch 'em with the drugs. Which somehow they never seem to do. Well, they do, but not enough to matter. And when they do, so what, the kid's a juvenile anyway. And the kids never rat on the pushers. Not if they want to stay healthy. Not if they want to stay alive.

I looked at Sheila Webb and I could see the pain and embarrassment in her face. So that was what she was edgy about. Not child abuse. This.

I wanted to do something to help her. But, as I said, there was nothing I could do. Anyway, hell, it wasn't my problem, it wasn't my fault. Jesus Christ, I shouldn't have been there to begin with, I didn't want the assignment, why the fuck did Richard have to pick this day over all others to be in court, damn it to hell, it just wasn't fair.

Suddenly, I just wanted to get out of there. That was the quick and easy solution—be less painful for all of us. A typical Hastings decision—the coward's way out.

I stuck my clipboard back in my briefcase, brought the interview to a close. I picked up my camera and snapped off a few shots of Raheem's bandaged face, then took him downstairs to shoot the scene of his accident.

Having one eye didn't slow him down any, or maybe he was just eager to get away from mom after the beeper bit, but when I said, "Let's go," he got up and scooted out the door. I grabbed my briefcase and followed him out, mumbling something at his poor mother. I still couldn't quite catch up, and I was only halfway down the stairs when he went out the front door.

I'd just reached the bottom of the stairs when I heard a loud voice from outside, "Hey, nigger, I beep you, where the fuck you been?"

I went out the front door. Raheem was at the bottom of the front steps, standing with the group of kids I'd seen on my way in. Then, I'd just seen them as a potential threat. Now, I noticed two of them also were wearing beepers.

But it wasn't any of them whose voice I'd heard. 'Cause they, like Raheem, were all looking out in the street. Naturally, I looked too.

Standing there was a large black man, about twenty-five years of age, muscular, a skin-head, with a moustache and goatee and scowl on his face that made my stomach jump through hoops.

He saw me at the same time I saw him. His eyes widened, then narrowed, then flicked to Raheem. The scowl that had been frightening before was murderous now.

"Motherfucker!" he growled.

Then he turned on his heel and walked away. Not slow, but not fast either. Head high, arrogant, insolent.

Jesus Christ.

Like I said, it was none of my business on the one hand, and there was nothing I could do on the other.

And I said nothing about the incident. I just walked over to a rather shaken looking Raheem and asked him to show me where he fell. After a few moments, he showed me a crack in the sidewalk and I duly shot a roll of film of it.

Raheem had no problem pointing out a crack in the sidewalk—the block was sure full of 'em. And it didn't matter which crack he picked. He knew and I knew no crack in the sidewalk had ever tripped him.

After the scene I'd just witnessed, it didn't take any genius to figure out where he'd got those forty-four stitches in his head.

4

"HE'S AFTER HER MONEY," ALICE SAID.

I didn't want to hear it. I was tired, frustrated and angry. It was later that night, and Alice and I had just finished a spirited argument about practicing birth control. Don't get me wrong—we're both for it. We have no religious, ethical or moral problems with birth control. Our son Tommie is all the children we can possibly afford to raise, and we have long ago come to the agreement that we are never going to have any more. So the argument, as always, was not over whether we *should* practice birth control—we both agree we should. The argument was over whether we should practice it *tonight*.

I, as always, was in favor. Alice cast the dissenting vote. I think basically that's the difference between the sexes. Alice, with the passing years, has become mature, calm, adult. I, on the other hand, seem to retain my adolescent instincts.

I suspect that this disparity between the sexes is one of the causes of mid-life crisis, one of the things that drives men my age to start running around chasing hopelessly younger women. Don't get me wrong—I have no idea to go out chasing teenyboppers or whatever the hell they call them these days. No, basically, I'd just like to win the argument a little more often.

This night I'd lost, which was not surprising. It was that sort of day. What with the Raheem Webb case, which I could do nothing about, and the Melissa Ford case, which I hadn't had time to work on, I was in a really foul mood. And having just lost the great birth control debate, it really riled me to hear Alice say that about my client Melissa Ford.

Because that was my view too. And it was, as I've said, a wholly sexist view, and one I chided myself for. And now here was Alice expressing it. And what was really frustrating as hell was, Alice is so good at arguments, I knew if I called her on it, told her what she'd expressed was a totally sexist opinion, she'd be able to talk her way out of it and prove that it wasn't.

I just couldn't help myself. I frowned. "Why do you say that?"

"Come on," Alice said. "The way you describe the woman, why else would he be interested in her?"

"Maybe he likes her for her mind," I said innocently.

Alice turned on me. "What an obnoxious, sexist thing to say."

My mouth fell open. "What?"

"You heard me."

"That's not a sexist thing to say. Just the opposite."

Alice shook her head. "No, no, no. Not the way you said it."

"What's wrong with how I said it?"

"You were ridiculing the concept. You didn't mean

that, you were just saying it to show me how stupid it sounds.''

"*Does* it sound stupid?''

"Of course.''

I don't know if I sounded stupid, but I sure felt stupid. Alice always reduces my brain to Jell-O. "Wait a minute. Time out,'' I said. "You're the one saying if this woman isn't attractive the guy must be interested in her for her money.''

Alice smiled. "I'm saying that based on your assessment of her. You're the one who told me this woman had nothing to recommend her except money.''

"No, I just said she wasn't physically attractive.''

"Didn't you say she couldn't even look at you and carry on a simple conversation?''

"That's part of what made her unattractive.''

"No, no. That's part of her personality. Her mind. The very concept you were ridiculing. How can he like her for her mind if she *has* no mind?''

"She has a mind.''

"Not the way you tell it. You describe a mindless nit who can barely get the words out.''

"That's not fair.''

"Why not?''

"You're making all kinds of value judgments on the woman, and you don't even know her.''

"I know one thing.''

"What's that?''

"She hired you.''

"Thanks a lot.''

"Not you personally. I mean, she hired a detective.''

"Yeah. So?''

"So that's the bottom line. Any woman who would

25

hire a private detective to check on her boyfriend and see if he's after her money, he's probably after her money.''

''You're in good form tonight.''

''Stop that.''

''And you don't seem the least bit tired.''

''I'm exhausted. I'm going to sleep.''

With that, Alice rolled over and buried her head in the pillow, effectively ending the conversation.

Leaving me alone with my thoughts. I didn't like my thoughts. I picked up the remote control and switched on the Carson show.

I'd missed the opening monologue—wouldn't you know it, that's the part I like best—and Jay Leno was guest-hosting and not doing his headline bit so there was no sketch and he had already started in on the guests. First up was Armand Assante, which is one of those names that always sounds more like a crime than a person—''You are charged with armand assante in the first degree, how do you plead?'' ''Not guilty, Your Honor.'' (The charge was later plea-bargained down to a misdemeanor count of patty hearst.)

I watched Armand Assante claim he never did talk shows and show a clip from his new picture, then switched the set off, switched the light off, and lay there in the dark.

I was really depressed. There was the Raheem Webb situation, which I could do nothing about. That I could deal with. In my work for Richard, I came up against a lot of heart-breaking situations I could do nothing about. And I'd learned to harden myself, push them from my mind and get on to something else. Not admirable, to be sure, but not that hard to do when you're working three to four cases a day. New problems arise, take focus, shove yesterday's bummer onto the back burner where it simmers away, recedes and is forgotten.

But the Melissa Ford case. That was the real bummer. Distasteful as it might be, I had taken it on because I wanted the money, and I hadn't done it.

Because I wanted the money. That was the problem. That was what was hanging me up. I had two hundred bucks of Melissa Ford's money for the work I'd done today, and I hadn't done any work.

What did I do, give it back? Say, today's a washout, I start the case tomorrow? Melissa Ford was gonna be in my office first thing Monday morning to hear my report. What could I do? Say, I only had time to work one day on this, come back tomorrow? Or say, I only had time to work one day on this, here's two hundred bucks back and here's your report? Or did I say nothing at all, do one day's work for her and keep the money?

I'm sure there are people who would not hesitate to do that, and I had to admit, boy, what a temptation it was. But I have to live with myself. And if the truth be known, I do not see myself as the best of all private detectives. I don't even work much, except for Rosenberg and Stone. And if someone should hire me, even if I did all the work, I'd still have the nagging suspicion I wasn't giving full value for their dollar. So to stint on that? Not possible. Attractive though it might be.

It occurred to me I could work one day over the weekend. An unattractive proposition, but it would solve my problem. And I probably would have done it if there'd been anything I could do. But everything's closed on the weekend. At least, anything that could possibly help me. To putz around ineffectively on Saturday or Sunday just to be able to say I did it would be pretty shoddy practice. Hell, Melissa Ford had paid me for two days and expected a report by Monday. Nothing ambiguous in that. The weekend didn't count. I'd been paid for Thursday and Friday.

But that was the least of my worries. The real thing bugging me was, I'd never checked out anyone's boyfriend before, and when you came right down to it, I wasn't really sure how to go about it. I mean, even if I called Rosenberg and Stone first thing in the morning and told them not to give me any work, what the hell did I do then? I had the guy's home address and I had his work address—he was an advertising executive with one of the Madison Avenue firms. What did I do, call on him at work and ask him what his intentions were toward Melissa Ford? Probably not the smoothest of approaches. No, I needed to find out if he was married and check his credit rating.

Well, married, I go to the Bureau of Vital Statistics, right? Wherever the fuck that is. I'll look in the phone book in the morning. But credit rating? How the hell do you do that?

I had no idea.

I lay there in the dark feeling worse and worse, like I'd dug myself into an impossible hole that I was never going to get out of.

It was just as I was dropping off to sleep that it came to me.

Fred Lazar.

5

FRED LAZAR, IF THE TRUTH BE KNOWN, was the guy who'd gotten me into this whole mess in the first place. Not the Melissa Ford mess—I mean the whole private detective bit. Fred and I had gone to the same college, Goddard, and played together on the soccer team. I'd run into Fred at a party a few years back and been surprised to learn he ran a private detective agency in Manhattan. I'd been between acting and writing jobs as usual, and looking for a job-job to tide me over. And at the time detective work had sounded absolutely fascinating. It turned out, however, there was no chance of my working for Fred. His detectives all had two to three years experience at least—in fact, most of them were ex-cops. But I got to talking to Fred, and damned if he didn't get an idea.

It turned out his agency had just turned down an offer of steady employment from a law firm. The firm was cheap, and was only offering ten bucks an hour and thirty cents a mile, which wasn't worth Fred's time. He was paying more than that, for Christ's sake, which actually made it a losing proposition. But for a guy who needed a job-job and was willing to work for that kind of money, it would at least be flexible hours, and was I interested?

Well, at that point with nothing else on the horizon, I was, but I didn't feel I was qualified. Fred told me to relax, it was only ambulance chasing, there was nothing to it, he could teach me in a day.

He did, and I called Rosenberg and Stone and I got the job and the rest is history.

And now Fred Lazar was the answer. He ran a real detective agency, one that did not do just ambulance chasing but all kinds of stuff. Surveillance and investigations and security guard work and the whole bit. Fred could give me advice. More than that, his agency could do some of the work. His rates would be prohibitive, but as professional courtesy and a favor I was sure he would help. Besides, his agency had computers and modems and stuff like that, and the whole thing would be easy. The way I saw it, I'd pay Fred two hundred bucks to give me everything he could on David Melrose. And I'd put in the day chasing around getting everything *I* could on David Melrose. And Melissa Ford would get her money's worth, two days' work done in one day by two people, and the job would be finished when she came for her report. Plus she'd get better than I would have given her, because Fred was a professional and would know what to do.

And, if the job hadn't been completed in that time— which I rather doubted it would be—since I was giving her such professional work and all, she'd be inclined to keep me on for a few more days. So my two hundred dollar loss wouldn't really be a loss, it would be a gain, and she'd feel good about it, and I'd feel good about it, and it was the right thing to do and everything would work out.

Having made that decision, I felt a lot better about the whole thing. Besides, it would be nice to run into Fred Lazar again. I hadn't seen him in a while.

It turned out I hadn't seen him in a long while. When I called Lazar Investigations, I found out the number had been disconnected. I called his apartment and got an answering machine giving me a number to call during working hours. I called it and got a McDonald's. I was about to hang up when I realized I was talking to Fred.

I met Fred for breakfast at a small coffee shop on Broadway in the 70s. Fred hadn't changed much, aside from his job. He was still handsome and cocky as ever. Fred was my age, of course, but while my hair was now showing a touch of gray, his was as jet black as when he'd been in college. Fred had always fancied himself quite the ass-man, and while with a lot of guys who come off like that it's just an act, I recall Fred always did very well with the ladies. Somehow, I just couldn't imagine Fred Lazar managing a McDonald's.

"It's the snake that swallowed its own tail," Fred said. He smiled, shook his head. "Damn shame."

"I don't understand."

Fred grimaced. "You see all that shit on TV about security guards turning out to have criminal records and wind up rapin' the people they're supposed to protect?"

My eyes widened. "Was that you?"

Fred waved his hand. "No, no, no. I check my guys out, believe it or not. That was the point of the whole piece—it takes a couple of months to run the checks, a lot of firms won't wait for it, hiring guys, putting

31

them into buildings and on the street with no idea who they are. No, that wasn't none of my guys, but a bad rap like that reflects on us all."

"I see," I said. "You're saying that cut into your business so much—"

"No, no," Fred said. "That's the tip of the iceberg. That's the sensational stuff you hear about. Actually, I had no problem in that area."

"So?"

"It's the negligence shit. The stuff you do. That's the killer. You know there's doctors won't do stuff now because the malpractice insurance is too high?"

"Yeah, I know. So?"

He shrugged. "The same all around. This mass market negligence shit. Everybody's suin'. I got no security guards rapin' people, but that don't matter. People get it into their head and they sue. A guy gets mugged, it used to be he went to the cops. Now a guy gets mugged, I got a security guard working anywhere in the area, they turn around and they're suin' *me.*"

"You mean . . . ?"

"Sure I do. I do negligence work too, you know. Or I did. If the work's there, you can't turn it down. And look what happens. I'll never forget, I'm sittin' in the office one day and the investigator comes in with his cases. I thumb through them, I come upon a case. A woman gets beaten, raped in a hallway of a building. Big mess. I saw the pictures. Aside from bein' raped, she's got stitches in her forehead and a broken arm. I check out the fact sheet—there's cops on the scene, police report, ambulance and the whole bit. Solid case. No problem.

"Then I look at the blank where it says DEFENDANT

and my investigator's filled in the landlord of the building and F.L. SECURITY.''

I frowned. ''What?''

''F. L. Security. That's me. Lazar Investigations, that's my agency. But F. L. Security, that's me too. That's how I'm listed in the yellow pages under Guard and Patrol Services.

''So what's the upshot? I'm suin' myself. The snake that devoured its own tail.''

''Didn't you have insurance?''

''Sure I did. And I lost a couple of cases and the insurance company paid off. And you know what happened to my rates?'' Fred raised his thumb up in the air as high as it would go. ''Just like the medical malpractice insurance. The upshot is it's too expensive to operate and I'm outta business.''

I felt bad. And for good reason. I couldn't be sure, but with all the hundreds of cases I'd done, I had a feeling I'd filled in the words ''F. L. Security'' on a fact sheet myself.

I told Fred. He shrugged it off. ''Don't sweat it. You're suin' me. I'm suin' me. Everyone's suin' me. It'll come around. You watch out they don't start suin' *you.*''

That startled me. ''What?''

''Hey, it gets in the blood. You get some wise-ass client sues the city of New York, loses, gets pissed off and finds another attorney to sue the first attorney for losin' the suit. They sue Rosenberg for legal malpractice and they sue you for bunglin' the investigative work.''

I stared at him. ''Son of a bitch.''

Fred grinned. ''I'm kidding, of course. But what the hell you want, anyway?''

I wanted things to be back to normal, with Fred Lazar running his invsetigative business, and me not obsessed with the thought that, despite Fred's assurances, someone somewhere was gonna sue my ass off.

But that wasn't what Fred meant, so I told him about the Melissa Ford case. He listened intently, and when I finished he nodded his head.

"Well, whaddya think?" I said.

"It's a gold mine," Fred said. "If you can't milk it for a grand, you're an amateur."

"I *am* an amateur. I'm not worried about milking it, I'm worried about doing it. Frankly, I was gonna hire you to help."

"What do you need?"

"I wanna run a computer check on the guy."

Fred cocked his head. "Great. Whaddya expect to pay me for that?"

"I figured you'd have a computer setup, I was gonna ask you to run whatever you could for two hundred bucks."

"Gee, that would've made my day. And what did you expect me to run for that?"

"I don't know. Credit check. Bank accounts."

Fred winced. "You *are* an amateur. You think a computer can just tap into that?"

"I thought if you had a computer and a modem you could plug in and get anything."

"Well, not bank accounts. Private citizen's got rights too."

"So what *can* you do?"

"You can get anything that's a matter of public record. Does the guy own property, pay taxes on any land? You must have done shit like that for your negligence suits."

"Yeah, I have."

"Well, that you can do. But you gotta do it county by county and it's gonna cost you six bucks a throw. Same thing with a criminal record. If the guy's got a criminal record you can find it, but it's either gonna cost money or it's gonna take time."

I sighed. "Jesus Christ. All right, look. If it was your case, what would you do?"

"Pad my expenses and bill her through the nose."

"No, I mean really."

"I'm telling you, that's what I'd do. It's a piece of shit case, and nothing's gonna help. If this broad's like you say, the guy's after her money, but nothing you can tell her's gonna change her mind."

"Even so, I gotta do the job."

"So you wanna be a straight arrow, here's what you do. Check Vital Statistics, make sure he hasn't got a wife kickin' around somewhere. Then tail him."

"Shit."

"Hey, there's two reasons. All the paperwork in the world isn't gonna tell you who this guy really is. You gotta check him out yourself and see what makes him tick."

"What's the other reason?"

"For surveillance you can bill more."

I sighed, shook my head. "I hate surveillance."

"Then you're in the wrong line of work."

"You advising me to get out?"

"No, just making an observation."

I sighed again. "I know that. I hate this shit. I'd love to get out. The thing is, with my liberal arts degree, what the hell else can I do?"

"I dunno." He looked at me, cocked his head. "How are you at makin' burgers?"

6

Sergeant MacAullif wasn't glad to see me. He looked up from his paperwork, frowned and said, "Who died?"

"What?"

He shrugged. "You come in here, someone's dead and you're in trouble. Who is it this time?"

"No one."

"Really? Let me mark that on my calendar. Stanley Hastings came to see me and no one died. So this is a purely social call?"

"Not exactly."

"No kidding." MacAullif grimaced. "Hell, you did me a favor once, I'll be payin' it back the rest of my life. What is it this time?"

I told him about the Melissa Ford case. I can't say he was too impressed.

"Christ," he said. "You're really sinking low, aren't you?"

"How much lower can you get than ambulance chasing?"

"You have a point. So whaddya want?"

"I'd like to know if David Melrose has a record."

"That's something you could find out yourself."

"I know. But it would take me all day. And I gotta report on this Monday morning."

MacAullif must have been in a good mood, 'cause he didn't get that upset. "Is that all you want?"

"I'd be grateful for any advice."

"I'd advise you to find another line of work."

"You're the second person today who's told me that."

"Sort of makes you start to think, doesn't it?"

I shook my head. "Not me. You're always advising me *not* to think. Just gets me in trouble."

"Damned if it doesn't." MacAullif picked up the phone, punched a button. "Daniels. Get me a rap sheet on—. What's the guy's name again?"

"David Melrose."

"David Melrose. Rap sheet and a Motor Vehicle check. Find it and bring it in." He hung up the phone.

"Motor Vehicle check?" I said.

"Hey, why not? You'll get a birth date and address. And if the guy's got no convictions, it's better than nothing."

"Thanks a lot."

He shrugged. "Hell, it's the easiest way to get you out of my office. And it happens to be a piece of cake. Now, you really want some advice?"

"Yeah, I do. It's a piece of shit assignment, seems stupid to me, but I want to give the woman value for her money."

"Then you're doin' the right thing. If the guy's got a criminal record, that ought to do it. If he doesn't, there's only a few other things that matter. You check if he's married?''

''Not according to Vital Statistics.''

''Yeah, well it ain't always accurate. He own any property?''

''I haven't checked, but according to his girlfriend he doesn't claim to, so there's not much point.''

''Yeah, unless he owns a *lot* of property he don't want her to know about. Like property he screwed other women out of.''

''Shit.''

MacAullif grinned. ''Hadn't thought of that? You have much too trusting a nature.'' He thought a moment. ''You check up on his work?''

''No. What's to check?''

''You won't know till you try. Where's he work?''

I gave him the address of the advertising agency David Melrose worked for. MacAullif picked up the phone, called information, got the number and punched it in.

''What you doin'?'' I said.

''Just checkin'.''

''Checkin' what?''

MacAullif held up his hand. ''Yes, could I speak to David Melrose, please? . . . David Melrose. Is this the Breelstein Agency? . . . Fine, could I speak to David Melrose?'' A pause, then, ''David Melrose, please?'' MacAullif grinned and hung up the phone.

I looked at him. ''What the hell did you just do?''

''Saved you a couple of hours of work and got you something you can use.''

''What?''

''Whatever David Melrose told your client, he is not a big wheel at this agency. The receptionist has to double-check to place the name. Then she says, ''Oh, yes,'' puts me on hold, and the next thing I know a voice answers sayin', 'Mail room.' ''

''No shit.''

''None. So David Melrose is not an executive at this agency, he works in the mail room. If he's told your client anything different, that's one thing you've found out and one strike against him.''

''Why didn't I think of that?''

''Because it's too simple and direct. You were probably workin' on some scheme to go to the agency posin' as an executive from some company lookin' for someone to handle a big advertising account.''

I said nothing. In the course of the morning, I'd considered exactly that. ''So now you don't have to,'' MacAullif said. ''Score one for the home team.''

The phone rang. MacAullif scooped it up. ''Yeah?'' He listened a few moments, said, ''Thanks,'' and hung up. ''Well, we drew a blank.''

''Oh?''

''I got rap sheets on three David Melroses, none of them yours.''

''You sure?''

''Absolutely. One's sixty-eight, one's black, and one's a juvenile.''

''Not mine.''

''No shit. Motor Vehicles shows four David Melroses, not yours either.''

''Verified?''

''Trust me. Two of them are the same as the rap sheet, the other two are out of the age range.''

''Shit.''

''Hey, it's good and it's bad.''

''What's good about it?''

''No record at all means maybe David Melrose isn't the guy's right name.''

''That's good?''

''Sure. It would mean he's a creep, which is what you want to find out.''

''Right. But there's nothing to go on. I mean, how the hell can I tell if it's his right name or not?''

MacAullif shrugged. ''Only one way I can think of.''

''What's that?''

''Tail him.''

7

I HATE SURVEILLANCE. I hate it because it's what TV detectives do, and on TV it looks so easy. But in real life it is such a pain in the ass. Because the TV detective is following a script, and unless the script calls for him to lose the subject, he doesn't lose him. And unless the script calls for the subject to spot the detective, he doesn't spot him. And, worst of all, eventually the subject will go someplace and lead the detective to something useful, because otherwise the scene wouldn't be in the damn script. In real life, even if the surveillance is performed perfectly, and the subject doesn't lose the detective or spot him, there is still no reason to believe he will ever lead the detective anywhere.

Which makes the whole thing a less than attractive proposition. I mean, if you were to check the forms of people applying for career guidance, I doubt if you would find many of them had indicated a preference for something difficult, tedious, and most likely futile and pointless.

But that's what I was up to later that afternoon. There I was, the tough P.I., stakin' out the Breelstein Agency.

I was across the street with a picture of David Melrose waiting to spot the bum when he came out the front door. *If* he came out the front door. If they didn't have a side service entrance for mail room employees.

Not to worry. He came out the revolving door promptly at five o'clock wearing a spiffy suit and tie, just as if he really were a high-level executive.

I didn't like him at once. I hadn't liked his picture, and I liked him even less in person. He was young and handsome, with curly black hair and a pretty boy face, medium height and a thin, youthful build. But there was something sharp about him. Something smooth, something slimy. I could tell all that from across the street.

Unless, of course, I was projecting it. Which was quite possible. Because I looked at him and I looked at my client, and I thought, Jesus Christ, why is the sleazo son of a bitch messing around with her?

Just as I had that thought, bingo, there she was, gingham, calico and all, throwing her arms around his neck and giving him a big kiss on the cheek.

Which I really wasn't ready for. A mousy Melissa Ford I could deal with. An animated mousy Melissa Ford was something else. I couldn't see from that far, but I could tell the eyes behind those wing-tipped glasses must be shining.

He put his arm around her and walked her down the street.

So far, the picture I had envisioned was checking out—David Melrose, mail room employee posing as advertising executive does not let girlfriend come up to the office to see where he really works, but meets her out front in the street. Davey-baby, I got you pegged.

I followed them from a discreet distance. Of course, Melissa Ford showing up had complicated the situation. There was no immediate danger of David spotting me, but Melissa Ford knew who I was. I hadn't told her I was going to tail David, and I had no idea how she would take to the idea. If she spotted me, there'd be hell to pay. Even if she didn't outwardly disapprove, I couldn't imagine her being cool enough not to let on.

They walked up to the corner and stepped out in the street to hail a cab.

On TV there's always a second cab for the detective to hail. Piece of cake. Right. Just hop in and say, "Follow that cab." I guess none of those TV shows were shot at rush hour in midtown Manhattan.

However, for once, luck was with me. They'd walked up Madison, and since Madison is one-way uptown, any cab they hailed would have to pass me first.

"Not through the Iron Duke," I muttered, stepping out into the street. It was a phrase left over from my bridge playing days, sometimes uttered when playing a king on a trick. It worked on cabs too—when a vacant one came along, I got it first. I hopped in, and as usual made the cabbie's day when he found out what it was I wanted.

We sat there another five minutes until Melissa and David got a cab, then followed them uptown to a small restaurant on Third Avenue. Which, of course, was a big pain in the ass because I had to hang out on the sidewalk while they ate their way through a leisurely two-hour dinner.

While they did, I began to have serious doubts. Shit, maybe this *was* a match made in heaven, maybe I was wasting my time. What bothered me most, was what I was gonna have to tell Melissa Ford Monday morning. "Yeah, the guy's a real sleazeball. I checked him out. You know what he did? He went out and had dinner with you."

What was also bothering me was wondering if after dinner she'd go back with him to his apartment. If she did, I didn't want to know it. Hell, I didn't even want to think about it. It was none of my damn business. But I'd taken the job, so it *was* my business. I just didn't *like* my business.

When they finished dinner, we went through the same cab routine again, and I followed them to an apartment building on York Avenue. So she wasn't going up to his apartment. He was going up to hers. I wondered if that was better, worse, or just the same.

He didn't though. They got out of the cab, she gave him a hug, he kissed her discreetly on the cheek and she turned and went inside.

He got back in the cab. I, like a schmuck, had let mine go.

I looked around frantically in a blind panic, but fortunately rush hour was over and, just like on TV, a vacant cab was coming down the street. It was on the wrong side, but what the hell, beggars can't be choosers. I sprinted across the street and flagged it down.

The cabbie was a little startled by the request. "What?" he said.

"Make a U-turn and follow that cab."

"You shitting me?"

I flashed my I.D. at him. "Not at all. This is legit, and I'll pay the tickets. Just don't let the guy get wise."

"Say, what is this?" the cabbie said.

"Just boring, sordid, domestic surveillance."

It didn't sound boring to him. "Son of a bitch," he said, and wheeled the cab into a U-turn and took off after David's cab, which had already started down the street.

"Don't crowd him," I said.

"Don't worry," the cabbie said. "Will he be lookin' for a tail?"

"He shouldn't be."

"Then it's a piece of cake. Just leave it to me."

The cabbie was young, white, long-haired, probably an unemployed actor working a job-job, and he was obviously getting a kick out of the whole thing. I can't say that I was. I'd realized the direction we were heading in was the direction of David Melrose's address, and in all likelihood he'd pay off the cab and go home and that would be that.

But he didn't. A half a dozen blocks down York the cab pulled into the curb and David Melrose got out and went to a pay phone.

That was something. There'd been a pay phone on the corner in front of Melissa Ford's building. But David Melrose hadn't used it. Instead he'd driven out of sight of her building to make the call.

I'd sure have liked to know who he was calling, but there was no chance of me hopping out of my cab and getting close enough to overhear. Not without him spotting me. And even though he didn't know who I was, him seeing me at the phone booth would blow my cover and kill my chances of ever getting close to him later on.

I'm sure a TV detective would have had no such problem. He'd have walked by the phone booth, overheard just the part of the conversation that mattered, and got back in his cab without the guy spotting him and just before the guy hung up the phone and got back in his.

I can't begin to tell you how many ways that scenario would have fucked up if I'd tried it. For one thing, it was a very short conversation and he hung up the phone before I could have even gotten there. For another thing, he hopped right back in his cab and took off and in all probability I would have lost him. As it was, my cabbie had to pull out quick and run a red light to keep up. It's a good thing he did, because a couple of blocks later David's cab hung a left and headed for the East River. This, I knew, was not the direction of his apartment. My spirits brightened considerably.

The cab got on the FDR Drive and headed downtown, which depressed me again. David's apartment was in the East 20s, so maybe he *was* going home and the cabbie was just using the Drive to make time.

He wasn't, though. Traffic on the Drive was light, and in no time at all we sped by the 34th Street Exit and the 23rd Street Exit, and kept on going downtown. We curved around Alphabet City, where Manhattan gets wider to accommodate Avenues A, B, C, and D. I wondered if that was where he was heading. If so, a drug buy seemed likely. And that should be enough to clinch the case for Melissa Ford.

When we flashed by Houston Street, that theory

went out the window. We kept going downtown and finally got off the highway at Canal.

That set my mind racing. David Melrose, the Chinese connection? Tong wars? Illegal fireworks, for Christ's sake?

Not at all, thank god—even with all the proof in the world, I couldn't imagine getting Melissa Ford to swallow that one. But not to worry. The taxi drove across Canal Street, turned uptown for a block, and pulled up in front of a loft building on Grand. David hopped out of the cab, went to the front door and rang a bell.

The building where the cab had stopped was right near the corner, so our cab hadn't been able to turn onto Grand. We were on Wooster a few car-lengths back from the corner, looking across the intersection at the scene. I'll say this for my cabbie, he was taking the whole thing seriously—we had a good view from there and there was no chance at all of our being seen.

A few minutes later the front door of the loft building opened and a man came out. I tensed up immediately. The man was wearing ragged jeans, a filthy T-shirt, and sneakers with no socks. He was young, say mid-thirties, with long yellow hair and a stringy, wispy beard. He was thin, almost what you'd call emaciated, and he made quite a contrast next to David Melrose in his spiffy three-piece suit.

Unfortunately, when they started talking they turned the other way and all I could see was their backs. But I could see the guy take something out of the back pocket of his jeans, and I could see his arm move, handing it to David, and then David's arm move, tucking it into his jacket pocket.

My original theory started to look good again. Drug buy.

It looked good to my cabbie too. "Drug buy?" he asked.

"Damned if I know. But it sure is interesting."

"Yeah. What now? You take the new guy, or follow the cab?"

The cab was still waiting there with the door open.

"The cab," I said. "The other guy lives here, I can get him any time."

Prompted by that thought, I whipped out my notebook and copied down the address.

By the time I'd finished, scraggly beard was heading back inside, and David hopped into his cab and took off. We followed him back uptown, and I figured this was it. The guy scored some dope and now he's goin' home.

Wrong again.

We whizzed right by any reasonable exit for Davey-baby's address, and didn't get off the Drive until 96th Street. The cab cruised around a few blocks and pulled up in front of a brownstone on 89th. From our vantage point half a block away, the cabbie and I saw David get out, walk up the front steps and ring the bell.

The brownstone must not have had a buzzer system to open the front door. And I was sure glad it didn't, because about a minute later a knockout of a young blonde opened it instead. Davey-baby stepped right inside and the door swung shut, so I couldn't see if he gave her a big hug, big kiss or big whatever. But it didn't matter. By now it was getting on to ten o'clock. And why the hell else would a young stud who had just scored drugs in SoHo be calling on a young blonde in her apartment building at that time of night? No, unless Davey-baby popped right out again, I had him dead to rights.

He didn't. The cab he'd been riding in turned on its lights and drove off. So I paid off my young cabbie—who was mighty reluctant to go, and who only did so after I gave him a large tip to keep his mouth shut, which absolutely thrilled him—and I hung out on the sidewalk to see just how long Davey-baby would actually spend with the young blonde.

He was out at twelve-oh-five by the two-dollar Casio I got for going to Yankee Stadium on Watch Day.

Now I must admit, the Casio is not entirely accurate—what I do is, look at it and subtract eight.

But even so, I figured eleven fifty-seven was pretty late for David Melrose to be coming out of a young blonde's apartment when he was supposedly betrothed to the fair young Melissa Ford.

8

MELISSA FORD WAS PISSED. At least for her she was pissed. For anyone else, she would have sounded positively normal. But I knew her and I could tell.

For one thing, her voice was audible. For another thing, she occasionally actually looked at me. So I could tell she was really steamed.

"You *followed* him?" she said.

"Yes, I did."

"You had no right to do that."

"Don't be silly. That's what you hired me for."

"I hired you to check into his background."

"Exactly. That's what I was doing."

"No, you weren't. You were following him. Spying on him."

"Of course I was."

"I didn't tell you to do that."

"You didn't tell me *not* to do it, either. You hired me to get the dope on this guy and that's what I did."

"I didn't tell you to spy on him. I would never do that. That's terrible."

I took a breath. Melissa Ford certainly drew a thin line. She had no compunction at all about hiring a private detective to investigate her young suitor's past. But she was horrified I might check up on his present.

"Well," I said. "Then we seem to have a misunderstanding. But what's done is done. I'm sorry you didn't approve of my following David, but I did, and would you like to hear what I learned from it?"

"I'm not sure I should," she said.

Jesus Christ. And I'd thought this was going to be a piece of cake.

I'd gone into the Melissa Ford interview in a very good mood. My good mood was partly because I'd actually gotten something on the young man, and partly because I'd solved my moral dilemma over the money. See, I'd started working on the case by calling Fred Lazar at 8:00 A.M. Friday. And I'd put in a full day on it, what with checking the Bureau of Vital Statistics and calling on MacAullif and checking the Tax Assessor to see if he owned any property. And that, coupled with my surveillance of him Friday night until midnight, added up to a total of sixteen hours. So I had in effect put in two days work in one day. Hell, it even occurred to me most private detectives would say I did one sixteen-hour day and the second eight hours was overtime at time and a half and you owe me another hundred bucks. I certainly wasn't gonna push for that. I just figured I'd given her her money's worth and we were even.

It also occurred to me that since I'd done such good work and got her exactly what she needed, she'd be inclined to keep me on for a few more days to investigate the situation. Which I was sure she would do as soon as she heard the true facts.

Only she didn't want to hear it.

I took a breath. Jesus Christ, here I was, once again, a private detective caught in a shaggy dog story, doing an impossible task for people who didn't want it done. What should I do, tie her up and gag her and force her to listen to me?

I used reverse psychology. "You're right," I said. "These are things I shouldn't have learned, and there is no reason for you to hear them. I assume, since you are displeased with what I've done, that I am fired. That's perfectly understandable. I hope *you* will understand that since I discharged the work, although you are not satisfied with it, I am keeping the money, because there are no guarantees in this business. I'm sorry we had this misunderstanding and I hope there are no hard feelings."

I stood up.

It worked. A first for me. Mark it on the calendar. Private detective's bluff succeeds.

Because she didn't get up too. Instead, she looked down at the floor and blinked her eyes behind her glasses a couple of times. "Oh," she said.

"I take it I am fired?" I said. "I mean, you certainly wouldn't want me to continue working for you when you are so displeased with my services."

Her lips moved, but nothing came out. She seemed to be trying to figure out what to say next. "Well," she said, "I don't want to be hasty about this. I suppose you acted in good faith. But I have to tell you, you were dead wrong."

"I don't want to argue with you," I said. "I accept your assessment of the situation, I apologize and I'm sorry I offended you."

That didn't please her either. Behind those glasses I

could see her mind going, trying to figure some way out of the predicament. Then I saw a glint come in her eyes that might have been indicative of an idea.

It was.

She raised her head slightly, opened her mouth and said, "I do not approve of what you have done, and I'm sure the information you have obtained is false. But you'd better tell me what it is, so I can explain it to you, so you do not go away with a bad opinion of David."

I had to hand it to her. That saved face and covered the situation beautifully. I couldn't have thought up a better way out myself.

"Okay," I said. "Here's what I've got. There's no record of David ever having been married before."

"Of course not," she said.

"Nor does he own a motor vehicle, have a driver's license or own any property."

She nodded her head. "That's right."

"Here's where I may surprise you. David Melrose is *not* a big advertising executive at the Breelstein Agency."

She frowned. "What?"

"I'm sorry," I said. "I know this may hurt you. But that's why David has you meet him on the sidewalk outside the office. He doesn't want you to see where he works. The truth is, no matter how he dresses, he is not an executive at all."

"Right," she said. "He works in the mail room."

It was my turn to frown. "What?" I said.

Her chin came up defiantly. "Now, it's nothing to be ashamed of. He works in the mail room. He's a young man, and he had to start at the bottom. But he doesn't intend to stay there. He dresses well, he works hard, and he intends to move up.''

I'm afraid all I could think of to say was, "He does?''

"Of course he does,'' she said. "He's young and he's personable and he's intelligent. And he's a hard worker. He's learning the business and making contacts. Believe me, he won't be in the mail room long.''

"Fine,'' I said. "I'm glad that's cleared up. Let me tell you what happened next.''

"Next?''

"Friday night,'' I said. "I'm talking about Friday night.''

"Oh,'' she said. One bra strap was showing. She covered it irritably, then set her lips in a firm line. "Go on.''

"Well, like I said, you met David outside his office, took a cab to a restaurant uptown.''

I paused there, in case she wanted to jump in again, but she merely maintained her look of cold disapproval. The fact that she directed it at the corner of my desk made my task easier.

"After dinner, you took a taxicab back to your apartment. You and David got out and you went inside.''

"I know that,'' she said.

"Of course you do. But you don't know what happened next. David got back in the cab, drove for five blocks and stopped at a pay phone.''

I paused to let that sink in.

She actually looked up a little. "So what?''

"There's a pay phone on your corner,'' I said. "Surely David could have used that, instead of getting back in the cab and driving five blocks to find one.

Unless, of course, he didn't want you to know he was making the call."

She sighed and shook her head pityingly. "The pay phone on our corner is broken," she said. "It's been broken for a week. Vandals pulled the wires out. David lost a quarter in it just the other day. I called and reported it, but of course no one came."

"I see," I said. I must say I was rapidly losing my confidence. But I still had a lot of ammunition to shoot. "Well, it might interest you to know that after the phone call, David drove to a loft on Grand Street and a rather scraggly looking disreputable type met him on the sidewalk and slipped him a package."

She must have been really worked up now. I could tell because both bra straps were showing and she made no effort to cover them. Instead, she sat up straighter in her chair and addressed a spot just south of my chin.

"You're pretty quick to make value judgments, Mr. Hastings. I assume the scraggly, disreputable gentleman you describe is Charles Olsen."

I blinked. "Who?"

"Charles Olsen. He's a free-lance sketch artist and does a large part of the agency's design work. David often picks up art copy from him."

I was beginning to feel slightly sick. "What?" I said.

"Because David wants to get ahead. He doesn't charge the company for doing it, or even bill them for his cabfare. But they know he does it, and they're grateful. Plus David's in good with Charles Olsen, whom it can't hurt to know. And he's in good with the art director who's getting the stuff. David usually makes pickups in the course of the day. But if it's a rush job, and they want it first thing in the morning, well, David will come walking in at nine o'clock in the morning and lay it on the art director's desk. David won't say a word about it, but the art director will know, and he's grateful. He's even told David a couple of times.''

Melissa Ford paused, sighed, and her eyes gleamed with admiration for a moment. Then she suddenly realized her exposed position, and hurriedly and angrily covered her bra straps. Then, as if to make up for the embarrassment, snuffled and said haughtily, ''Do you have anything else?''

I did, but I had lost my will to continue. This mousy, repressed little woman had beaten me to a standstill. And somehow I knew, as sure as the sun would come up tomorrow, that the tale about the attractive blonde would be another total fizzle. She'd turn out to be the agency's ace editor and head writer, who had to add the copy to the pictures before they hit the art director's desk the next morning. But I had to go through with it, so I did.

''Well,'' I said, ''after that he took a taxi up to East 89th Street, went up to a young blonde's apartment at ten o'clock and didn't come out until midnight.''

I was ready for Melissa Ford to take my head off on that one. In fact, I was ready for any reaction except the one I got.

Because her head came up, and this time she actually looked me in the eyes, and when she did, her own were blazing.

''He did *what*!?''

9

I WAS IN A FOUL MOOD as I drove to Metropolitan Hospital the next morning to sign up an accident victim who'd been hit by a car. I was in a foul mood for a lot of reasons.

For one thing, I'd been fired. Melissa Ford had fired me for gross incompetence, for exceeding my authority and for making an unauthorized investigation which I had no right to do. At least, that's the way she phrased it. Basically, she fired me for telling her something she didn't want to know.

Which was infuriating. Any other woman would have kept me on a few days and had me dig out all the dirt. But Melissa Ford was not another woman. The *young blonde* was another woman. Melissa Ford was *the* woman, and the young blonde was the *other* woman, just your typical, normal, messy domestic triangle, just as Alice and Fred and MacAullif and I had all predicted. David Melrose was a slime and a shit who was after her for her money, and savin' all his lovin' for another gal. And so the grand and glorious

Melissa Ford case came to a close. And yours truly went back to his appointed rounds.

Only not right away. Reason-For-Foul-Mood-Number-Two. Because, wouldn't you know it, after Melissa Ford had slammed out the door and I had sat there sulking for a while for doing the job right and losing my two-hundred-dollar-a-day meal ticket, when I called Rosenberg and Stone, Richard was in court again, and Wendy/Janet, in her incomprehensible yet predictable wisdom, wouldn't give me any cases until she heard it from Richard that I was back on the job.

Which was just the kick in the balls I needed. I not only lost my two-hundred-dollar-a-day client, I also lost my eighty-dollar-a-day Rosenberg and Stone job.

Somehow that figured. I'd had a four-hundred-dollar day on Friday, so it was only fitting on Monday I'd get totally dorked and make zip.

And, Reason-For-Foul-Mood-Number-Three, on top of everything else, I woke up this morning with a violent case of diarrhea. Which, as far as I know, is a first for a private detective. At least it is in the books I've read. I can't recall a private detective ever having diarrhea. I don't think they even have assholes. Well, welcome to the real world. I had the runs pretty good. And the thing is, in New York City there are virtually no public toilets. And of the few there are, the ones I'd be willing to sit on you can count on the fingers of no hands. There are a few McDonald's and Burger King rest rooms that, if pressed, I would pee in, but sit down, never. So my minor infirmity was a major pain in the ass.

So in that respect, I was lucky that my first assignment was Metropolitan Hospital, calling on a client who was laid up there with his leg in traction. I walked into his hospital room, said, "Hi, I'm from the lawyer's office," and immediately ducked into the john. When I came out the guy looked at me a little funny, but otherwise the signup went swimmingly. I filled out the fact sheet and signed him up, no problem, took out my camera and fired off a few shots of his broken leg, being careful to close the door so I wouldn't get my camera impounded by some passing hospital security guard, went out and picked up my car where I'd left it at a meter on First Avenue, and headed out for my next assignment in Brooklyn.

The client lived on Euclid Avenue, which always reminds me of a joke I made up once: "My wife wants me to study non-Euclidean geometry. I love my wife, but, oh, Euclid." Unfortunately, like most of my jokes, it is the type that amuses only me, which is probably one of the reasons I never made it as a writer.

Realizations like that, reminders of my inadequacies, happen to me all the time, and most days they would roll off my back. But today I was in a foul mood, and seeing the sign for Euclid Avenue just made me more depressed, angry and frustrated.

So did the fact I couldn't find a parking space. Alternate side parking was in effect, and I could have double-parked and left a sign in the window, but I hate to do that when I'm not in my own neighborhood. You're sitting there talking with the client and there'll come a knock on the door, and god knows who's on the other side. Maybe someone asking me to move my car. But maybe not. And believe me, I'm not looking for trouble. Anyway, there was half a space by the hydrant on the corner, not entirely kosher, but in a neighborhood like this and me going in and out fast, I shouldn't get a ticket, should I?

Worrying about whether I would or not did not improve my state of mind. Neither did the fact the client's apartment was so filthy I could not bring myself to use his bathroom, which I sorely needed to do. So, my needing to get to a john coupled with my worrying about getting a parking ticket made for the fastest signup in history. The guy never knew what hit him. I had the fact sheet filled out, retainers signed and pictures taken before the poor guy even had a chance to ask me who I was. Nor did I let him read the retainer. Good thing I'm an honest guy. For all he knew, I could have just sold him an encyclopedia.

I got out of there and rushed down the stairs, visions of porcelain bathroom fixtures dancing in my head.

I hit the street and stopped dead.

Jesus Christ. Wouldn't you know it. On this draggiest of all possible days, there was a police cruiser pulled up right next to my Toyota and one of the cops was already out and looking at the plate.

I was tempted to turn and walk the other way, just so I wouldn't have to listen to the cop lecture me for parking there. Believe me, I was in no mood to hear it. But I realized that was stupid. Besides, the guy hadn't written the ticket yet. Maybe, just maybe, I could talk him out of it. Yeah, and maybe some day I'll get elected president. Still, a guy in my position's gotta take the shot. A ticket here would wipe out the whole morning's work.

I walked up to the car, expecting the cop to turn on me and demand to know who the hell I thought I was, parking my car there.

He didn't. Instead he said the last thing in the world I ever would have expected him to say.

What he said was, "Stanley Hastings?"

10

THEY DROVE ME TO ONE POLICE PLAZA, a building I
knew well. I just didn't know it as One Police Plaza.
Oh, I knew that's what it was, it's just that no one had
ever referred to it that way before. The other times I'd
been taken in, the cops had just told me I was going
downtown. But this time, after the cops had bundled
me into the back of the cruiser and taken off and I had
screwed up enough courage to ask where we were going, one of the cops said, "One Police Plaza." Maybe
it was because we were in Brooklyn, and from there
it made no sense to call it "downtown". At any rate,
whatever you called it, I certainly knew where One
Police Plaza was. It was the same place I'd called on
MacAullif not two days before.

I figured MacAullif had to be the answer. For the
cops picking me up, I mean. He'd done me a favor,
and now it was payback time. I had no idea what he
wanted, and I couldn't imagine why it was so urgent
he'd sent two cops to pick me up. I also couldn't imagine why he hadn't just called Rosenberg and Stone and

had them beep me. That was the scary thing. That had to mean whatever was up was something he didn't want generally known.

Which didn't make any sense. Because how the hell would he have found me *without* calling Rosenberg and Stone? But these two cops knew where to look for me. Unless there'd been an APB out, and these were the guys who scored. But in Brooklyn? What a long shot that would be. So the whole thing just didn't make any sense.

I'd like to think I could have figured things out if I'd been in a better mood, but like I said, I wasn't. And to be picked up by two cops and hauled in for no reason was really the last straw. And of course they wouldn't tell me anything. In the whole ride, "One Police Plaza" was the only response I got. Not that I expected any more, knowing cops, but still I couldn't help asking.

The way I saw it, there was only one saving grace in the whole thing. The place we were heading for, One Police Plaza, or downtown, or whatever the hell you wanted to call it, would have a bathroom.

We went over the Brooklyn Bridge, pulled up in front of One Police Plaza and the cops marched me in. I expected them to march me straight to MacAullif, but they didn't. Instead they took me down the hall to a small interrogation room. When I saw that, I made the most eloquent speech you have ever heard on the rights of private citizens to avail themselves of the use of police lavatory facilities. I don't know whether it was my eloquence or the fact that I made the speech bouncing up and down and teetering back and forth from one leg to the other that convinced them, but in any event they granted my request, and I was in a

slightly better mood by the time I finally took the indicated seat in the interrogation room.

Which was all wrong. Interrogation? Give me a
break. MacAullif was a hard ass, and despite our quote
friendship unquote, he was not above busting my balls
if I fucked up an investigation of his or did something
illegal. But I hadn't done anything, for Christ's sake.
And even if I had, surely he'd have dragged me into
his office instead of in here. No, the interrogation room
was all wrong.

So maybe it wasn't MacAullif at all.

Maybe it was Sergeant Clark.

What a frightening thought. Sergeant Clark was a
homicide officer I'd met a while back during the course
of another investigation. He was a methodical,
straight-laced, by-the-book son of a bitch, who'd stick
me in an interrogation room as a matter of course.

Holy shit. That was probably it. My worst nightmare. To be hauled in and interrogated by Sergeant
Clark.

Wrong again.

Sergeant Clark would have been a cakewalk, a god-
send, a breath of fresh air.

Because at that moment the door opened and in
walked Sergeant Thurman.

11

IF YOU READ DETECTIVE FICTION, you know the police are usually depicted as inept bumbling plodders, who couldn't solve a thing if it weren't for the genius of the private detective working on the case. In real life, I'd found the reverse to be true. Sergeant MacAullif was sharp as a tack. Sergeant Clark, though not to my taste, was none the less brilliant. In point of fact, almost all the cops I'd run into in the course of my investigations had been intelligent, resourceful, and good at their jobs.

Sergeant Thurman was the exception that proved the rule.

Thurman was a bad cop. Don't get me wrong—I don't mean he was corrupt. He was on the side of the angels, and he believed in what he did. He just wasn't particularly good at it. In short, Sergeant Thurman was exactly what you've been reading about in detective fiction all those years—a cop too stupid to solve a case without help, and too dumb to know he needed it.

Sergeant Thurman looked at me and scowled. He was a big man, with a crewcut and a broken nose that made him look like an army drill sergeant. His speech, crude and guttural, made him sound like one too. He was, in short, so stereotypically dumb one might think this rough exterior must hide a mind of some intelligence.

One would be wrong.

I could think of no reason why Sergeant Thurman wished to see me. And I could think of no reason why I would ever wish to see him. All I knew was, the moment I saw his face I felt nausea, revulsion and despair, coupled with a strong desire to return to the men's room.

Thurman scowled again and shook his head. "Dumb schmuck," he said. "Don't you ever answer your beeper?"

That startled me. I reached instinctively for my belt.

Son of a bitch. My beeper was on silent switch. I'd put it on silent when I'd gone into Metropolitan Hospital because a beeper is a no-no there. And I'd been in such a bad mood I'd forgotten to switch it back on when I'd come out. I did so now, and it began beeping like crazy, meaning the office had tried to reach me. I pushed the button, switched it off.

Well, that answered a lot of questions. About how the cops had found me, I mean. They'd called Rosenberg and Stone and asked them to beep me, which Wendy/Janet had done. When I hadn't answered the beeper, they'd found out where I was working and sent cops to that address. Yeah, that answered that question.

But it still didn't answer the big question, why I was there.

Sergeant Thurman was looking at me with a mocking grin. "Great," he said. "The ace detective. Switch it on now."

"What's this all about?" I said.

He smirked. "As if you didn't know."

I hate that. That has to be one of the most annoying statements in the English language. If I knew, I wouldn't be asking, schmuck. So much for my participation in this conversation. Anything else you want you can ask for yourself.

I sat and waited. So did Thurman. It became boring. I wondered if he'd forgotten why he'd brought me there. From what I knew of the guy, it was entirely possible. Then the door opened and a stenographer came in, and I suddenly realized that was what we'd been waiting for.

When the stenographer had sat down and opened his notebook, Sergeant Thurman said, "Name?"

I took a breath. "My name is Stanley Hastings, and I have no idea why I am here. I was dragged in here without a warrant and without explanation. If I am charged with anything, I demand to see an attorney. If I am *not* charged with anything, you have no right to keep me and I want to go home. You are violating my rights by this irregular, unorthodox, illegal interrogation."

I admit irregular and unorthodox might be slightly redundant, but I think under the circumstances I spoke pretty well.

Sergeant Thurman didn't think so. He looked like he had just smelled a fart, which considering my state of health was possible, but I think it was just what I'd said.

"Mr. Hastings," he said. I could tell he was controlling himself with a great effort and solely for the benefit of the stenographer. "Mr. Hastings" was not indicative of his usual mode of address. "You dumb fuck" would be a little more like it.

He took another breath, repeated the distasteful words again. "Mr. Hastings. You are not under arrest. You are here as a material witness. You are here of your own volition, and you are free to leave at any time. I assume that you wish to cooperate with us in our investigation. I should point out that if you do not, you will be subpoenaed and dragged in front of the grand jury. But that's up to you."

For Sergeant Thurman, that was a long speech. By the end of it he looked out of breath and slightly red in the face.

It was also a good one. He had smacked the ball cleanly in my court. If I didn't cooperate after that, it was entirely my own fault.

"As I say, I have no idea why I'm here. Of course I'd like to cooperate with the police. But I don't know how I can until I know what this is all about. Now, you wanna tell me, or you wanna play guessing games all day?"

Sergeant Thurman frowned. "Mr. Hastings, we are investigating the murder of David Melrose, who was shot to death in his apartment some time last night."

I'm afraid my jaw dropped open. "What?"

"I see that means something to you. For your information, at the present time we have a suspect in custody, one Melissa Ford. I believe she is also known to you."

My heart sank. Jesus Christ. "At this time I have no statement to make, and I would like to call my lawyer."

I can't say Sergeant Thurman looked too upset. He nodded, as if that were exactly what he'd expected and said, "That concludes the interrogation of Mr. Hastings at this time." He jerked his thumb at the stenographer. "You can go."

The stenographer folded his book, got up and walked out.

As soon as the door closed, Sergeant Thurman turned back to me. "All right, asshole. Let's you and me have a little talk."

That sounded more like the Sergeant Thurman I knew. After his stiff formality in front of the stenographer, it was almost a relief.

"I have nothing to say," I said. "I wanna call my lawyer."

"Sure, sure, you can call him at any time. But I don't wanna wait for it. If you don't wanna talk, you can still listen."

"To what?"

"The facts of life."

The facts of life according to Sergeant Thurman? Not an attractive proposition. But David Melrose was dead and Melissa Ford was in custody, and I wanted to know all I could. "Go on," I said.

"All right. Here's the facts of life. Melissa Ford hired you to check up on her boyfriend, David Melrose. You did, and found out he was playing around with a young blonde. You told her that yesterday morning. Yesterday afternoon she confronted him in the mail room where he works and they had a screaming fight. We have three independent witnesses to that. She said he was a cad and a cur and a fucking asshole and anything else you wanna think of, and she said she'd kill him."

"That doesn't mean she did."

Thurman smirked. "Grow up, willya. This is an open and shut case. I'm telling you what the story is so you'll talk straight to the grand jury. And I tell you, if you don't corroborate it, it's gonna be your ass."

"I'm sure glad you sent the stenographer out before you started making threats."

"What threats? I'm tellin' you how it is, so you see you gotta talk. You choose not to, it's your funeral. We don't need your testimony anyway."

"Then why am I here?"

"Give me a break. You're a witness. Before you go on the stand, the prosecutor'd like to know what you're gonna say."

"I told you I'm not talkin'."

"And I told you to listen. So shut up and listen."

I shut up. As long as he was dishing out the information, I'd be a damn fool not to take it.

"Okay," he said. "They had a huge fight and she storms out sayin' she'll kill him. That's around three o'clock. Melrose gets off work at five, then we start tracing his movements. No one knows where he goes from five till nine, but at nine o'clock he shows up at the apartment of some broad named Melony Tune, if you can believe that."

"You're kidding. Melody Tune?"

"No. Not Melody. *Melony*. As in tits like melons. Blonde bitch on East 89th Street."

So, that was her name. Melony Tune. If I hadn't been fired, I'd have investigated and discovered that.

"He goes in there at nine o'clock, he's out at eleven-thirty. According to the Tune dame. That, as far as we know, is the last time anyone sees him alive."

"According to her."

"Sure, but why should she lie? Anyway, this morning there's a call to nine-one-one. Logged in at eight-oh-five. Melissa Ford calling to report her boyfriend's been killed."

"You're kidding."

"Not at all. Cops go to the address, check it out, find one stiff on the floor. Gunshot in the chest. Gun, twenty-two, lying next to the body. Ford bitch sittin' in a chair.

"I get there, she's still sittin'. I can't believe her. Dumb cunt with a capital D. She's not hysterical, she's not cryin', she's just sittin' there, no expression at all.

"I ask her what happened, she said, 'Someone shot David.' Just like that. No expression. No nothin'. Just like I asked her what time it was."

"She was in shock."

"Shock, hell. She's like that. You met her. You know."

"What about the fight in the mail room?"

"I call it a fight, but the way I get it, he was the only one raisin' his voice. She was calmly, matter of factly cutting his balls off—'Who's this woman? You lied to me. How could you do that?'—simple, direct, like she was ordering a pizza. No wonder he started shoutin'. It would be enough to drive anyone up the wall."

"What about the death threat? I thought she said she'd kill him."

"She did, but same way. Simple, direct. I'll kill you. Flat, just like that. Turned out she meant it."

"Oh, yeah?" I said. "What makes you think she did?"

He grimaced. "Give me a break. Who do you think did it? Anyway, I read her her rights—you can be damn sure of that—but she don't care, she talks. She says she's up all night feeling bad—though how you can tell how she's feelin' one way or another is beyond me. So she comes by his apartment this morning to apologize and finds him dead.''

''How'd she get in?''

He grinned. ''With a key.''

I frowned. ''What's the big deal with that, in this day and age?''

He waved his hand, but kept grinning. ''Nothin', nothin'. No big deal. She had a key, she let herself in. Found him dead and called the cops. See, at this point I don't know about the fight or this Melony-tits dame or any of the rest of it.

''But she tells me. Tells me about the fight. Tells me about the dame. Tells me about hiring you.

''Which makes for a nice little picture, don't it? Motive, method and opportunity, all wrapped up with blue ribbons on it.''

''Method?''

''Gun's there, registered to him. Right in the apartment. Whoever used it, just picked it up and plugged him with it.''

''What aren't you telling me?''

''What do you mean?''

''Well, it doesn't sound like such a solid case to me. What is it about the gun?''

''Well, for one thing, her prints are on it.''

''You're kidding.''

He shook his head. ''No. They're hers, all right. We told her that, she said, yes, when she found the body she picked up the gun and looked at it before she called the cops.''

''Jesus Christ.''

"Hey, she had to say something. Then there's the key."

"What about the key?"

"Well, the key was brand new. Like it was just made. Stuck out on her key ring like a sore thumb. Anyway, we checked around the neighborhood and found a locksmith open seven-thirty in the morning."

"Don't tell me."

"You got it. The guy shows up to open up, there's a woman standing there waiting to get an apartment key copied."

"He I.D. her?"

"What do you think? You know what she looks like. You think she'd be that hard to I.D.?"

I sighed. What a fucking mess.

"We confront her with that and she changes her story. She got there at seven o'clock. The entrance door was open. It's a small apartment building with a buzzer system, no doorman, so there's no confirmation there. Anyway, the door was open so she went in and went up. The apartment door was ajar, she went in and found him dead."

"And the key?"

"She says she panicked. Hard to believe, lookin' at her, right? She says she was afraid the cops wouldn't believe her story—about the door being open. They would think the guy had to be alive to let her in. So she took his key ring out of his pocket, found his apartment key, and went out and had it copied so the cops wouldn't think that."

"It could be the truth."

"Yeah, sure. Anyway, she told us that as if that should be the end of it. I think she was rather surprised—of course it's hard to tell with her—but I think she was surprised we didn't buy it and let her go.''

I shook my head. ''Jesus Christ. Is that it?''

''More or less. When it finally dawned on her we didn't believe her, she clammed up and called a lawyer. Big deal. Too little and too late, huh? I tell you, she gotta be the dumbest killer I ever caught.''

I held up my hand. ''Look, sergeant, let's take it easy here. Just 'cause she lied don't mean she did it. I mean, her story sounds bad, but from her point of view maybe it makes sense. I gotta tell you, knowing this woman, I just can't see her killing anyone.''

He grinned. ''Are you kiddin' me? It's these mousy, repressed types do it every time. And sex, hell, that's always the motive. You take a husband/wife, a girl-friend/boyfriend, it's always the other one who did it.''

''Maybe so, but that doesn't mean it happened here. I have to tell you, from what I've seen of him, this David Melrose was a sharp character, probably involved in some shady stuff. We know he was playing Melissa Ford for her money. He probably had some other scams going too. I'd say drug running, gambling, maybe industrial secrets. I think one of those probably fits him, and you could dig it out with a little work.''

He snorted. ''Give me a break. I got my killer. It's open and shut. We have her statement to the cops, and your testimony to corroborate it. You're getting a subpoena and you'll be on the stand. From what I told you, you know how important your testimony is, and you know you'll be up shit creek if you don't give it. So you stick around, you be available, and when the time comes you talk. Got it?''

''Yeah, but—''

He held up his hand. "Hey, I know you think you're a hotshot private eye and you'd love to help me solve this case. But this time do me a favor—don't. Thanks, but no thanks." He grinned and jerked his thumb at the door. "On your way, hotshot."

12

I walked down the hall to MacAullif's office. He was on the phone when I came in. He waved me into a chair and proceeded to chew the shit out of whoever the hell was on the other end of the line. I figured that did not bode well. I figured right.

MacAullif finished his tirade, slammed down the phone and turned on me. "Jesus Christ, what a fucking day. I got detectives screwin' up in the field, I got the brass on my ass cause the crime rate's up, and now I got you a material witness in a murder case I got nothin' to do with, but you're gonna bug me about it anyway."

"You heard?"

"Yeah, I heard, and it made my day. I said, shit, the asshole will be in here before the day's out, and the fact it's got nothing to do with me won't faze him one bit. Nor will the fact it's an open and shut case."

"You heard that?"

"Come on. It's your typical sordid little domestic tiff. A man and a woman and another woman, bang.

The way I hear it, you gave your client the goods on the guy and she went out and popped him. I suppose that makes you feel bad, but there's nothin' you can do about it, so why don't you give it a rest?''

"I don't think she killed him."

"Of course not. You have a storybook mentality. Anything that obvious couldn't be true."

"Maybe, maybe not. But it needs to be checked out. And there's a problem with the investigation."

"What's the problem?"

"You know who's in charge of it?"

"Yeah. Sergeant Thurman. So?"

"Thurman's an asshole."

"He may be an asshole, but that don't make him wrong. Odds are, the broad popped him."

"Yeah, but what if she didn't?"

"Who gives a shit!" MacAullif controlled himself, took a breath, blew it out again. "I'm sorry, but what the hell has this got to do with me? You got a theory, talk to your client."

I frowned. "Well, that's the thing."

"What?"

"She fired me."

He stared at me. "What?"

"When I told her that her boyfriend was playing around, she got pissed off and fired me."

MacAullif shook his head. "Jesus, what a moron. You got no obligation to this woman at all."

"If she's innocent—"

"If she's innocent, I'll kiss your ass in Macy's window. You're in here to sell me on the theory the woman's innocent and Sergeant Thurman hasn't got the brains to see it. Well, it's no go. You bring in a perp and we'll talk. You got a perp?"

"No."

"Then we won't. You take your business else-where."

"Like where?"

He grimaced. "I gotta do all your thinking for you? The broad hired a lawyer, didn't she?"

"Yeah."

"So talk to him."

13

MELVIN C. POINDEXTER LOOKED LIKE A LAWYER. At least my idea of a lawyer. He was middle-age, balding and wore a three-piece suit. The perfect picture of conservative respectability.

But the image wasn't quite right. Something about it bothered me. After a moment, I knew what it was. Poindexter looked like a *corporation* lawyer. The type of lawyer who would summon the relatives together for the reading of the will. But I couldn't quite see him defending a murder case. Somehow, he did not exactly inspire me with confidence.

I didn't impress him much either. He looked me up and down and said, "Well?"

"I'm Stanley Hastings. I'm here to talk about your client."

"As I understand it, you're a witness for the prosecution."

"They intend to subpoena me."

"I'm sure they do. So you're here to tell me how much harm I can expect you to do?"

"Not at all. I'm here to help."

"You can help by getting hit by a truck. Then you won't have to testify. The way things stand, you'll do a fine job furnishing motivation."

"That's hardly my fault. They only want me to corroborate what your client already told the police."

"Well, don't blame me for that. She made the statement before she called me. Nothing I can do about it now."

"Well, whoever's fault it is, the fact is she made it. So the fact I back it up doesn't mean much."

"Don't be silly. Clients confess all the time. That doesn't make them guilty. And there's ways of getting around it. Maybe I can find a way to suppress her statement. It isn't that hard to do—maybe she wasn't advised of her rights. Well, that's fine, but the prosecution's still got you."

"I see your problem."

"Do you? Good. Then you understand why I'm not jumping up and down at your offer of help."

"Fine. I understand it. Now can we get beyond it and discuss the case?"

"Why? So you have some more information to spill to the cops?"

"Give me a break. In the first place, I haven't told the cops a thing. Now, they can subpoena me and make me talk about the work I did for your client, there's not much I can do about that. But that's another matter. That's something I did. What you tell me is hearsay. I can't testify to that."

"I'm not telling you anything."

"I know that. I'm here to tell you."

"Tell me what?"

"I have information that may help your client. I may be able to get more."

"What do you mean?"

"The surveillance I conducted. Aside from turning up the unfortunate relationship with Melony Tune, I found out enough things about David Melrose to feel he's not entirely kosher and warrants further investigation."

He frowned. "What sort of things?"

Damn. I knew he was gonna say that. The thing was, I had nothing specific. "Well," I said. "There's every indication the man was leading a double life and living above his means. How much could he make in the mail room, for Christ's sake? And he's dressing like a king and entertaining an attractive blond on the side. I wouldn't be surprised to find out he was involved in drugs, gambling, what have you."

"You have no evidence of this?"

"Not at the present time. Your client fired me before I could turn up anything."

"So that's your tack. I must say, your argument is somewhat less than convincing."

"I don't understand your attitude. If your client didn't kill him, someone else did. It behooves you to look for the reason."

He nodded. "Of course. Raise an inference. Create reasonable doubt. I assure you I will do that."

"I'm not talking reasonable doubt. If we can find out who really killed him, the case would be dropped."

He looked at me for a moment, then smiled at me in a rather patronizing way. "Yes, yes, of course."

I studied his face. My eyes widened. "Son of a bitch."

"I beg your pardon?"

"You think she did it, don't you? You're going through the motions, but as far as you're concerned, she did it. You don't believe her story at all."

"I resent that."

"Did she *tell* you she did it?"

"What I discuss with my client is none of your business."

"If she says she did it, I'll walk out that door and never bother you again."

"That would be a blessing."

"Is that the case?"

"No. Her story is exactly what she told the police."

"Fine. Well, what if it's true?"

"What if it is?"

"I would think you would want to check it out."

He smiled. "I see. And you would like me to hire you to do that?"

"Well, you should hire someone. I happen to have the inside track."

"My client fired you."

"She was upset. And that was before this all happened. I would imagine she feels differently now."

"I'll ask her."

"What?"

"I'll ask her. Look, I don't mean to be unreasonable. I've got my own problems. Right now I'm concerned with the matter of bail. If I can get a judge to grant it, she can afford to raise it. That's my main concern at the moment. As for you, my client's a grown woman, and she can think for herself. If she wants to hire you, that's her business. I'll tell her what you told me and she can decide. But *I'm* not hiring you. As far as I'm concerned, you're a prosecution witness.''

''When will you ask her?''

''I'm seeing her this afternoon.''

I took out one of Richard Rosenberg's business cards and passed it over. ''When you do, call this number. They can beep me and I'll get back to you.''

I can't say he seemed thrilled by the prospect, but he took the card.

I got out of there and went back to work. Which wasn't as easy as it sounds, seeing as how the cops had picked me up and left my car in Brooklyn. By the time I took the Eighth Avenue IND out to the Pitkin Street stop, it was getting on towards three o'clock, rather late in the day to be starting a new assignment. Not that I had one to start. Wendy/Janet hadn't assigned me anything, seeing as how the cops wanted me and all. And even my solemn assurances that the police were finished with me and I was free to work cut no ice with her. When I called in before hopping on the subway, Wendy/Janet told me she'd have to check with Richard and beep me back.

So when my beeper went off as I walked up the street toward my car, I assumed she'd gotten his O.K. and was giving me a case.

Not so. The message was to call Mr. Poindexter.

Well. That was something. I'd hardly expected him to call me at all, and certainly not this fast. Something must be up.

It was. Poindexter had had me beeped to report that he had conferred with his client and she had asked him to tell me in no uncertain terms that I was fired, that I could stay fired and that she would be perfectly happy if she never saw my face again.

It was not exactly what I needed to hear at the end of a long, depressing day on a bleak, deserted street corner in Brooklyn, standing under a street sign that said Euclid Avenue.

14

IT WAS INFURIATING. Melissa Ford wouldn't have anything to do with me. Me. The one person who might have helped her. The one person who was on her side. The one person who thought she was innocent.

Everyone else in the world thought she was guilty. Sergeant Thurman. Sergeant MacAullif. Even her own lawyer.

Even Alice.

"Don't be a damn fool," Alice said. "Of course she did it."

"I don't think so."

"You don't *want* to think so. Because then you think it's your fault. That's stupid, but that's the way you are."

"Thanks a lot."

"It's not your fault. You were just doing your job."

"That doesn't sound good."

"I know, but it's the truth. The way you have to look at it is, even if you hadn't, if she's this type of woman, eventually she would have found out and she'd have killed him anyway."

"I don't think she killed him."

"Right. Then what you did doesn't matter, and you don't have to feel guilty at all. Of course you want to think that. That's understandable. But it's not logical. You're letting your emotions cloud your judgment."

"Maybe I am, but the fact remains, at this point I'm the only one who can help her."

"She doesn't want your help."

"I know, but people don't always know what's best for them."

"Funny you should say that."

I took a breath. "Alice, I have to live with myself. The way I see it, no one believes this woman, and no one is going to help her. If I do nothing and she goes to jail for murder, how do you think I'm gonna feel?"

"You're telling me you're going to work on this for no money?"

"What else can I do?"

"I don't know." She thought a moment. "I assume you mean work on this *in your spare time* for no money. I mean, you're not going to call Rosenberg and Stone and ask for time off, are you?"

The thought had crossed my mind. I hadn't decided to do it, but I hadn't decided not to do it either.

I decided now. "No, I know we need the money. I'll do it in my spare time."

Alice looked at me in weary resignation. "But you *are* going to do it?"

"Yes, I am."

15

ONE OF MY FAILINGS AS A PRIVATE DETECTIVE is to be a little too credulous, to believe what people tell me. I've tried to break myself of the habit, to be a little more skeptical and not to take things at face value. I have to keep telling myself that when someone tells me something, whether it's a witness or a suspect or a friend or even my own client, it doesn't necessarily have to be true.

Melissa Ford had told me David Melrose sometimes made late night pickups for the art department.

Winston Peel, the art director for the Breelstein Agency, was a middle-aged man with curly white hair, chubby cheeks and steel-rimmed glasses with such thick lenses one wondered if the man could see any art at all. He was an amiable sort, however, and was perfectly agreeable and cooperative when I showed up at his office the next morning. He just wasn't quite sure why I was there.

"What's this all about, officer?" he asked.

I was in fact impersonating a police officer, though

in a strictly legal way, or at least one no one could nail me for. The method consisted of flashing my I.D. and using the pronoun "we." The only nonkosher thing I was doing was not correcting his use of the word officer, but, hell, nobody's perfect.

"It's about David Melrose," I said.

He frowned. "Yes, I assumed it was." He shook his head. "Terrible thing. But what has this to do with me?"

"Absolutely nothing," I assured him. "We're just checking into the background. I understand David Melrose worked for you."

"Well, not for me directly. For the company. He worked in the mail room."

"Yes, but I understand he made pickups for you. Sometimes after work."

He frowned. "You'd have to check with the mail room on that. I certainly never asked him to."

"No, I'm not saying you did. But isn't it true he sometimes showed up first thing in the morning and put copy on your desk? Work you'd asked for the previous afternoon?"

Peel nodded. "That's true. Sometimes he did."

"And you thanked him for the extra effort?"

He frowned. "Yes, I can recall that happening once or twice. Why?"

I ignored the question. "Now, yesterday, in the morning, naturally that didn't happen because David Melrose was dead. But I'm wondering if you were expecting anything from him?"

"No, I wasn't. Why?"

"We're trying to trace his movements the night he died. We know he left here at five o'clock. I was wondering if there was any art or copy that was due to be turned in that he might have gone to pick up?''

''I see. Well, no. Not that I know of.''

''And as art director, if there *had* been you'd have known it?''

''Yes, I suppose I would.''

''And there was nothing that you know of. But you do know that David Melrose was in the habit of picking up art copy from time to time.''

''Yes, that's true.''

''Who would he pick it up from?''

''I beg your pardon?''

''Who were the artists? Where would he go?''

He frowned. ''I really fail to see what this has to do with anything.''

''You say as far as you know, David wasn't picking anything up that night. Well, that's fine as far as you know. But we have to check from the other end.''

He nodded his head. ''Well, I guess you know your business. We get art from a Donald Phelps, a Julius Blackburn and a Charles Olsen.''

''But you say David hasn't made an early morning delivery in some time?''

He shook his head. ''Not that I can recall.''

''Now, the day before. Monday. His last day of work. Did he deliver any art copy to you that morning?''

''As I said, no.''

''Are you sure?''

''Absolutely. I told you. He hadn't done anything like that in some time.''

''There was no art work that you were expecting that morning? No rush job, something you needed to see?''

"No, there wasn't. And what difference could it possibly make?"

"We're trying to establish a pattern of movement. So, as far as you know, David Melrose would have had no reason to make a pickup from any of these names you've given me over the weekend? Nothing to be picked up Friday night and turned in Monday, for instance?"

He shrugged his shoulders helplessly. "Not as far as I know. You can check with the mail room if you like."

I did check with the mail room and verified the fact that David Melrose had been assigned no after hours pickups in the last few weeks.

Then I got the hell out of there and beat it down to MacAullif's.

He looked about as thrilled to see me as you would expect. He told me I was a schmuck and a fool and a moron and a pain in the ass and other things too numerous to mention. I stood it all patiently and, when he was finished, told him what it was I wanted, at which point he proceeded to run down the whole list of my attributes again, even finding new ones. What saved the day was my firm resolve not to leave coupled with the fact that my request was actually a very simple one. MacAullif hated to give in, but he wanted me out of his office. Only he did not give in gracefully, and you would not believe the sarcasm with which he finally made the call.

The call back five minutes later changed his tune. Donald Phelps and Julius Blackburn had no record at all, but according to his rap sheet, Charles Olsen had a number of priors, including the possession and sale of narcotics.

16

SERGEANT THURMAN SCRUNCHED UP HIS FACE. "Drug paraphernalia?"

"Yeah. Was there any drug paraphernalia in the apartment? Gram scale. Straws. Any drugs, for that matter."

Sergeant Thurman squinted at me. "You workin' for the woman's lawyer?"

"No."

"You workin' for her?"

"No."

"Then what the hell you doin'?"

"A man is dead. I don't like thinkin' it was because of me."

"That's dumb. A broad plugs her boyfriend, it's not your fault."

"Maybe not. What about the drugs?"

"You sure you're not workin' for her lawyer?"

"No. Why?"

"It's just the sort of stuff he'd use. Paint the guy as

a dope fiend. Make the jury think it was a public service to kill him.''

''That's not the idea at all.''

''The hell it isn't. Well, it's no go. No drugs. No equipment. Nothin'. The guy was clean. The only mistake the guy made was havin' a little blonde number on the side. Big deal. You think a jury's gonna feel that gives a mousy little twerp like her the right to shoot the guy for puttin' the pork to something better?''

''No, I don't.''

''Me neither. They take one look at her and, bye, bye, baby. Well, anyway, there you are. No drugs. Nice idea, hotshot, but it's no go. Guess that shoots that theory of yours right out of the water, huh?''

''Not at all.''

17

I staked out Charles Olsen's apartment at five that evening. I'd have done it earlier, but I got beeped and sent to Harlem and beeped again and sent to Queens. I have to tell you, it sure was a pain in the ass having to work for a living and do the Melissa Ford investigation on the side. Particularly for a stupid bitch who'd fired me. Still, my guilt was great and my resolve was firm.

And, I had a genuine bona fide lead. In spite of what Melissa Ford had said, David Melrose had not picked up anything for the art department from Charles Olsen Friday night. And Charles Olsen had a history of drugs. Now, I could have written that off, said big deal, so David Melrose picked up a gram of coke to party with his girlfriend, the Melony-tits broad. But David Melrose had no drugs or drug paraphernalia in his apartment. And you would think a guy who was into recreational drugs would. The way I saw it, David Melrose was a sharpy and a hustler, probably working a lot of different scams. So what if the packet Charles

Olsen slipped David Melrose that night wasn't dope? What if it was money to *buy* dope? What if David Melrose wasn't making pickups from Charles Olsen, he was making deliveries *to* him?

Well, that made for a nice little picture. David Melrose picks up the money that night. Because Monday after work is when he's gonna score. That's what he's doing from five till nine, when the police can't account for his movements. He goes out, scores the dope, then calls on Melony Tune. By the time he's done with her, it's too late to make the delivery and he goes home. So now he's home and he's got the dope, and someone who knows he's got the dope calls on him, kills him and rips it off.

I had to admit there were holes in that theory, but of course there would be since I didn't have all the facts yet. But I had enough to know all that had to add up to something. Hence the firm resolve.

By nine o'clock, that resolve had begun to weaken. If you can't understand that, try standing on a street corner sometime doing absolutely nothing for four hours. At any rate, by nine o'clock the thrill of doing surveillance had greatly worn off, and I was rapidly coming to the opinion that I was wasting my time, that the theory I had was a lot of idle speculation that in reality added up to nothing, and my former client was almost undoubtedly guilty. I wasn't entirely convinced of this, but I think a fair measure of my conviction 'long about nine o'clock would have been that if I'd still had diarrhea today, that would have tipped the scale and I'd have hung the whole thing up and gone home.

It's a good thing I didn't, because at nine-thirty Charles Olsen came out the door large as life and scraggly looking as ever, and set off down the street. I followed him down to Canal, over to Broadway and into the subway. BMT, uptown side.

Not that many people ride the BMT that time of night, but there aren't many trains either, so there were about a dozen people in the station who had obviously been waiting for some time. That was good, because it made less chance of Olsen spotting me. Not that he was likely to anyway. He seemed to take no interest in his surroundings, just shuffled through the turnstile and leaned himself up against a pole. I must say, for an artist the guy wasn't particularly observant. But it made life easier.

A train came by about ten minutes later and everybody got on. I got in the same car, opposite end, plunked down in a seat and sat back to enjoy the ride.

He got off at 42nd Street and so did I, but there was nothing in that to make him suspicious of me. Times Square is the transfer point to about a dozen trains, and at least half the people got off.

Olsen walked to the uptown end of the platform, shuffled up the long ramp there. I paced myself, managed to dawdle along behind. I followed him through the labyrinth of the Times Square station and eventually found myself on the platform of the Broadway uptown line.

If you're not from New York City, I know that makes no sense. I'd just gotten off the Broadway line. But Broadway's a funny street, twisting and curving and cutting across Manhattan as it wends its way downtown. The Broadway IRT follows Broadway downtown to 42nd Street, then continues straight on down Seventh Avenue while Broadway itself veers east. The Broadway BMT, originating in Queens, crosses Manhattan from the east, hits Broadway at 42nd, and then swings back to the east again and follows it on downtown. Don't worry if you haven't got that—there will be no quiz later. At any rate, I'd just transferred from one Broadway train, the uptown N, and was now waiting for another, the uptown 1, 2, or 3.

It was the 3 we wanted. I knew that because the 1, the Broadway local, came and went. So did the 2, which is an express. So he either wanted the 3, or else Charles Olsen was a stone freak who liked to hang out in subway stations.

He wanted the 3. It came, he got on, so did I, and up we rolled.

The car was only about half full, most of the people who'd been on the platform having already opted for the 1 or the 2. But there was still no danger of Olsen spotting me. He sat down, leaned back, and actually closed his eyes.

It was too good to be true. Jesus Christ, was this guy so smooth that he'd spotted me already and was attempting to lull me into a sense of false security before ditching me but good?

Not at all. We stopped at 72nd Street, but he didn't get off. No surprise there. If that's where he was going, he could have taken the 2. Same thing with 96th. Ditto 125th.

At that point I began to get alert. See, the subway map on the wall of the car had given me a clue. The 2 and the 3 run identical routes up to 135th Street. After that, the 2 hangs a right under the East River into the Bronx, while the 3 goes two more stops up Lenox Avenue to the end of the line. So with him passing up the 1 and the 2, I knew ever since I checked the map way back when we pulled out of the station at 42nd Street, that we were going to Harlem.

We were. 145th Street, he opens his eyes, gets up and gets off the train. So did I and so did half a dozen other people, none of them white. That seemed like a good reason for him to spot me, but, as I say, he wasn't spotting anything. He just plodded up the stairs, through the turnstile and out to the street.

The street light on the corner was out and it was dark on Lenox Avenue. And by now it was after ten. I don't know about you, but walking around Harlem alone at night is not my idea of a good time. It didn't faze Olsen any. He just plodded ahead, looking neither left nor right. If he did this often, why he hadn't been mugged by now was beyond me.

He just kept walking and I kept tagging along behind. It would have made a strange picture to anybody watching, him in his tattered T-shirt, sneakers and no socks and me in my suit.

The thought occurred to me about then, maybe the guy never gets mugged because he doesn't look like he has any money.

And I do.

That thought did not sit well.

I followed him two blocks up Lenox Avenue, where he hung a left on 147th Street. That didn't cheer me either. The street was much darker than the avenue and virtually deserted. Not the sort of place I'd like to hang out.

He walked about halfway down the block and went into a tenement. It was a large building, twice as wide as the other buildings on the block. It would have a lot of apartments. That was bad—it would make it twice as hard to figure out where he went. Because, of course, I couldn't walk into the building right on his heels. And I couldn't let him get too far out of sight either. Not that I wanted to go in at all. The lobby was dark and foreboding.

There must have been a staircase in the back and off to the left because that's the direction he went, but I couldn't see it from the street. I counted one, two, three from the time he left my line of sight, gritted my teeth and stepped in the front door.

Damn. A short, narrow hallway. Alcove off to the left. Probably for mailboxes, though it was too dark to tell. The perfect place for someone to hide in, if that was their want. Not a happy thought. Worse, in that I couldn't see where he went until I walked down the hall.

I did, not liking it a bit, and reached the end where the lobby widened out. Again poorly lit, but that shadow in the far corner must be a stairwell. I went over, discovered it was. I stopped, listened for footsteps. I couldn't be sure, but I thought I heard a faint tread overhead. Of course the guy was wearing sneakers, which didn't help—why couldn't he be clompin' along in army boots? The thought flashed through my mind, you're not getting paid for this, as I took a breath and started up the stairs.

Nothing on the first landing. A long, narrow hallway with several doors. None open. Light under the cracks of half of them. Muffled sounds of talking, music, TVs. Could he have knocked on one of those doors and gone in before I got there? Not likely. Any sound of footsteps going up the stairs? Impossible to tell with the noise from the hall.

I hesitated. Schmuck. The longer you wait, the bigger the lead.

I turned and headed up the stairs.

Next landing, same thing. No sign of Charles Olsen, no open door. Quick decision time here. Move on, pick up ground.

Next landing, pay dirt. An open doorway halfway down the hall. A rectangle of light spilling out across the floor. Son of a bitch. Got him.

I'd just had time to think that when a young black kid came giggling out, slammed the door, jerked the door on the other side of the hall and went in, slamming that door too and leaving the hallway in darkness. Shit. Wrong again, and lost some time.

I went up the next stairs fast, reached another hallway of closed doors. By now I couldn't be sure if Olsen had had time to get into one of them. There were no immediate clues, nothing to go by. The easiest choice to make was up.

I climbed a flight and discovered I'd reached the top floor. That narrowed my choices. Another hallway, just like the rest. And, once again, no open door.

But this hallway was a little better lit than the others. A bare bulb in the ceiling at the far end was on. And it showed me something I hadn't seen before. The end of the hallway wasn't the end of the hallway. There was another hallway off it at right angles to the left.

That knocked all my previous deductions into a cocked hat. Charles Olsen probably wouldn't have had time to knock on a door and get admitted before I came up the stairs. But he would have had plenty of time to walk down the hallway and turn left out of sight before I got there.

And he could have done it on any fucking floor.

That was enough to piss off the Good Humor man. So what the hell did I do now?

Well, I could go floor by floor around the bend in the hallway and try to listen for the sound of voices. But what would I listen for? I'd never heard Charles Olsen's voice.

Schmuck.

He's white.

Shouldn't be too hard to distinguish.

I didn't want to do it. But it was either do it, leave, or stand there like a schmuck.

Anything beat standing there like a schmuck. I went down the hall, turned the corner.

A short hallway with four doors. Could be worse. I listened at them. TV, stereos, and the rumble of voices, none white.

Down to the next. Same thing. No obvious honky.

Next floor, same thing again. Except one door produced a sound that could only be a couple making love. That was all I needed to make me feel truly foolish. Unless *that* was Charles Olsen. Which was more than my brain could handle on the one hand, and would not have helped my investigation one whit on the other.

No go on any of the other floors, and suddenly I'm back in the dimly lit lobby feeling somewhat like a schmuck. Also feeling somewhat relieved that I'd gone up and down without incident.

So what the hell did I do now?

Well, one thing for sure. I wasn't going back up again.

I crossed the lobby, went out the front door. The street was deserted, or at least appeared to be—it was dark and hard to tell. I crossed the street, stood behind a parked car, looked back at the door.

I also looked at my watch. It said ten fifty-three,

which meant it was ten forty-five. I'd been inside some time, what with checking all the floors. If Charles Olsen had gone to a lower floor, he could easily have been in and out again. One more persuasive reason for opting for the depressing prospect of giving it up.

Well, what the hell, I'd come this far. I decided to give him half an hour.

It passed. So did several black men, most of whom looked at me kind of funny. After the first few I found myself crossing the street every time I saw someone coming so they wouldn't pass right by. It was like a chess game—the black knight would threaten the white king, who would move across the street out of check. I ought to patent it. Three-dimensional, Harlem Paranoid Chess.

I'd just moved white king to queen's bishop three, when Charles Olsen came out the front door. That was bad, because queen's bishop three was on his side of the street. Fortunately, he walked the other way. And fortunately, once again he plodded ahead without appearing to notice anything.

The white king conceded the game. The hell with chess. Too intellectually taxing. Let's try follow the leader.

And there was a point to the game. Because the leader was carrying a small package. A paper bag. Just about large enough to hold a kilo.

I have to tell you, if that's what it was, Charles Olsen had to be the coolest character I ever knew. To be walking through Harlem in the dead of night, alone, unarmed, carrying a kilo of dope.

Wait a minute. Unarmed. Did I know that? That dirty T-shirt hanging down over the front of the jeans. Was there room there for a gun to be stuffed in the front of the pants? I couldn't tell from this angle. I'm not sure I could tell from any angle. I hadn't thought to look before. And even if he *had* a gun, what the hell difference could it make if he wasn't looking around for anyone to use it on? They could mug him and take his dope before the poor schmuck even knew anyone was there.

No one did. He walked over to Lenox Avenue, down to the subway station and down the stairs on the downtown side. So did I, and this time it was a little hairier. There was only one other person in the station, an old black man sleeping on a bench. I bought my token, then hung back, not wanting to go through the turnstile and find myself on the platform, virtually alone with Charles Olsen. I figured that would make the token clerk suspicious, but he didn't seem to be. Then I realized, at this time of night it was only natural for a white man in a suit and tie to wait by the relative protection of the token booth until the train came.

Which is what I did. When the train came into the station ten minutes later, I stepped smoothly through the turnstile and got on board.

The train was nearly deserted, so this time, Charles Olsen's apparent indifference notwithstanding, I didn't risk the same car. I got in the car behind and kept watch on him through the window.

Not that there was much to watch. He just sat there, oblivious, the paper bag resting casually on his lap, just as if it held a couple of pounds of sugar.

We clanked back through Harlem, stop by stop. No one got on my car or his. A few people got on at 96th and a few more at 72nd. As we rolled into 42nd I got ready to move, figuring he'd switch back to the BMT again.

But he didn't. At 42nd Street he just sat there while the doors opened and closed and the train pulled out. Well, that was something. We were going somewhere else. Unless the guy had just fallen asleep and missed his stop. From my vantage point it was impossible to tell. I glanced at the sign on the wall. The Number 3 to Flatbush Avenue. Shit. Wouldn't that be a kick in the ass, to ride this train to the end of the line in Brooklyn 'cause the guy I was tailing fell asleep.

Not to fear. 14th Street he stands up and gets off. I get off too, and so do a bunch of other people. 14th Street Manhattan is racially mixed and there's not a chance of him spotting me now.

When we came out on the street I realized I was only a couple of blocks away from Rosenberg and Stone. Right here on 14th Street was where I usually parked my car at a meter when I went there. We were headed in that direction now, and it occurred to me wouldn't that be the ultimate irony if that's where Olsen was going. Not that Rosenberg and Stone was open at that hour, of course, but if he went into that building, I was going to think the gods were fucking with my mind.

He didn't, of course. Instead he walked to an apartment building on West 13th Street and went inside.

Which presented a whole different problem from the tenement in Harlem. Here was a well-lit lobby with an elevator and a doorman. How the hell was I gonna get past him?

From my vantage point on the street I could see Charles Olsen confer with the doorman, who nodded and stepped to a phone and a series of buttons on the wall. He pushed what appeared to be the third button down on the left, then talked into the phone, after which he waved Charles Olsen up.

All right. Cold, hard facts.

I took out my notebook, wrote down the address of the building plus third button down on the left.

All right. Now, did I risk the doorman?

I thought it over and decided not. Third button down on the left would always be third button down on the left. There's no reason taking the shot and risking blowing it now. And there wasn't a chance the doorman was gonna let me go up, so there really was nothing to gain.

I stood on the street and waited. It was now after eleven, so I hoped I wouldn't be waiting long.

I wasn't. He was down at eleven-twenty by my watch, or eleven-twelve Eastern Daylight-Savings Time.

And he didn't have the package.

A pickup and a delivery.

Jackpot.

I figured I had what I wanted, but I followed him just the same. He walked back up to 14th Street and headed east. I figured he was heading for the subway, and I figured right. He walked over to Broadway to the BMT line.

I knew he was going home and there was no reason for me to follow him anymore, only I needed to pick up my car which I'd left downtown on Grand Street. So I caught the BMT too. I was real careful doing it. It would have been a real kick in the ass to have followed him successfully all night all over town, and then have him spot me after I'd actually given it up.

He didn't, though. He walked straight home and into his loft building without even a backward glance.

Fine with me. I got in my car, switched off the code alarm that had kept it safely there all night, and drove home.

I must say I felt pretty good. I hadn't pinned down either of the people Charles Olsen had called on, but I had both of the addresses, and in one case I had a potential apartment number. It wasn't much, but in this business you don't usually get much. Nothing, would be the more likely outcome. So all things considered, I had to admit I'd really done a hell of a job.

18

Poindexter wasn't impressed.

"So?" he said.

I stared at him. "What do you mean, so? The man has a record of drug arrests. He made a pickup and delivery last night."

"I fail to see what that has to do with the present case."

"You don't? David Melrose was involved with this man. He made pickups and deliveries for him or from him. Now he's dead, and the man is making pickups and deliveries himself."

"So you say."

"I saw it with my own eyes. A pickup in Harlem and a delivery downtown. There is every reason to believe David Melrose worked that route himself. If he did and it was drugs, his getting shot could be a natural consequence.

Poindexter waved his hands. "Yes, yes, yes. I understand your theory."

"What's wrong with it?"

"There's nothing wrong with it. It's just, that's all it is. A theory."

"And that's all it will be until it's checked out. That's all I'm suggesting you do. Check it out."

He frowned. "It's not much to go on."

"Well, whaddya want?"

"And my client has no intention of hiring your services."

"That's what she said. But she didn't know about this then."

He sighed. "Are you asking me to talk to her again?"

"Could it hurt?"

"I don't think it would help. She was most adamant."

"That leaves you."

"I beg your pardon?"

"As her attorney you have the right to hire anyone you want."

"Not against my client's wishes."

"You're supposed to act in her best interests?"

"Yes, of course."

"Don't you have clients who don't know what their best interests are? As a lawyer, don't you sometimes have to protect them from themselves?"

He smiled and shook his head. "You really need the work this bad?"

"I feel I have a moral obligation to *do* the work. Not getting paid for it is a bitter pill to swallow."

"It's a tough life."

"You're not particularly sympathetic."

"Of course not. I'm concerned with my client's problems, not yours."

"Of course you're being paid."

"Yes, or I wouldn't be doing it. Maybe there's a lesson to be learned there." He paused, frowned. "But perhaps I'm being too hasty. Perhaps there's something in what you say. Why don't you fill in some of the blanks and we'll see if your story has any merit."

"The blanks?"

"Yes. Who is this man you're talking about?"

I shook my head. "You want names, you hire me."

"From what you've told me, my client could probably tell me who he is."

"Maybe, but not where he went."

Poindexter shrugged. "If that's the way you want to play it. Of course, you're a prosecution witness."

"We've been over that."

"Not in this context. As a witness, you will be cross-examined by me on the stand."

"Yes, I know, but—" I broke off, stared at him. "You're telling me why should you pay for the information when you can simply demand it in court?"

"It's probably not proper cross-examination, but I would, of course, subpoena you as my own witness."

"Son of a bitch."

"Sorry you feel that way. I have to protect my client's interests. Now, are you sure you don't want to tell me what you know?"

Yeah, I was sure. The Melissa Ford case could go hang. Poindexter could go fuck himself. And if a year from now I should happen to read in the paper how a young woman just got found guilty of murder, I would shrug and think, gee, that's too bad.

Of course, I said none of this. I just stood with as much dignity as I could muster, said calmly, "Thanks for your time," and turned and walked out the door.

19

IT WAS NOT A GOOD DAY.

After I left Poindexter's office I got beeped and sent out to Bed-Stuy to call on a client who had no phone. He also had no *home,* which was a bit of a shock, since he was supposed to. But the street number on Herkimer that Wendy/Janet gave me did not exist. Needless to say, this made it difficult to find the gentleman in question.

I called Wendy/Janet to report the wrong address, but she gave me no satisfaction, just another signup with a client in Montefiore Hospital in the Bronx. That was gratifying in that Brooklyn to the Bronx was a lot of time and mileage, but when I got there the client was in surgery and I couldn't see him and I had to wash that one out too.

Then I got beeped and given a picture assignment to go back and shoot shots of Raheem Webb. His mother had called in to say that his bandages had just come off, and, while I already had shots of his bandaged head, Richard was all hot to get gross-out shots of the forty-four stitches in his forehead while they were still fresh as possible.

Any other day I would have taken that as a matter of course—naturally that's what Richard would want to show to the jury. But today it just struck me as ghoulish. Plus, it was Raheem Webb, a case I didn't want to be reminded of. A case I knew in my heart was bogus. A case where Richard was gonna dun the city of New York for umpty-thousand dollars, knowing damn well that kid had never tripped on any crack in the sidewalk. I'd told him as much when I'd handed in the case—about the crack and the pusher and the whole mess. And Richard had told me that wasn't his problem. He couldn't go by what I inferred, he could only go by what his client said. He'd file the case, and if it was without merit, the city shouldn't settle.

Easy for him to say. I was the one who'd have to go back there and shoot the shots. Look the mother in the eye again. Look the kid in the eye again. Pretend the whole thing was legit and pretend I didn't care. And then live with the guilt. And for what? Twenty bucks for the photo assignment? While Richard stood to make thousands. Yeah, Raheem Webb was about the last person in the world I wanted to see.

And I couldn't see him either. When I called his mother he wasn't home. Thank god for small favors. Though all that did was make it a pending assignment which would hang over my head and haunt me for days to come. Great.

The whole day was like that, just one fruitless annoyance after another, and even though I wound up with zero on my pay sheet, it was still a blessed relief

when it was finally over and I found myself on the
West Side Highway heading home.

Only I got beeped again. I figured no sweat, it would
just be an assignment for tomorrow, but when I called
in Wendy/Janet told me Richard had a summons he
wanted served and I was to stop by the office to pick
it up.

That was all I needed to hear. I used to get a lot of
summons work, but I don't anymore. That's because
Richard has a service that does the work a lot cheaper.
So the only summonses I get now are the ones the
service failed to serve, which made them a less than
attractive proposition.

Great. It was all I needed to cap off a beautiful day.
The unservable summons.

By the time I fought my way through midtown traffic
down to the office, it was after five o'clock, and while
Wendy and Janet were still there, Richard had gone
home, which was too bad, because I had a few choice
things to tell him about the functionings of his office.
I wasn't going to waste them on Wendy and Janet,
however. I just accepted the summons and got the hell
out of there.

As I walked back to 14th Street where I'd left my
car at a meter, it occurred to me I was exactly where
I'd been last night not twenty-four hours ago, doing
yet another job that I wasn't going to get paid for.
And if Poindexter and Melissa Ford weren't so stupid, I'd be following up that lead right now. But they
were, so I wasn't. Which was a damn shame, with
the address just blocks away, at the end of a long,
draggy day where I'd accomplished absolutely nothing.

I stopped dead in the middle of the sidewalk, furious

with myself. Asshole. Don't even think it. Poindexter made his decision perfectly clear.

Only a moron would even dream of doing anything else now.

20

I WASN'T SURE IF THE DOORMAN was the same one I'd seen last night. For one thing, he was wearing a uniform jacket and cap, which tend to make people look alike. For another thing, last night I'd mainly been concerned with his finger and which button it pressed.

I walked up to him, smiled and prayed.

My prayer was answered. The name next to the third button down on the left was legible enough to read. So when the doorman said, "Yes?" I said, "Mr. Harrison, please."

The doorman nodded and said, "And who shall I say is calling?"

"Mr. Hastings."

The doorman picked up the phone and pressed the third button down on the left next to the name Harrison. After a moment he said, "Mr. Hastings to see you." He listened a few moments, then turned back to me. "What is this in regard to?"

I flipped open my I.D. "I'm an insurance investigator. I've been given Mr. Harrison's name as a witness to an automobile accident. I'd like to ask him a few questions.''

The doorman relayed that information, then the phone squawked for a while. The doorman turned back and said, ''Mr. Harrison knows nothing about any automobile accident.''

I nodded. ''That may well be, and his name may have been given to us in error. If that's the case, I'd like to clear it up.''

Mr. Harrison must have already given the doorman an earful, because he didn't even bother relaying that one. ''Well,'' he said, ''if that's the case, you have no business bothering one of our tenants.''

I smiled good-naturedly and shrugged my shoulders, but raised my voice. ''I know,'' I said. ''I'm only doing my job. I work for an attorney. And he wants the facts. If there's been a mistake and this guy can clear it up, fine. But if not, we gotta subpoena him and drag him into court and clear it up there. It doesn't matter to me one way or another, I get paid for my time. But do the guy a favor and tell him there's money involved, and there's no way the lawyer's just gonna let this go.''

The doorman didn't even have to relay that message, the phone had begun squawking before I'd even finished. The doorman listened, hung up the phone and said, ''Mr. Harrison will be right down.''

I can't say he seemed particularly cordial. I was about as popular in that building as a cockroach.

Minutes later the elevator door opened and a young man came out. Thirties, large-boned, solid, short blonde hair. He looked like he could have played linebacker somewhere. Except for his wire-rimmed glasses. They belied the image. Made him look more like a college student who just happened to be large.

He was wearing some slacks and a sweater which were probably fashionable, if I knew what fashion was. Did that make him a yuppie, whatever the hell they really are?

His attitude was almost laughable. He was obviously put out, but was doing his best to be agreeable and conciliatory. I understood perfectly. No one wants to get dragged into court.

He came bustling up to us. "Mr. Hastings?" he said.

"Yes. And you're Mr. Harrison?"

"That's right. What's this all about?"

I shrugged. "As I say, your name has been given as a witness to an automobile accident."

"That's impossible. I didn't see any automobile accident."

"Ever?" I said.

He frowned. "What?"

"I haven't told you when the accident happened. Some of these cases drag on for years."

That threw him. "Oh."

I smiled. "But, as it happens, you're right. The accident took place Monday night."

"Then I didn't see it."

"That's odd, since your name was given as a witness."

"I don't understand that."

"Well, the driver of the car may be in error. Your name is Harrison?"

"Yes, it is."

"What's your first name?"

"Alan."

I whipped out my notebook, flipped it open, checked a random page. "Well, that could be it. I have it as Albert."

He shook his head. "Not me."

I flipped my notebook closed, stuck it back in my pocket before he could think to ask to look at it. "Well," I said, "let's make sure, and maybe I can write you off."

"I tell you, it isn't me."

"I believe you, but I have to satisfy the attorney. If I can convince him, he'll let you go. If not, he's not gonna take my word for it and you'll get a subpoena."

He actually flinched at the word. People do. "You got the name wrong," he said. "What more do you need?"

"Monday night. The 25th. Eleven thirty-five P.M. Were you in the vicinity of 14th Street and Sixth Avenue?"

"No."

I grimaced and shook my head. "You're too quick to say no. You live in the neighborhood. You could pass that intersection just walking to the store."

"But I didn't."

"How can you be sure?"

"If I saw an automobile accident, I think I would know it."

"Yes, of course you would. But you're not just saying you didn't see the automobile accident. You're saying you were nowhere near the location."

"No, I wasn't."

"How do you know? See what I'm getting at? I can tell the attorney, no, the guy didn't see the accident, which isn't gonna satisfy him. Or I can say, no, the guy wasn't there, at the time of the accident he was uptown just getting out of a Broadway play. I know you can't see the distinction, because you didn't see the accident and that's all that matters to you. But you're dealing with an attorney, and that's not all that matters to him.''

He frowned. "I see."

"So where were you on the 25th at eleven thirty-five P.M.?''

He frowned, and I could see his mind going. He didn't want a subpoena, but how much of this shit did he have to take?

He decided he'd had enough. "Frankly," he said, "I don't think that's any of the attorney's damn business. I keep telling you I was nowhere near the corner of 14th Street and Sixth Avenue. I was not even in the neighborhood at the time. If the attorney wants to put me on the stand, that's what I will testify to. It's not gonna do him a damn bit of good, and if I'm dragged into court I'm going to point out to the judge that I'm not Albert Harrison I'm Alan Harrison, and that the attorney knew that, and then I'm gonna ask the judge if I have any legal recourse for being illegally subpoenaed.''

I smiled and nodded. "Good for you. And just between you and me, if that happens, I hope you win."

He looked at me. "Oh, yeah?"

"Hey, this is a job. You think I like it? You beat the system, more power to you. Anyway, if I'm the guy winds up serving the subpoena, I hope there's no hard feelings.''

He frowned. "Hell."

"Hey," I said, "I'm gonna try to talk him out of it. Your not wanting to tell me where you were at the time won't help, but I'll do the best I can. For what it's worth, I believe you."

Harrison hesitated. He wasn't sure if he wanted to let it go at that. And he wasn't sure if I was his friend or not. Probably not, but no reason to antagonize me. A tough call for him.

He looked at his watch. "Well, if that's it, I was getting ready to go out."

I put up my hands. "Don't let me hold you up. I'll do the best I can."

He gave me one more look, then turned and got back in the elevator.

I turned back to find the doorman looking at me. Alan Harrison's feelings may have been ambivalent, but the doorman's sure weren't. I was as popular as pond scum.

I got the hell out of there and beat it down to the corner where the doorman couldn't see me. Because I'd learned two things useful from my interview with Alan Harrison. One, he hadn't been home and didn't have an alibi for the night David Melrose had been killed.

And two, he was about to go out.

21

It was tougher than following Charles Olsen. Harrison knew me. And he wasn't nearly as obliging and unobservant as Olsen had been. He came out the front door of his apartment building at six thirty-five—six twenty-seven, real time—and looked up and down the street as if he expected to be followed.

If he had looked across the street at the far corner, he might have seen yours truly, standing behind a phone booth. But he didn't, and moments later he set off down the street toward Sixth Avenue. As I followed him from across the street, it occurred to me, maybe he was going to check out the scene of the accident. Though it also occurred to me there was no earthly reason why he should.

He didn't. At Sixth Avenue he walked out in the street and faced downtown, obviously looking for a cab.

That was a bummer. I couldn't let him get one first, but I couldn't walk by him to head one off.

I took a gamble. He was on the southwest corner of

13th and Sixth, and I was on the north side of 13th, natch, having been following him from across the street. I beat it to the corner and crossed Sixth Avenue. There was no reason for him to see me, since he was facing downtown. I glanced down Sixth, saw no cars in the near future. Then I turned and looked east on 13th.

And there it was, a deus ex machina in yellow and black, a Checker cab, one of the few dinosaurs left in the city, coming down 13th with its light on. I flagged it down, hopped into the spacious back seat, whipped out my I.D. and made the cab driver's day.

Only I didn't. The cabbie, Mr. Walsh, according to his posted license, was a quarrelsome old cuss who wasn't about to listen to me. "I ain't doin' nothing illegal," he insisted.

"Of course not," I assured him, but it cut no ice with him. He wasn't waitin' on no street corner to follow nobody in no cab. Just tell him the destination and he'd take me there. No destination, no ride.

I was trying to think of the all-pervasive argument outside of cash, of which I was running low, when I spotted another cab coming up behind us. I hopped out of the cranky Checker and flagged that cab down.

Follow that cab, take two. With much better results. The cabbie was a young black man who seemed quite pleased with the prospect. Pull up to the corner and wait for a man to hail a cab? No problem. He switched on the meter and did just that.

As we reached the corner I looked out the window and saw something that made my blood run cold.

Alan Harrison had just crossed the street and flagged down the Checker cab.

"Oh, my god," I murmured.

"What's the matter?" the driver said.

I filled him in, which wasn't that easy to do. Don't get me wrong, he had no trouble understanding, I just had trouble explaining. It was a new one on me—a private detective tailing a suspect who happened to be riding in the very cab the private detective had tried to tail him in. I wondered if the cranky Mr. Walsh was giving Alan Harrison an earful about the private detective who had tried to get him to tail a cab. It seemed entirely likely. What would Alan Harrison make of that? Would he put two and two together and say, gee, I wonder if that's the same private detective who just called on me? Not if he swallowed the bit about being mistaken for an accident witness. But what if he was involved in something heavy and hadn't bought that bit at all? That could be dangerous. Very dangerous. After all, David Melrose had wound up dead.

The black cab driver—Jones on his license—didn't know all the details, but he read my paranoia correctly. "Don't sweat it, bro. Just sit back and enjoy the ride. Keep your head down, if it make you feel better. I let you know if he's wise."

The cabbie was so agreeable and reassuring I had a sudden flash of paranoia. They're all in it together. Charles Olsen, Alan Harrison, the cranky Mr. Walsh and my guy. After the scene in the lobby Harrison had gone upstairs, called Olsen and said, "Some private dick's wise. He's waiting to tail me when I leave." And Olsen said, "No problem. Go out to the corner of 13th and Sixth. I'll have Walsh and Jones pull the two-cab scam on him. Take care of him good."

All right, so I didn't really believe that. But I have to tell you, I sure felt jinxed.

If Harrison was suspicious, he sure wasn't showing

it. The Checker was just sailing along, straight up Sixth Avenue. That was good. I figured if Harrison was suspicious, he's have the cab make a few figure eights. Then I realized, no, he wouldn't. The cranky Mr. Walsh wouldn't make them. No destination, no ride.

I wondered what the destination was. Most likely nothing helpful. He said he was going out. Most likely he was picking up a girlfriend and going to the movies. Or maybe a Broadway show. If they did, they could see it alone. I wasn't forking out fifty bucks to watch him watch a play. I didn't even *have* fifty bucks.

That started an unsettling chain of thought about whether I could cover the meter. I checked my cash, figured I could. Unless the guy went out of town. That would be the ultimate indignity. "Let me out here, cabbie, before the meter clicks."

We tooled uptown through the forties and fifties, washing out the Broadway play theory, and hit Central Park South. We crossed it, drove into the park and kept on heading uptown. We were now on the drive that makes a huge ragged oval around the perimeter of Central Park. It's a one-way road running uptown on the east side and downtown on the west. I never use it myself, because during certain hours it's closed to traffic to accommodate the bicyclers and joggers, and I can never figure out just when. That's too bad, 'cause it's a very convenient road if you want to get from midtown to the Upper East Side.

Only we weren't going to the Upper East Side. When the cab didn't get off at 90th Street and kept tooling uptown toward 110th, I started to get excited. It seemed too much to hope for, but it sure looked like we were going to Harlem.

We were. We came out of the park at 110th, went straight up Lenox Avenue and hung a left on 147th. The cab went halfway down the block and stopped in front of the building Charles Olsen had gone to the night before.

It was too good to be true. On the other hand, it occurred to me since Poindexter and Melissa Ford didn't want my help, it was only natural every lead I followed would happen to pan out.

Alan Harrison didn't want the cab to wait. Well, actually that's a conclusion on my part—he might well have wanted the cab to wait, only the cranky Checker driver wouldn't do it. At any rate, when he got out, the cab drove off.

But did I want my cab to wait? That was the question. If Harrison was going in and out again, I sure did. But with him dismissing his cab it didn't look like he was. Unless, as I say, that was just Mr. Walsh being persnickety. But should I really gamble on that?

The click of the meter turning over made up my mind. I wasn't gonna sit here and piss away any more unredeemable expense money. I paid off the cab, shuddering at the amount, and got out. The cab drove on down the street, turned the corner and was gone.

So. Just like that. The cranky Mr. Walsh and the agreeable Mr. Jones, my two imagined potential saboteurs, were out of my life and gone just like that. And here I was, once again, hanging out on the street in Harlem with night coming on.

Yeah, I was hanging out in the street. Much as I would have loved to know where he was going, I wasn't following Alan Harrison in. Now that may seem chickenshit to you, but the guy knew me. And if I were to run into him on the stair, what the hell could

I say? Sorry to bother you, Mr. Harrison, but are you *sure* you didn't see that accident? Somehow, I couldn't imagine that was gonna play. At any rate, I hung out on the street.

He was out in twenty minutes. Carrying a paper bag. Just like the one Charles Olsen had. But that wasn't the half of it.

He wasn't alone.

I took one look and gasped.

The man was black. All black. Black T-shirt, black jeans. Full-length, black leather coat. Black boots.

He was also huge. He wasn't as tall as Alan Harrison, but he probably outweighed him. Massive chest, protruding belly, tree trunks for arms. A bull-neck. And then the head. Black hair, black beard, black skin. The hair an irregular Afro with spiky points. A hell of an apparition coming at me out of the twilight.

Well, not exactly at me. I was across the street behind a parked car. I ducked down behind it so Harrison wouldn't see. He didn't, but the two guys coming down my side of the street had to wonder what the hell I was doing. If they raised the alarm I was sunk. But they took it as a matter of course. They passed right by me without breaking stride, and as they did I heard one of them say, "Drug bust." No sweat for them. Just another routine day in Harlem.

Harrison and the Black Death, as I dubbed his companion, walked down the street toward Lenox Avenue. I gave them a good head start before tagging along behind. It would be one thing to have Alan Harrison spot me. I didn't even want to imagine what it would be like to have the Black Death on my case.

At Lenox Avenue they parted company, Alan Harrison downtown and the Black Death uptown.

Decision time. Who do I take?

No problem. I know where the Black Death lives. I want to know where Harrison goes.

I followed him about a block down Lenox when he stepped out in the street and hailed a cab. That caught me up short. He'd made no sign he was gonna do it, and I hadn't been looking for any, expected any, really, cruising Harlem. But there one was, a yellow with its light on and Alan Harrison climbing into it. And no other cab in sight.

Ever try to follow a cab on foot? I did, for about half a block, then stood there watching to see where it went. No apparent help. Down Lenox Avenue till it went out of sight.

All right. Change of plans. I've blown Alan Harrison, let's settle for the Black Death.

I hotfooted it up Lenox Avenue as fast as I could without actually running. I was trying to be inconspicuous, but I could almost swear I heard the words "drug bust" at least one more time.

I crossed 147th, headed uptown in the direction the Black Death had gone. "Had" was the operative word. So was "gone." By the time I reached the corner of 148th, it was clear the gentleman in question was nowhere in sight.

So what did I do now? Look for him. A black man in Harlem, shouldn't be that hard to find.

Fuck that. I was right by the subway station. That was for me. I wasn't taking a cab if I wasn't following anyone.

I went down in the station, bought a token. There was a train coming in. I went through the turnstile and got on. It was the number 3 express, of course. There were no tunnel delays and we hit 96th Street, which was my stop, in record time.

Only I didn't get off. Because I was on the express. And without tunnel delays, going uptown and downtown an express train can usually beat a cab.

I rode the express down to 14th Street, got off, sprinted out of the tunnel up to the street and flagged a cab. It was a Checker, and if it had been cranky Mr. Walsh again I'd have nearly died, but it wasn't. I hopped in and said, "Grand and Wooster."

The cabbie made good time and we pulled up on the corner five minutes later.

It was a hell of a long shot, and I figured I'd just wasted the six bucks I'd just handed the cabbie, but as I closed the door another cab drove by us and pulled up in front of the loft on Grand.

Holy shit. Was it possible?

My cab drove off, leaving me exposed for all to see. I shrank back into the shadows around the corner.

It's a good thing I did, because Alan Harrison, still carrying the paper bag, got out of the cab, walked up to Charles Olsen's loft and rang the bell.

22

How many times does a guy have to get kicked in the face before he learns? I don't know what the answer is, but what I'm trying to say is, I knew calling Poindexter again wasn't going to do me any good. But I just couldn't help myself. I didn't beg and plead this time, though. Just dropped the bomb and hung up.

"Yes?" Poindexter said.

"This is Stanley Hastings," I said. "Just calling to tell you another drug deal went down last night."

"What?"

"Just wanted to let you know. Incidentally, it was a different party this time. I have now I.D.'d two separate drug runners, plus I can personally I.D. the connection they're scoring from. It's been nice talking to you, beep me any time."

And I hung up the phone.

I felt pretty good about the whole thing. Of course, it occurred to me if Poindexter could put me on the stand and make me talk, I was just telling him what questions to ask. But at the moment I didn't care. At the moment it was fun just twisting his tail.

And anyway, what the hell *could* I say on the stand? I mean all that shit about dope deals and connections, that was pure speculation on my part. I had no hard evidence. At least, nothing I could testify to. I mean, what had I seen? A guy carrying a paper bag. If that was all it took, you could bust half of New York City. No, when it came right down to it, the whole Charles Olsen, Alan Harrison, Black Death drug connection was nothing more than idle speculation, and there was no reason for me to testify to it when I got on the stand.

Which would be Monday. I found that out right after I talked to Poindexter. I got beeped, and when I called in Wendy/Janet told me the cops had called and wanted to know where they could find me so they could serve me with a subpoena.

I wasn't looking for trouble. I called right in and spoke to Sergeant Thurman himself, told him I wanted to cooperate. He was pleased to hear it, but wasn't about to take my word for it. They were putting together a grand jury to indict Melissa Ford, they'd be calling witnesses on Monday, and they wanted to subpoena me to be sure I'd be there. I told him that wasn't necessary, but he allowed as how it was, and wanted to know just where the hell I was gonna be. So I gave him the address of my first signup in Queens, and when I pulled up in front of the building an hour later, damned if there wasn't a process server standing right there.

I'm always apologetic about serving subpoenas, but this guy wasn't. He was a tough son of a bitch who looked like an ex-cop, most likely one who retired from the force after being shot a few times. When I admitted to being Stanley Hastings, he slapped the subpoena in my hand and glared at me in a way that might have made sense if I'd been the defendant in the case instead of just a witness. Then he hopped in his car and drove off, leaving me standing there on the sidewalk holding the subpoena.

Son of a bitch. There it was, all official and everything. Nine-thirty Monday morning, Criminal Court building, 100 Centre Street, Stanley Hastings is hereby ordered to appear.

I sighed, shoved the subpoena in my pocket, went inside and signed up Delbert Cross, who had had the misfortune to ride his bicycle into a pothole, resulting in a broken wrist. I signed him up, fired off some pictures of his cast, then went out with him to scout the offending pothole. I can't say I was too impressed. It was a simple indentation in the street—no cracks, no break in the asphalt—just a smooth, rounded dip, none of which was gonna show up in the picture. I took them anyway, knowing even if they stunk I'd still get paid for the job. Hot damn. It occurred to me it was about time I got paid for a job.

I bid a fond farewell to Delbert Cross and headed up to the Bronx to sign up Harold Burlson, who'd been the victim of a hit and run.

I was not happy. Not that unusual a condition for me, but this time my unhappiness had a specific focus. The subpoena in my jacket pocket.

A grand jury. What the hell was a grand jury? I mean, I knew what they did, they handed down indictments. That was the way you always heard of them. "The grand jury handed down an indictment today in the Gotsagoo case." Handed down? Handed down to whom? A younger brother? No, that's hand *me* down. But that's how they say it on the news: handed down an indictment. Why handed? Was it a slip of paper, this indictment, something they could hand? And why down? Because they're a grand jury, a lofty jury, way up there, that they have to hand something down? No, I'm confusing them with a *high* court. Not to be confused with a supreme court. Supreme court, high court, grand jury. What the hell did all that mean?

Well, I knew who made up a grand jury anyway. I knew that from my stint on jury duty. I wasn't called for a grand jury—which was a miracle, since I was called for everything else—but I heard other prospective jurors being interrogated by the lawyers, and one of the questions they all asked was, did you have any previous jury experience, and if so, was it criminal, civil or grand? And several of them stated they'd served on grand juries. So that was something. This would not be a star chamber with a panel of high judges listening to me testify, it would be a panel of my peers.

How big a panel, I didn't know. A criminal jury's twelve, a civil jury's six, but a grand jury I had no idea. As to the rest of the personnel, the prosecutor would be there, but not the defense attorney—Poindexter had said that much. And the prosecutor would call me to the stand and start asking me questions about my relationship with Melissa Ford. About the work I did for her. And I would have to answer.

But what about the work I *didn't* do? The work I did for myself. Would I have to answer about that? I had no idea. On the other hand, the police didn't know about the other work I'd done, so they wouldn't be asking about it, would they?

Or would they? Would they ask for a blanket statement giving everything I know? Surely they couldn't do that. But what about specifics? I have to tell 'em about David Melrose meeting Charles Olsen. Suppose they ask me if that's the only time I ever saw Charles Olsen? Well, it sure wasn't, but could they ask me that? And if they did, would I have to answer?

And what about the stuff I told Melissa Ford? I suppose I'd have to state it. After all, that was the crux of the matter. I gave her the information and she acted on it. Yeah, they could ask me about what I told her.

But what about what she told me? Would that be hearsay? Or would it be an admission against interest? Aha, my years of reading murder mysteries pay off.

No, they don't. Schmuck. You don't *want* to be able to testify about that, and if it's an admission against interest you can.

So, my years of reading murder mysteries dork me. A much more natural consequence.

But was it true? Was that the case? As a witness before the grand jury, just what the hell were my rights anyway?

It was right about then that two things occurred to me.

One was that I was in the EXACT CHANGE ONLY lane of the Triboro Bridge, and I didn't happen to have exact change, and even if I did, I wouldn't want to pay it because I'd get dorked out of it because I couldn't get a receipt.

The other was that I really ought to consult a lawyer.

23

ANYONE WHO HAD NEVER MET RICHARD ROSENBERG would probably have trouble thinking of him as small. He was certainly a giant in the industry. In terms of settlements, he was second to none. That's percentage of settlements, by the way—I'm sure there are larger firms that handle more volume, and Richard's a one-man show. Even so, his volume ain't bad either. But of the cases he takes, the percentage he wins is phenomenal.

And for good reason. For one thing, Richard is very sharp at weeding out clients and turning down cases that aren't worth his time—when Richard files suit, it's there. For another thing, Richard is the consummate showman. Put him in front of a jury, and nine times out of ten that jury is going to give him exactly what he wants. The tenth time, while it won't do that, it will still give him something. Though only in his thirties, his exploits are already legend.

But I was talking about size. See, Richard Rosenberg is actually rather small. He is short and slight of build. But you would never know it. Even people who have met him have trouble thinking of him as small. Because Richard compensates so well. If that's what you could call it. If you can imagine an intelligent pit bull on speed, that's Richard. His mind is going a mile a minute, his body is going a mile a minute, if he gets hold of something, forget it, he ain't never gonna let go. So talking to him is always a challenge. There's no use trying to keep up. All you can do is watch and wait and hope somehow, some way, some part of what he's doing relates to you.

Richard had helped me out in the past when I'd had trouble with the police. Partly because he's a frustrated Perry Mason who would love to take part in a murder trial, and partly because he just naturally loves bopping cops around.

But in this case I wasn't accused of anything, so I couldn't count on him giving a shit. In fact, that was the first thing he said to me when I walked into his office and asked for his help.

"Are you accused of anything?"

"No," I said.

"Then who gives a shit?"

I knew I had to hook him right away or I was out the door. I took out the subpoena and threw it on his desk.

"They're hauling me in front of the grand jury and forcing me to testify against my own client. I don't wanna do it."

Richard picked up the subpoena, looked at it. "They subpoenaed you?"

"They sure did."

"Well, what do you want me to do, quash the subpoena?

"What does that mean, get me out of it?"

"That's right."

"Absolutely. Can you do it?"

"No."

"Then why did you bring it up?"

"To see if that was what you wanted me to do. If it was, it would end the discussion."

"Okay, then that's not what I want you to do."

"What *do* you want me to do?"

"I need advice."

"Legal advice?"

"Of course."

"You know what my rates are?"

"No, I don't. Do you know what mine are? Ten bucks an hour and thirty cents a mile."

Richard frowned. "What's that got to do with it?"

"Well, I do an awful lot of your work. If I go to jail, you're gonna have to get someone to replace me."

"You're not going to jail. You're a witness, not a suspect."

"Yeah, but I don't wanna testify. If I don't get some good legal advice, I'm apt to find myself in contempt of court for refusing to answer questions."

Richard thought that over. He nodded approvingly. "Very good. Very good. You've come up with a very logical argument why I should help you."

"So, you gonna?"

Richard picked up a pencil, drummed it on the desk. He cocked his head. "You shoot the shots of that kid's forehead yet?"

"You mean Raheem Webb?"

"If that's the kid with the stitches, yeah."

"I haven't reached him yet."

"I want fresh shots."

"I called but the kid wasn't home."

"Was that today?"

"No. Yesterday."

"You haven't tried today?"

"Not yet."

Richard scooped up the phone, pushed the intercom. "Yeah," he barked. "Call up . . . what was the name again?"

"Raheem Webb."

"Yeah, call Raheem Webb's mother, find out if he's there, tell him to stay there because Stanley's coming by to take the shots."

Richard slammed down the phone, looked back at me.

"It's a bad case, Richard," I said.

"So you say."

"I'm telling you, it is."

"Bad case, good case, the shots are still the shots. If I go ahead with it, I want 'em fresh."

I had to hand it to Richard. He knew damn well I didn't like the Raheem Webb case, and he must have suspected I was dragging my heels on the photo assignment—which wasn't actually true, I just hadn't been able to do it, but he didn't know that. At any rate, without actually saying so, he had managed to set up the situation as an if-then proposition. He would "give in" and advise me about my grand jury testimony, if I would stop making a stink about the Raheem Webb case and go take the accident pictures.

It was a big victory for Richard. No, not the Raheem Webb case—he could bully me into doing that anyway. But now he could act put upon while pontificating about grand juries, which I'm sure was something he secretly wanted to do anyway.

"Fine," I said. "I'll take your pictures. Now tell me what I can do."

"You'll have to be more specific."

"How specific do I have to be? They're gonna ask me to testify and I don't wanna."

"Yeah, but to what? What's the story?"

I told him the whole thing. From Melissa Ford hiring me, to Melissa Ford firing me, to the cops picking me up and Sergeant Thurman questioning me. A lot of that he already knew, of course, what with the cops calling the office to have Wendy/Janet beep me, first to pick me up and second to serve the subpoena. But most of the details were new.

And I told him about my post-murder investigation. From Charles Olsen's drug record, to tailing him, to tailing Alan Harrison, to finding the Black Death. I told him about my conversations with Poindexter, and Poindexter's apparent lack of faith in his client.

He never interrupted once. He just sat there, hunched over at his desk, his brow furrowed in concentration, his fingers occasionally drumming a tattoo on the desk as if to accent something I'd just said.

When I was finished, he cocked his head at me and said, "So. No wonder you don't have time to take pictures for me."

"All of that was on my own time, Richard."

He waved it away. "Sure, sure. So whaddya want?"

"I told you. I don't wanna testify."

"You have to testify. You're a witness."

"Yes, but to what? The way I see it, I only know what I told her and she told me."

"What you told her is what you personally observed."

"True."

"And what she told you is an admission against interest."

"Shit."

"You didn't know that?"

"Actually, I did. I hoped I was wrong."

"Well, you're not. But what's the big deal? I thought you said she already told all this to the cops."

"Yeah, but the lawyer thinks maybe he can suppress her statement."

"Perhaps he can. But not before the grand jury."

"Why not?"

"Because he won't be there. The prosecutor can do any damn thing he likes. He can call the officers and have them testify she made that statement."

"Will the judge allow it?"

"What judge?"

"The judge in charge of the grand jury."

Richard looked at me. "There's no judge on a grand jury."

I blinked. "What?"

"There's no judge. There's just the prosecutor and the grand jurors."

I stared at him. "Richard, that makes no sense."

"Why not?"

"Well, it's unfair."

He shrugged. "Who said anything about fair? That's why an indictment's not like a conviction. It doesn't mean anything. Because, the way it's set up, basically a prosecutor could get anybody indicted for anything at all if he really wanted to. The defendant isn't there, the attorneys aren't there, the judge isn't there. The only one there is the prosecutor, telling the grand jurors what he wants them to do. Callin' only the witnesses he wants to call and askin' them only the questions he wants to ask.''

''Aren't the grand jurors allowed to ask questions too?''

''Sure. They have that *right*. But with the prosecutor moving things along, you think they ever get a chance? It's not like he ever says, ''Well folks, any of *you* got any questions of this guy?'' They'd have to *interrupt* him to get a question in.''

I could feel my heart sinking. This meeting was supposed to calm me down. To allay my fears of going in front of the grand jury. Instead, it was as if my worst nightmare were coming true.

I took a breath. ''Richard.''

''Yeah?''

''Come with me.''

''What?''

''Come with me to the grand jury. Represent my interests.''

Richard chuckled, shook his head. ''You don't want me.''

''Yes, I do.''

''No, you don't. See, you don't understand. That's the only good thing about a grand jury hearing. A witness before a grand jury has immunity.''

''Oh?''

''No matter what you testify to, you can't be prosecuted. Oh, if you lie, they can get you for perjury. But if you tell the truth, they can't get you on any count whatsoever for this crime.''

''That's not what I'm worried about.''

''Maybe not. But get this. If you have a lawyer there when you testify, the only way you can do that is if you *waive* immunity. And why would you wanna do that just to have a lawyer there when he can't do anything anyway?''

"He can't do anything?''

"No. He can't ask questions, he can't object, all he can do is sit there and watch his client testify.''

"So what's the point?''

"There isn't any. That's what I'm trying to tell you. Look, you're making a big fuss over nothing. If they wanna indict, they're gonna indict. That's a given. So what you testify to doesn't matter. And if it's hearsay and inadmissible, then when you get into a courtroom it won't be admitted. The jury won't hear it and there's no big deal.''

"Yeah, but . . .''

"But what?''

"There's other stuff I don't wanna talk about.''

"What other stuff?''

"The stuff I did after. Charles Olsen, Alan Harrison and the Black Death.''

"Yeah, but they don't know, so who's gonna ask you?''

"I don't know, but it might come up.''

"So what if it does? That don't hurt your client any. In fact, it helps her. It's evidence someone else might have committed the crime.''

"I know that. But . . .''

"But what?''

"Well, Poindexter won't be there, but he'll get a transcript of the testimony, right?''

"Not necessarily. Only if they go to trial. Then he'll get it as part of the Rosario material.''

"The what?''

"Rosario material. Like Miranda decision. It's a

precedent. Someone named Rosario got to see some material, now everyone gets to see it. See?''

''Yeah. Well, then he'll see it. And it's work I did for him, and I don't want the son of a bitch getting the information unless he pays me for it.''

Richard spread his hands wide. ''Aha! A purely selfish, mercenary motive. I love it.''

The phone rang. Richard scooped it up. ''Yeah?'' He listened a moment, said, ''Good, make sure he stays put,'' hung up the phone and turned back to me. ''The kid is home. You can go take the pictures.''

''Yeah, but—''

''But what? You got nothing to worry about. As far as you're concerned, you got immunity. As far as that other shit's concerned, they're not gonna ask you about it. As far as what you told your client and your client told you, don't sweat it, just testify to it. They're gonna indict anyway, so what's the big deal? When they get into court they'll have to ask those questions again, and then her attorney will be there objecting to every one.''

''Yeah, maybe, but—''

''But nothing. Look, I'm glad you're greedy and I'm sorry you're paranoid, but there's nothing I can do about either one. If you got a problem, a legitimate problem, give me a call. But the fact is, you don't. The fact is, you worry too much.''

Richard smiled benevolently, as if he'd just solved all my personal problems. Then he leaned back in his chair and cocked his head.

''Now,'' he said, ''if it's not too much trouble, you think you could get some shots of that kid's forehead before the damn thing heals?''

24

I WAS IN A FOUL MOOD DRIVING UP TO HARLEM to take the shots of Raheem Webb. I think I've said that before—about being in a foul mood, I mean. In point of fact, practically ever since I met Melissa Ford I'd been in a foul mood. And, ever since I met Raheem Webb I'd been in a foul mood. Either of those cases alone was enough to make me less than happy. Taken together, they were almost more than I could bear.

My interview with Richard had not cheered me. Despite his assurances, I was convinced my appearance before the grand jury was going to be a total disaster. Everything pointed to it. I had information I wanted to conceal. Somehow, someway, they were gonna ask some question that called for it. And what was I gonna do then? Answer? Refuse to answer? Challenge the prosecutor on procedure? That would be great—I wonder if anyone had ever done that before. And if I did, what would happen then? Well, I know what would happen—the prosecutor would say I was out of line and to shut up and answer the damn question. And if

I didn't answer it, they'd find me in contempt of court. But wait, *who* would find me in contempt of court? There's no judge.

But that didn't matter, did it? Because Richard said they could find me guilty of perjury. So if they could find me guilty of perjury, they must be able to find me guilty of contempt. So who cares how they do it, the fact is they could do it. The only thing they couldn't find me guilty of was the murder itself, because I had immunity.

Well, that started a train of thought. Son of a bitch. I had immunity. Immunity for the murder. So what if . . . ?

Immediately in my mind I began playing out a movie scenario. I'm on the stand and the prosecutor is questioning me and I say, "No. no, you've got it all wrong. Melissa Ford didn't commit this crime. I ought to know, because I shot the son of a bitch myself."

Wow! That would rock 'em in their sockets. I'd clear Melissa Ford of the crime, and they couldn't prosecute me for it because I'd have immunity.

My bubble immediately burst. For the murder, yeah. But they could prosecute me for perjury. And that's what I'd be committing.

Of course, they'd have to prove it. That would be a neat case. The prosecutor would have to prove I *didn't* commit the murder. "Your Honor, ladies and gentlemen of the jury, I intend to prove that the defendant, Stanely Hastings, did not kill the decedent, David Melrose." Wow. Tough assignment, proving a negative. I wondered if he could do it?

I was still wondering about it when I pulled up in front of Raheem Webb's building. That snapped me out of it. Bye bye, daydreams, hello, harsh reality.

There were a couple of kids hanging out on the front steps. They might have been some of the ones who'd been hanging out there before, but I wasn't sure because I hadn't noticed them particularly at the time. But I did notice one of them was wearing a beeper.

I looked around when I got out of my car, but Raheem's pusher was nowhere in sight. That was good. I had enough problems without dealing with him too. I locked up my car and went in, receiving my usual creature-from-another-planet stares from the kids on the front steps.

Sheila Webb let me in. If she'd been uncomfortable at my first visit, this time she was even more so. She had trouble even meeting my eyes. She led me into the living room, said, "I'll get Raheem," and went off to do that.

I was wearing my camera on a strap around my neck, or on my shoulder, actually. I put my left arm through and pull it over my head so the strap is on my right shoulder and the camera hangs down my left side under my jacket, useful for hospitals and places where I'm not supposed to have it. It always strikes me as sort of funny—I wear it where most private detectives would wear a gun.

I reached under my jacket, tugged the camera out, slid the lens cover open, checked the film. I had twelve pictures left on the roll. Good. That should be more than enough for simple injury shots.

I realized I was fiddling with the camera so I wouldn't have to think about Raheem Webb—just as his mother had gone off to get him so she wouldn't have to deal with me.

From the bedroom I heard, "Raheem, lord, what is

the matter with you?'', then some indistinguishable mumbling, then, ''Get along now, the man is waiting.'' Moments later Sheila appeared, prodding Raheem along. Her manner was irritated, but at the same time more relaxed than when she'd opened the door. Raheem's stubbornness had given her a focus, allowed her to deal with the boy rather than with me. She indicated me, of course, but only as the man who was waiting, then turned back to glare at Raheem in exasperation.

On the other hand, I had to admit her impatience with the boy was totally warranted. Standing in the doorway, his head down, his chin set, his lips curled into a sneer, his eyes focused somewhere on the floor, he certainly looked like a sullen punk.

I had a sudden wild impulse to raise the camera and fire off a shot of the two of them together. A family photo. I restrained it. Get a grip on yourself. Just get the shots and get out of here.

I still hadn't seen the wound. Raheem's bandages were off, but he now wore a blue knit cap which was pulled down over his forehead. The cap now drew his mother's ire. She batted at it, said, ''Come on, boy, get that off and let the man see.''

He batted back at her, all loose-limbed and ungainly, reminding me how young he was for one so tall. He kind of slumped on his tailbone on the door frame, reached up and tugged off the cap.

Jesus Christ.

The bandages were off, but the stitches were still in. Forty-four of them, in two jagged rows. From just over his left eye all the way to the hair line on the right. The scar tissue was still fresh, a mottled red and pink, crosshatched with the black stitches, an ugly inch-wide headband cutting across three-quarters of the fore-head, a brutal contrast with the coal black skin. It was enough to turn your stomach.

Richard would love it.

I wasn't gonna ask the kid to move, pose, stand in the light or anything else. I just walked up to him, raised the camera and fired off shot after shot.

I finished the roll, lowered the camera, hit the button to rewind the film.

I said, "Thanks, Raheem," then turned to his mother, said, "Thanks, Mrs. Webb. That's all I need."

She still wasn't ready to deal with me. She nodded an acknowledgement, but her eyes were on her son. "Raheem," she said, "walk the man down to his car."

I put up my hand. "That's not necessary."

She put up hers. "No, no. Raheem will walk you down. Raheem?"

Raheem casually kicked one foot lazily against the floor, waggled his head a few times, then reached up and pulled on the cap. He pushed himself away from the door frame and shuffled loose-limbed and gangly across the room, never once glancing in my direction.

His mother sighed, shook her head as if to say, "Boys," then looked down at the floor.

There was no use protesting any further. I nodded my farewell to the top of her head and followed her son out the door.

It was on my way down the stairs that the whole thing hit me. The scar on his forehead. The beeper on his belt, which I assumed he was still wearing, though with his T-shirt pulled out I couldn't tell. And the mother who couldn't meet my eyes.

Why the hell had she called us? Why had she demanded my presence, which obviously embarrassed her so much? I mean, she knew as well as I knew his story about falling down was bullshit. Anyone would know that. She knew it wasn't a legitimate case. And yet, here she was, calling a lawyer, filing suit. Why? Just to get the money? I couldn't buy that. Not that woman. It wasn't in her nature. It wasn't the sort of thing she would do. And yet, here she was doing it.

It was going down the stairs that I realized why. *Raheem, walk the man down.* Why? Like I couldn't get out of the building myself? Like I couldn't find my own car? In all the hundreds of cases I'd handled, no parent had ever asked their child to see me out. Except for Sheila Webb. And in that sickening moment, I understood why.

It was a cry for help. Sheila Webb was a single mother with a lying, dope-dealing ten-year-old kid she didn't know how to handle. Then he got hurt and told a stupid lie. So what did she do? She called a lawyer. She called a lawyer because the lawyer wouldn't believe Raheem's story any more than she did, and the lawyer would know what to do. The lawyer would protect her, protect her son. Any lawyer would. No lawyer could be so stupid as not to see. Imagine her chagrin when I showed up, appeared to take Raheem's story at face value. That must have been a shock. But then a second chance. The accident photos. Surely when I see the scar on his forehead I won't be able to just let it go.

But I do. So what's the upshot? "Raheem, walk the

man down to his car.'' One last stab. One last desperate hope. A chance for me to question the boy. A
chance for the boy to open up to me.

And what made me sick, of course, was the fact that
it wasn't gonna happen. I couldn't do it. It wasn't my
job. Because I wasn't the lawyer, as Sheila Webb assumed, I was merely the private detective investigating
the case. Richard was the lawyer. And Richard didn't
give a shit.

But that was a lame excuse. I might be working for
Richard, but I was still my own man. I shouldn't do
anything to undermine Richard's case, no, but aside
from that, whether I helped Raheem Webb out was
entirely up to me.

And I wasn't gonna do it. As I tramped down the
stair, watching the back of Raheem's knit cap bobbing
down in front of me, I knew that bad as Sheila Webb
might need help, bad as Raheem Webb might need
help, and bad as it made me feel, there was no way in
hell I was getting involved in all this.

Raheem reached the front door, pushed it open,
stepped outside.

I half expected to hear a voice yell, ''Hey nigger,''
but none did. I stepped out on the step next to Raheem.

They were right at the bottom of the steps. Raheem's
pusher and one of the kids who'd been hanging out on
the step when I went in. The kid had just handed
something to the pusher.

The kid saw me first. He said, ''Oh, shit!,'' turned
and ran.

The pusher looked up then. He saw me and our eyes
met. I don't know how to describe the look he gave
me, but I have to tell you, it was hard to keep from

pissing in my pants. The guy looked like he would have loved to squash me like a bug.

I did my best to stare him down. That was the best I could manage at the moment—to stand still without moving. I doubt if I did that good a job, but the net result was it worked. I was a white man in a suit and tie, probably a cop. The guy was obviously carrying, had obviously just taken drugs from his mule, and didn't want to mess with me.

He wasn't about to run, though. That wasn't his style. He just stared back, haughty, proud, insolent. Then he looked from me to Raheem. He shook his head, slightly, slowly, deliberately, glaring straight at Raheem. He looked back up at me, shook his head again. Then he turned and walked away, slowly, insolently, as if daring me to follow.

Naturally, I didn't. I just stood there watching until he went around the corner and out of sight. Then I turned to look at Raheem.

He looked like he'd just seen a ghost. He stood there swaying slightly, his eyes blinking. He wet his lips, blew out a breath.

One of the kids at the bottom of the steps looked up and said, "Shit, man, you done it now."

It wasn't my problem. And there was nothing I could do. If Raheem's pusher beat him up again because he thought I was a cop and Raheem had sicced me on his case, damn it, that wasn't my fault. And even if it was, what the hell could I do?

Nothing. That was the answer, and it was the only answer. I'd been doing this job for a while, and if there was one thing I'd learned in all the cases I'd handled, it was that a private investigator can't let himself get involved. Because if you did, you'd go nuts. You just harden yourself, put it out of your mind, and get on to the next case. And bad as it made me feel, I knew damn well that was the only thing to do.

Like hell.

I took Raheem Webb by the shoulders, turned him around, and piloted him back upstairs to his mother.

●

25

NOTHING PROPINKS LIKE PROPINQUITY. Now there's a phrase you don't hear too often. Like you're sitting in a bar watching a Mets game, and the guy next to you leans back on his stool and says, "Nothing propinks like propinquity." It just doesn't happen. Though, to be honest, I don't sit in bars watching Mets games. I gave up drinking years ago, and I'm a Red Sox fan. But if I ever *did* sit in a bar watching a Mets game, I'd be willing to bet you that phrase wouldn't come up.

Nonetheless, that's what occurred to me as I walked down the street away from Raheem Webb's building. Which was strange, 'cause to be honest, I don't know what those words mean. I don't even know where they come from, though most likely I read them in an Agatha Christie novel. But maybe not. Anyway, what I *think* they mean is something like if you put a man and a woman together on a desert island they'd fuck each other's brains out. But that's a rather vague definition, and probably not the one found in Webster's. Or in

Agatha Christie, for that matter. And I'm not sure getting friendly is the intended meaning either. Maybe it really means they'd *beat* each other's brains out. But either way, I figured it had something to do with nearness. But then again, it occurred to me maybe I was just confusing propinquity with proximity.

No matter. The simple fact is, as I walked away from Raheem Webb's building, the phrase "Nothing propinks like propinquity" flashed in my brain.

The reason was simple. I had just realized something. Raheem Webb's building was only a block and a half from the Black Death's.

You might think it strange I hadn't realized this before, but it wasn't really. The first time I'd called on Raheem Webb was before I'd tailed Charles Olsen to the Black Death's. And the night I did that there was no reason for me to think, gee, I must be really near Raheem Webb's. Because *he* wasn't important. The only way I would have realized it would have been the other way around.

And the reason I didn't realize it today, when it *was* the other way around, was I was daydreaming. I was so preoccupied with Richard and the grand jury and fantasizing about confessing to the murder and getting away with it because I had immunity, that I was driving on automatic pilot and had no idea where I was until I pulled up in front of Raheem Webb's door. At which point I was too concerned with my problems with him to stop and realize where I actually was. So it was only after I came downstairs again after a half-hour session with Raheem and his mother and started to get in my car that it suddenly occurred to me.

A block and a half from the Black Death. And my

beeper quiet as the grave and no pending assignment for Richard to do.

Now I knew there was no use doing any more work for Melissa Ford. There was no way on earth I was ever gonna get paid for it. But I had that grand jury appearance hanging over my head. And all that information I had that was so close, that was almost there. And I couldn't help thinking it would be really nice to wrap things up, to nail it down before Monday, to come walking into that courtroom with every ace in the deck.

Not that I really thought that possible. It was just that, hell, a block and a half. It was almost like a free shot. Almost like it had been planned that way. As part of the grand design.

Plus, I was psyched for it. Psyched up by my half-hour meeting with the Webbs. Which was, after all, not the sort of thing that I'd usually do.

But I'd done it. I'd taken Raheem back upstairs and I'd called his mother in and I'd said, "All right, Mrs. Webb, these are the facts of life."

I'd spelled it out for them plain and simple. If they wanted to file a claim that they knew to be bogus, well, fine, I couldn't stop them. But I knew what was going on. And they knew what was going on. And it was time to cut the shit and talk turkey.

I told them I wasn't the lawyer on the case, just the private detective. That lowered me some in Sheila Webb's eyes, but not in Raheem's. His actually grew wide. Holy shit, a private eye. I could thank TV for the buildup, but suddenly I was a lot more interesting than Raheem Webb had ever thought I was, and I played it for all it was worth.

I never got Raheem to change his story, we never

got as far as all that. But I left there with his beeper, which he had indeed been wearing under his shirt. And I left them with instructions that if that pusher (whose name Raheem still wouldn't tell me) ever hassled him again, they were to call the office and inform me right away.

Of course, I had no idea what the hell I was gonna do about it. But sayin' it sounded tough, and tough was what I was going for just then. I was playing macho private eye. Not that I'm good at the role. It was just that was what a ten-year-old kid needed to see.

Anyway, the point is, I was riding a high leaving Raheem Webb's. And while I was in a kick-ass mood, it seemed a good time to check out the Black Death. Besides, nothing propinks like propinquity. Whatever the hell that means.

I walked down the street, around the corner and down 147th to the building, the home of the Black Death. I stood there watching it from across the street.

I wasn't sure what I was gonna do next. I hadn't thought that out yet. But odds were, I was gonna go in. As I say, I was psyched for it. Plus it was broad daylight, which made it a far less scary proposition. And I sure wasn't gonna accomplish much on the sidewalk.

I'd just had time to think that when the front door opened and the Black Death came out.

Son of a bitch. What a fantastic, amazing coincidence. Did I need anything more than that to convince me that this was fated, that this was meant to be? That the gods had somehow decreed that I was to be the one to bring down the Black Death, to smash the drug ring, and free the fair Melissa Ford?

Damn. That fucked up the fantasy. Having to think

of Melissa Ford as fair. How about unfair? And free the unfair Melissa Ford. Doesn't quite have the same ring to it.

Believe it or not, the Black Death had not been standing in the doorway waiting for me to think all this. He'd come down the front steps and started down the street. I followed from across the street and slightly behind. I wasn't taking any chances of being spotted, but I sure as hell wasn't letting him get away.

One reason was, the Black Death was carrying a bag. A paper bag. Similar in size and shape to the one Alan Harrison had the night he'd come out the front door with him. And I sure wanted to know where that package was heading.

It headed over to Lenox Avenue, then down a block, then turned right, heading back west again. I ran to the corner just in time to see the Black Death cross the street partway down the block.

We were in a section with a lot of bricked-up buildings and empty lots. It was at the edge of one of the bricked-up affairs that the Black Death suddenly foxed me. Before I knew what he was gonna do, he suddenly turned and walked around the corner of the building out of sight.

I was about two building widths behind. Not wide ones, but still. And of course I was across the street. I sprinted to cover the distance. Stopped and peered out from behind a parked car.

There was the Black Death, walking casually down along the side of the bricked-up building. On the other side of the building was merely a rubble-filled lot. Where the hell he was going, I had no idea. All I knew was in that open area there was no way in hell I could follow him.

I crossed the street, got closer, to try to see where he'd go. I peered around the edge of the bricked-up building. He was still walking down along the side of it. In the direction he was heading there was nothing. Just the back of another bricked-up building that must have fronted on the next cross street.

As I watched, he walked up to this bricked-up building, suddenly turned right, and disappeared.

What!?

This was not like he walked out of sight. Around a corner, through a door or anything of the kind. Facing me was a blank wall with bricked-up windows. The Black Death had not gone anywhere, he had just vanished off the face of the earth like a magic trick.

A more prudent me would have let it go. But, as I say, I was all psyched up. And confronted with an optical illusion, it was too much not to check it out.

Not that it didn't take guts. Guts I didn't really have. Discretion is the better part of valor, and no one knows it better than I. But I just *had* to know.

I crept along the side of the building, slowly, looking all around. There was no one in sight. Nothing in sight. I was in a goddamned empty lot.

I kept going. Reached the bricked-up wall.

Sure enough, optical illusion.

There were two walls. Or at least two depths to the wall. With a difference of about four feet. The main wall ran the length of the building. But there was another wall about twelve feet long running parallel to it in the middle. In the distance these blended into one and looked like a solid wall. Between the two, perpendicular to the main wall, was a bricked-up doorway, the bricks of which had since been knocked down. And that was where the Black Death had disappeared.

Holy shit.

I could see the doorway from twenty feet away. Did I want to get any closer? If I stopped to think, I sure didn't. But I wasn't stopping to think, I was a bloodhound on the scent. I crept up to the open door, peered inside.

Black, but not pitch black. There was light coming from somewhere, obviously another bricked-up door or window that had been smashed in. I peered in, let my eyes grow accustomed to the light.

A small, empty room, rubble-filled floor, bare walls. No surprise there. A door on the far wall. And one on the side wall. Both apparent sources of light. Which way had the Black Death gone?

I froze. Listened for footsteps. Heard none.

I crept slowly into the room. Paused. Listened again.

I heard what sounded like a faint noise off to my right. That's pretty stupid—how does something sound like a noise? What I mean is, I *think* I heard a faint noise. It could have been a footstep. It could have been a rat. It could have been my imagination.

I chose the door in the direction of the sound. I crept to it, peered around.

Another empty room. A bricked-up window with two bricks missing, letting in light. A door on the far wall. A door on the left wall.

I stopped. Listened again. Another faint sound, this time to the left.

I crept in, made my way to that door. Peered in.

An interior room. No window, but three doors.

None bricked-up, of course, as they were interior doors. All wide open.

Shit.

It flashed on me then, it's a maze. I'm a rat in a maze and this is an intelligence test. I gotta get through the maze and get the cheese or the Black Death or out again alive or whatever the hell the goal is in this stupid game.

I crept into the center of the room, stood quiet, tense, looking around at the three doors. I thought I heard a sound, but by now I couldn't be sure. It could just be my ears playing tricks on me. And if it was a sound, I had no idea from where it had come.

Pick a door, any door. Just like taking an exam back in high school—multiple guess.

I crept to the center door, peered in.

Pitch dark. No light at all. Whatever the hell was in there, I didn't give a shit.

Backtracked to the door on the left.

A thin ray of light. Coming from where? Shit. Can't tell. Must be a bend in the wall somewhere. An L-shape, a corner. What the hell was it?

Another sound, like a crunch on gravel. Or rubble. A footstep. From where?

I felt a cold chill from head to toe.

What the fuck was I doing here?

Was I out of my mind?

Well, probably. The odds on insanity were running pretty high at the moment.

Well, what the hell did I do?

Schmuck. You need a written invitation? Get the hell out of there.

I crept out of the room with the unexplained source of light. Now I was back in the interior room with three doors. It really had *four* doors, of course, the three I'd encountered and the one by which I'd come in.

Which one was it?

I must have been really scared, because I was starting to lose it. Damn it, get your bearings! Which door did you come in?

This one. The one to the right. I checked out the one across from me first and then the one to the left. Coming from the one to the left, I have to want the one on the right. This is it.

Isn't it?

Shit.

I crept to the door.

Peered out.

Couldn't see a thing.

Dark. Pitch dark.

Damn. The wrong way? No, it had to be right. My eyes just aren't accustomed to the light yet and—

Wrong. It was lighter here than there. It should be lighter still. Something's blocking the light, and—

There came a sound like thunder, then a blinding flash of light. I felt a dull thud in my chest, then a sharp, searing pain.

Then nothing.

Ramblings in the Ether

bumping thumping crash smash turn me over turning turning widening gyre and gimbel in the wave storm seascape escape rap song rhapsody wrap me in white linen no hands helping hands hans brinker look ma no hands mutilated amputee get the picture gotta shoot it don't shoot no floating flying half-done half-finished half-baked whole loaf none what am I dizzy doing loony tunes shrieking reeking sirens wailing sirens failing sirens luring ships to rocks rough ride rough rider big stick boom streaking from the Dakota too late too late if not him how me misspent life poor wife we are the hollow men draining blood sweat tears what goes up must come down jackhammer fast in vain in vein insert qua qua qua in spite of the tennis six love lost love's labors bank and shoal of time jump the life to come jump jump jump it's all right ma I'm only bleeding bleeding leading punctured junctured sectioned like an orange peel peel peel bell peel bells toll for whom astronaut what your country can can can kick line kick back kick off kick the bucket kickstart false start fast start if only but no no no void avoid a void annoyed don't do that ow that hurts or does it who cares who dares who wears where's wares whoops goes whoops goes don't go do not go do not go gentle gentlemen gentle ben bear bare don't care don't wear not fair over over over easy scrambled sunny side funny side not really not real no deal into that good night

26

I opened my eyes to find MacAullif looking
down at me.

MacAullif?

That couldn't be right.

I closed my eyes and he went away and so did I,
and I drifted in a kind of warm and mushy place where
things weren't much fun but there weren't any respon-
sibilities either, which seemed a fair trade-off.

That was too good to last. I opened my eyes again
and MacAullif was still there. And when he was, I
wasn't sure if he was still there or if he was there for
the first time, 'cause I couldn't be really sure the other
time had actually happened. This was confusing at
best.

I blinked, almost closed my eyes again, didn't,
blinked again, and some of the fog cleared.

"Where am I?" I said.

"Harlem Hospital," MacAullif said.

"What?"

"Harlem Hospital. Surely you've been here before.

But not like this. Usually you come chasing *after* the ambulance.''

"What happened?"

"You don't know?"

"Not really."

"You got shot."

"Jesus Christ."

"You didn't know that?"

"That's what I thought."

"You were right."

Jesus. I didn't wanna ask. "Is it . . . ?"

"What?"

"Is it . . . bad?"

"Bad? Well, it isn't good. Do you mean is it serious?"

"Damn it, MacAullif—"

"Relax. You have what a movie hero would refer to as 'only a flesh wound.' "

"You're kidding."

"Not at all. A movie detective would have shrugged it off, kept going, taken the gun away from him, and pistol-whipped him with it. You, of course, fainted dead away."

"My god. What time is it?"

"More to the point, what day is it? It's Saturday morning if you really need to know. You were shot some time last night.

"My wife . . ."

"She's here. Your kid, too. They've been in but you wouldn't wake up. The nurse booted 'em out. I'm a cop and I'm hard to boot."

"How are they taking it?"

"The doctor told them it's nothing. Your wife believes it. Your kid's gonna have to see you up and around.''

Shit. Poor Tommie.

''I'll tell 'em you're conscious.''

MacAullif got up and I realized he'd been sitting in a chair by the bed. And I realized I'd been lying in a bed. I mean, I kind of knew that, but it hadn't all sunk in, if you know what I mean. My perceptions were hazy at best. But it was gradually all coming back. I followed the Black Death into an abandoned building and wound up getting shot.

Jesus Christ. Shot. Only a flesh wound. What the hell did that mean? From MacAullif's macho point of view I could be in intensive care on the critical list.

The door opened and Alice and Tommie came in. Tommie had been crying. Alice looked like she wanted to, but had been putting up a good front for his sake.

They broke my fucking heart.

Tommie came tentatively, hesitantly at first. Then he saw that I was awake, actually looking and smiling at him.

''Daddy!'' he screamed, and ran for the bed.

Alice headed him off before he jumped on my chest and set my recovery back a good week.

''I'm all right,'' I said. I said it again and again. Not having talked to the doctor, I didn't know if it was true, but it was the only thing to say.

I was still really in a fog and didn't know what to do. But Alice did, and Alice took charge. She's wonderful that way. When all the preliminary fumphering around was done, she said, ''Tommie has something he wants to ask you.''

I looked at Tommie, who looked positively frightened at having been put on the spot. He snuffled, stammered and said, "Dad?"

"Yes?"

"I wanted to ask you . . ."

"What?"

He started, then broke off crying.

Alice hugged him, took charge. "He has a soccer game tomorrow. He wants to ask you if you'll be able to go."

"Oh?"

"Well?" Alice said.

"I hope so, Tommie. I have to ask the doctor."

"But . . ." Alice prompted.

I looked at her.

"But," she said again, "what about next week's game?"

Slow me got it. "But next week I will definitely go. Okay?"

He snuffled. "Okay, dad."

Easy as pie, if you're not a big, insensitive boob who's just been shot. I was in the hospital, and the kid just wanted some assurance I was ever getting out. And, even without having talked to the doctor, it was an assurance I would readily give.

They left shortly after that, which was merciful, because I don't think I could have taken much more and I don't think Alice could have either. It occurred to me it was gonna be hell when I got home.

If I got home.

Fuck that. Don't even think that. It's not serious.

It was hard to convince myself. Because I was all doped up, but I still had a rather severe pain in my chest, which it occurred to me might be really intense if I *weren't* doped up. So how bad *was* it?

The door opened and MacAullif came back in.

MacAullif said, "Saw the wife and kid, got the family all squared away, now we can get down to business."

"Business?"

"Yeah," he said. "You know, I don't think I've ever seen anybody go to such lengths to get out of testifying before the grand jury before." He shrugged. "Not that it's gonna work. Not a scratch like that. Monday morning you ought to be able to testify just fine."

"Glad to hear it."

"Are you? Of course, you may have a little bit more to tell them now. About getting shot and all."

My mind was still sorting things out, and something occurred to me that should have occurred to me before. "MacAullif, why are you here?"

He shrugged. "Hey, I take it kind of personal when someone I know gets shot. Particularly if I have any idea why."

My mind was working better now, and one of the things it was telling me was there was a hell of a lot I didn't know. And a hell of a lot I might or might not want to spill. And in my groggy state, it was kind of hard to sort that out.

"MacAullif," I said. "Help me out here."

He frowned. "What do you mean?"

"I'm really at sea. I've lost half a day. I have no idea what's really going on. Who found me? How did I get here? What's going on?"

He scratched his head. "Trying to figure out how to play it, huh?"

"Give me a break. I'm doped up and I've just been shot."

"Sounds like you know *exactly* what's happening."

"If you don't wanna tell me, fine, then leave me alone and let me get back to sleep."

"You sleep anymore and your brain will rot. Coals to Newcastle." He chuckled. "See? Bet you thought I wasn't literate. Okay, I'll fill you in. Four thirty-five P.M., report of shots fired in the vicinity of West 145th Street. Radio patrol unit sent to investigate pokes around, finds no sign of disturbance, reports in and leaves scene.

"Six forty-five, report of body lying in empty lot in back of same address."

"Huh?"

"I'm just giving you what I got. That's how it came in. Body. No description. Sex, race, nothing."

"An empty lot?"

"Yeah."

"Where?"

"Like I said. Back of the building. Building is on One Forty-Fifth, I guess that would make the lot on One Forty-Sixth. As I understand, it's an abandoned building, which is one reason the cops got nothing the first time around. The address they went to's all bricked up. Anyway, the cops check it out, and this time, jackpot. One stiff as ordered. Only the guy ain't a stiff, he's just a chickenshit who passes out at the sight of a little blood."

"No sign of how I got there?"

"You weren't shot there?"

I was saved from having to answer by the arrival of the doctor. At least, that's who he turned out to be. He was so young, at first I thought he had to be an orderly or intern. But I guess they dress differently. Or maybe not, I don't know. To be honest, I couldn't tell you what the guy was wearing. All I know is, he struck me as young. He probably wasn't. It's probably just that I'm getting old.

He didn't kick MacAullif out, just nodded to him and walked up to me. I wondered if he knew who MacAullif was. MacAullif was in plain clothes, of course, and I wondered if the doctor knew he was a cop, or took him for a kindly relative. At any rate, he let him stay.

He nodded his head up and down in agreement with himself, smiled in the way doctors do, and said, "Well, well, so we've decided to rejoin the world of the living."

I hate it when doctors say "we." As if *he'd* been shot and out cold for a day.

"Who are you?" I said.

The question didn't offend him. "I'm your doctor. I saved your life."

"What?"

He smiled. "Just kidding. A little doctor humor. Your wound is very superficial and you were never in any danger. I'm glad to see you conscious. I want to check you out so we can send you home."

"Home?"

"I hate to rush you, but frankly we need the bed."

The doctor flipped on a stethoscope I hadn't noticed he was wearing and listened to my heart. He slipped it off his ears, took the thing they use to do blood pressure and put it around my arm. As he did, I noticed he was chewing gum, which seemed out of character for a doctor.

As if he read my mind, he said, "Please excuse the gum, I'm trying to quit smoking. Bad image for a doctor, right?"

He pumped up the blood pressure, squinted at it, nodded, unstuck the Velcro and slid if off my arm.

"Close enough," he said. "All right, Mr. Hastings, we're checking you out."

I stared at him. "Now?"

He chuckled. "You never worked in a hospital, did you?"

I had, but not in the context he meant. "No."

"Well, just between you and me, we had a bad night and we need the space. Ordinarily, I might hold you till tomorrow, but there's no real need. You didn't lose that much blood. You're down about a pint, same as a donor. You may be a little weak today, but that's it."

"A pint?"

"That's a rough estimate. I don't have a dipstick. You lost maybe two pints, we gave you one, you're fine."

Horror gripped me. "You gave me blood?"

He put up his hands. "Relax. Your wife's the donor. She may be a little weak today too."

"What about the shot?"

"Oh, the shot." He jerked his thumb at MacAullif. "Well, that may be a little more interesting to him than to me. The bullet went into your left chest." He ticked them off on his fingers. "Missed your heart. Missed your lung. Cracked a rib. Not bad, but cracked. Probably ache a bit. But you won't be able to tell, because the whole wound will smart. You're on Demerol now, you'll be on Percodan a few days, after that you take aspirin and grit your teeth. You got damage to some muscle tissue, but nothing that's not gonna heal. And nothing that's gonna permanently impair your gross motor function. It's your shoulder's gonna give you the trouble. Temporarily, I mean. I'm gonna give you a sling, keep your weight off your left arm for a while. Say a week or two. If you can use it, you can use it. Just try it out and see how it feels. I'm gonna recommend some physical therapy exercises you can do, and give you a pamphlet describing them. Whether you do 'em or not is up to you. No one will be checking up to give you demerits it you don't, or a gold star if you do.''

I squinted up at him. ''You sure you're a doctor?''

He smiled. ''Mister, I'm a surgeon. Just wait'll you get the bill.''

He grinned at me, nodded his head and went out.

I stared after him, then turned to MacAullif. ''Is he serious?''

MacAullif shrugged. ''Seems like a good man. It's standard procedure in posttraumatic situations to kid the patient along and try to minimize the trauma by making light of the episode. Happy medicine. I don't wholly disapprove, though this guy does push it a little far.''

MacAullif cocked his head. ''Before he came in, we were talking about this particular traumatic episode. I don't think we got very far.''

''Oh.''

MacAullif frowned. ''You're rather reticent. I understand you've had a shock and you're doped up and all the rest of it, but I would have to describe your attitude as less than forthcoming.''

''You were filling me in, MacAullif. Remember? All I know so far is, I was found in an abandoned lot with a bullet hole in me.''

''What more is there to tell?''

''You said the cops got a report. First of a shooting. Then of a body.''

"Right."

"What kind of report you talking about? Was there anything in that?"

He shook his head. "Routine calls to nine-one-one. I think they had a couple on the shots fired and one on the body. As far as I know, none of them gave a name."

"Is that unusual?"

"Hell, no. All the calls to nine-one-one, at least half are cranks."

"These weren't cranks."

"No, but half the real ones, no one leaves a name either. That's New York for you. No one wants to get involved."

"Great."

"Hey, it's par for the course. You got three, maybe four unidentified voices calling in nine-one-one. It's Harlem, so they're probably black. Male or female, nobody's sure. With overworked nine-one-one operators processing a lot of bogus shit, that's the best you can do."

MacAullif shifted in his chair. "Now, let's talk turkey here. I'm a cop, but this ain't my case. Whose is it, I don't know. Not that big a deal, nonfatal shooting in Harlem. But it *is* a shooting, and it *will* be investigated. When you leave here, you're going downtown and you'll have to make a statement."

"A statement?"

"Sure, whaddya think? It's just routine."

"And after that?"

"I don't know. It depends on your statement. There's not much of a case. All the cops got is the bullet and you."

"The bullet?"

"Sure. The bullet was in you. That hotshot surgeon who was just in here took it out."

"Oh, yeah?"

"Yeah. We got that, and if Doctor Kildare didn't mark it up too bad, we can match it up if we ever get the gun."

"Well, that's something."

"Yes, it is." MacAullif took a breath. "So, you know everything I know. And probably a lot I don't know. Last time I talked to you, you were messed up in this murder case and pulling rap sheets on drug runners, and pulling all kinds of fancy shit to try to get this woman off. Next thing I know, you're in the hospital and you've bought a bullet. I have to wonder if there's any connection."

I frowned. "I see."

MacAullif frowned too. "You're bein' a real pain in the ass today, and I don't think it's just 'cause you're shot. And I have to tell you, I'm gettin' a little pissed off. So why don't we cut to the chase?" MacAullif leaned in, looked me right in the eye. "Who shot you?"

Shit. He would have to ask me that. It was a question I knew sooner or later he was gonna ask, I was just really rooting for later.

The problem was, I knew the answer. Well, not the name of course, but I knew who. I just didn't know when. When he spotted me, I mean. Maybe it was just yesterday that he noticed me tailing him. And he had the stuff on him, and he spotted me, and I look like a cop, and that's why he took that bizarre route and led me into ambush. That much was certain, that he saw me and led me there. All I meant was, maybe that was the first time.

But maybe not. Maybe he saw me the other night, when he'd come out of his building with Alan Harrison. Maybe he'd spotted me then, so seeing me for a second time, he'd know for sure.

But maybe *that* was the second time. Maybe he saw me way back when, the night I'd stumbled around all over his building losing Charles Olsen.

But whenever, however, for whatever reason, the fact was he'd seen me and the fact was he'd shot me.

And the fact was I knew the answer to MacAullif's question perfectly well.

I frowned at MacAullif, shook my head.

"I don't know."

27

THEY SENT ME HOME. It was partly due to a lack of bed space, and partly due to MacAullif making a call downtown and persuading them there was no real urgency about taking my statement and I could go down and make it Sunday, but the bottom line was they sent me home.

I was not, in spite of what my jovial doctor said, in tiptop shape. In point of fact, I felt like shit. When I tried to get out of bed, I found I was terribly dizzy, my legs were rubber and I couldn't walk. That did not, however, slow up the process. When they want you out of the hospital, you go. Discharged patients get a wheelchair ride to the front door. I always wondered why, and now I know. It makes an inability to navigate no excuse to stay.

At the front door the wheelchair was, of course, repossessed, and Alice and Tommie had to get me into a cab, no small feat that. If I'd been lucky, MacAullif would have still been there with his car, but it was later in the afternoon and I guess the poor guy actually had work to do. At any rate, Alice managed it. She refused to relinquish the wheelchair until she had actually gotten a cab, not as easy as it sounds on either count. She had a screaming fight with a male nurse over the former, and close to ten minutes of standing out on Lenox Avenue on the latter, but the end result was that a cab eventually pulled up to the door and Alice and Tommie managed to wrestle me in.

We didn't have a wheelchair at the other end, of course. Alice left Tommie and me in the cab and went in and got Jerry, our elevator man, to come out and help, and Alice and Jerry walked me in between 'em.

Once inside, I stumbled into the bedroom and collapsed on the bed, utterly worn out from the effort of just getting home. Alice fluttered around, the ministering angel, removing shoes, pants and other encumbrances, fluffing pillows and tucking me into bed.

Tommie hovered discreetly in the background, and once Alice had flounced out to fill the prescription the doctor had written for me, he poked his head in the door and then came up to the bed.

"Were you really shot, dad?" he asked.

I hated to answer the question. But there was only one answer, and I gave it. "Yes, I was."

That didn't terrify him, as I'd expected. Quite the contrary. Having had time to think about it, and having realized I wasn't going to die in the hospital and was already home recuperating, Tommie had come to the realization that, gee, it was pretty glamorous to have a father who'd been shot. I could tell from his attitude that he'd already worked it out that he was bound to be the most popular boy in the East Side Day School. I could only hope he wouldn't try to bring me to show-and-tell.

Yeah, things got easier for Tommie, and pretty fast too. But Tommie's a kid.

Alice is a grownup.

Once Tommie was safely taken care of and out of earshot and playing Super Mario Three in the living room, Alice wanted to hear the whole thing.

I told her. Every fact, facet, nuance, without reservation.

She listened to the whole thing without interruption, nodded, and said, "What are you going to tell the cops?"

Leave it to Alice to cut right to the heart of the matter.

I shook my head. "I don't know."

"You gonna tell 'em all you know?"

"I don't know."

"You gonna tell 'em all you suspect?"

"I don't know that either."

"There's a big difference," Alice said.

"I know that."

"You make your statement to the cops, you gotta be careful. You go around accusing people of shooting you, you could be in a lot of trouble."

"What do you mean?"

"You're doped up, so I don't know how much of this you've thought out. This guy you call the Black Death—if you tell the cops he shot you, he could sue you."

"Or shoot me."

"I'm being serious."

"So am I."

"I know. Damn it to hell."

"It's all right, Alice."

"All right? How can it be all right? Just look at you. *Look* at you, damn it."

"I've felt better."

"Don't joke. Please. I'm not up to having you joke. I'm scared. I'm really scared."

"Alice—"

"You know, every day you're out there, you're going into those bad buildings, places you could get hurt, and that's scary too and I hate it. But that's part of the job, it's a general fear, it goes with the territory. You get used to it. You never like it, but you get used to it and you get by.

"But this thing." Alice shook her head. "I can't stand it and I want you out of it. I mean, Jesus Christ." Alice touched the bandage on my shoulder. "An inch or two to the right."

"Bible would have gone right through my heart if it weren't for that bullet."

"Damn it!"

"Alice, I'm only joking 'cause I'm really scared too."

"I know." Alice took a breath. "This has to end. This can't go on. One way or another, you have to be out of it."

"What do you mean?"

"This woman, this stupid fucking woman who won't pay you. You're not working for her. You got shot for nothing, do you realize that? For nothing."

"I know."

"But that doesn't matter. The money doesn't matter. There isn't enough money in the whole world to be worth getting shot for. It has to stop."

"That's a comical understatement."

"Don't humor me. What are you gonna do?"

"What do you want me to do?"

"I don't know. I just want you out of it."

"I'm out of it now."

"What do you mean?"

"If I don't go chasing this guy, he's not following me to my neighborhood. If I leave him alone, he'll leave me alone."

"Oh yeah? What about the cops?"

"What about 'em?"

"What's he gonna do when he finds out you sicced the cops on his case?"

I took a deep breath. The dull ache in my chest got sharper when I did. It occurred to me I'd better take a pain pill. My exhale was more of a sigh.

"He won't."

28

THE COP'S NAME WAS REYNOLDS. Sergeant Steve Reynolds. He looked too young to be a sergeant, just as my surgeon looked too young to be a doctor. In a way that was good, it made him less formidable somehow.

So did his manner. He was polite, courteous, almost deferential. I suppose that was to put me at ease. It didn't. Knowing cops, it only made me suspicious.

Of course, I was in that frame of mind anyway. Paranoid, edgy, afraid that everybody knew.

Knew I was holding back.

If that's what you could call it.

"Now, Mr. Hastings," Reynolds said, "this is just routine. I hate to put you through it, but you realize we have to. I know you don't feel well. If you get too tired, need a break, just tell me. Otherwise, let's just get it over with as quickly as we can and send you home."

"Okay, fine," I said.

I was once again downtown, at One Police Plaza, in a small interrogation room not unlike the one where

Sergeant Thurman had had a go at me. I was seated at a table with Sergeant Reynolds and a stenographer who was poised to take down what I had to say. I didn't like that, but there was nothing I could do about it. At any rate, my "fine" was somewhat less than sincere.

Sergeant Reynolds nodded to the stenographer to begin, got my name and address in the record and started in on the statement.

"Now, Mr. Hastings, we are concerned with the date, Friday, September 29th. Can you tell us where you were employed on that day?"

"I was working for the law firm of Rosenberg and Stone."

"Where are they located?"

I gave him the address, the name Richard Rosenberg, how long I'd been working for him and a general description of my duties as a private investigator.

"Now, Mr. Hastings," Reynolds said, "directing your attention to the afternoon of September 29th, did you have occasion to go to Harlem on that day?"

"Yes, I did."

"And why was that?"

I told him about taking the injury photos of Raheem Webb and gave him the Webbs' address on Adam Clayton Powell Boulevard.

"And what time was it when you left that apartment?"

"Sometime after four in the afternoon."

"And where did you go then?"

"I walked around the neighborhood."

His eyebrows raised slightly. "You walked around the neighborhood?"

"That's right."

"Where was your car?"

"In front of the building."

"The building you'd just come out of? The, uh, what is the name?"

"Webb."

"The Webbs' building?"

"That's right."

"You left your car there and walked around the neighborhood?"

"Yes, I did."

"Why did you do that, Mr. Hastings?"

I took a breath. "I was looking for potholes."

He frowned. "Potholes?"

"Yes, sir."

"Why were you doing that?"

"To register them."

His eyebrows raised. "Oh, you mean . . . ? The pothole law?"

"Exactly."

That did not particularly please him. He frowned. "Briefly, for the record, would you explain the pothole law?"

"Of course. In negligence cases against the city of New York, it is not enough to show that someone tripped on a defect in the street or sidewalk, it is also necessary to show that that defect was duly reported to the city of New York prior to the accident, and that the city failed to repair it in a reasonable amount of time. For this reason, it has become common practice for attorneys to employ people to go around the city locating and registering potholes."

"I see," Reynolds said. "And that is what you claim you were doing in this instance?"

"That's right."

"You were walking the streets in Harlem looking for potholes and defects in the sidewalk?"

"That's right."

"This boy you had just photographed—what's his name again?"

"Raheem Webb."

"This Raheem Webb—how was his injury incurred?"

"Well, now you're asking for hearsay information. I only know what the boy told me."

Reynolds frowned. "That is not at issue here. I'd like to move this along. How did the boy tell you he sustained his injury?"

"He tripped on a crack in the sidewalk."

"I see. And was this crack in the sidewalk in the vicinity of his building?"

I frowned. "I really don't think I should discuss the case without consulting Mr. Rosenberg. And I hardly see how this would be relevant."

"Perhaps not," Sergeant Reynolds said. His attitude towards me was no longer kind. He didn't believe me, but it was all right. Because what he *did* believe worked for me. He didn't buy the fact that I was just walking around Harlem looking for potholes to register. No, the way he saw it, Raheem Webb got injured, so I was checking out all the defects in the immediate vicinity to try to find a registered one to blame it on. Which was something, incidently, that Richard would never do. But it was also something that I was sure, if not widely practiced by negligence attorneys, was at least widely suspected of them by employees of the city. Which is what Reynolds suspected me of now, and why I'd suddenly plummeted from his good graces.

Which is why it worked. It was something I naturally wouldn't want to admit, but was a logical explanation of my actions.

Reynolds took a breath. His manner was decidedly cold. "So you say you were looking for potholes to register?"

"That's right."

"And where did you go?"

"I can't recall exactly. I walked several streets. 147th. Lenox Avenue. 146th."

"How about 145th Street? Did you walk there?"

"No, I did not."

"You were never on 145th Street?"

"No, I was not."

"Well, perhaps we're going about this wrong. Can you tell us, generally, how you came to be shot?"

I shook my head. "I don't know."

"You don't know?"

"No, sir."

"How is that possible?"

"The last I recall I was walking along 146th Street."

"Where?"

"Between Lenox and Adam Clayton Powell."

"Which side of the street?"

"South side."

"Looking for potholes?"

"That's right."

"And what happened?"

"I don't know. The next thing I know, I'm lying in the hospital with a bullet in me."

Reynolds held up his hand. "Wait a minute. You don't recall getting shot?"

"No, sir."

"You recall an empty lot, a lot filled with rubble and refuse?"

"I believe I walked by one."

"On 146th?"

"Yes, sir."

"Would that be the last thing you remember?"

"I'm not sure. It's all sort of a blur."

Reynolds took a breath. "Mr. Hastings, you were discovered in a rubble-filled lot on 146th Street. Actually, you were near the back of the lot, near the building that borders on 145th Street. That is an abandoned building that has not been occupied for years. Do you have any idea what you were doing in the vicinity of that building?"

"No, sir."

"Do you recall being in that building?"

"No, sir."

"I would like to refresh your memory on that point. There is a bricked-up door in the back of that building where the bricks have been knocked out. Investigators on the scene noticed a faint trail of blood leading into that doorway. It was faint, as I say, but there was enough to type, and that blood has been typed as yours. There is every reason to believe it *was* yours. That blood trail leads into the building to an interior room. The investigators found a small pool of blood, again not much, but enough to indicate that might have been the point of origin, the place where you were shot. If so, it would tend to indicate that you had lain there for a short period of time, and then either crawled or were dragged out of the building to the place where you were subsequently found. Now, with that to refresh your memory, do you recall ever being in that building?"

"No, I do not."

Reynolds frowned. On a less polite officer, I'd call it a scowl. The man was not happy.

"Mr. Hastings, you have no recollection of being shot?"

"No, sir."

"And you have no idea who shot you?"

"No, sir."

"Or why?"

"No, sir."

Reynolds took a breath. He blew it out again, slowly. He was a nice guy, Reynolds, politer than most. Even so, I would have to count his parting words as sarcastic.

"Thanks for your help."

29

THEY GAVE ME MY CAMERA BACK. That was good. I hadn't even missed it. Hadn't even thought about it. They gave me the film back too. They'd processed it, to see if there was anything on it that might have been a clue. There wasn't. Just some shots of a crack in the sidewalk and the shots of Raheem Webb. Lucky there. Richard would have flipped out if I hadn't gotten them back. Who knows how much the kid's forehead might have healed given an extra three days?

No, I got them back. I got my film back and I got my camera back, and I got the hell out of there and hopped on the subway, since the only thing I hadn't gotten back yet was my car.

That was next on my list. I took the Number 3 train up to Harlem, got off at 145th.

I walked up Lenox Avenue. A shudder ran through my body when I hit 146th. I'd planned to walk across it. I hadn't been thinking. I changed my mind. I didn't walk across 147th either. No way. I kept going, crossed on 148th.

I turned the corner onto Raheem Webb's block. He wasn't out front, but the pusher and two of his buddies were. They were looking at me real funny. They always did, but this time was different. Then I realized I was wearing a sling.

The pusher gave me a hard look, real hard, tried to stare me down. I gave it right back to him. Fuck him. He might be hot shit on this block, but he was small potatos compared to what I was dealing with.

I unlocked my car, got in, banged the code alarm off. God bless Harlem—I hadn't gotten a ticket. Today was Sunday, but they should have nailed me Saturday morning. Hooray for the lax meter maid. Small victory there. Bigger victory in that my briefcase was still on the floor of the front seat. Score one for the code alarm. Gee, things are really working out.

I started the car, took the brake off, shifted into first and pulled out. Tough driving one-handed with a floor shift, but not that tough. I'd done it before eating a cheeseburger, no different doing it with one arm in a sling.

And slightly doped up from Percodan. It occurred to me I could get pulled over, given a ticket for driving under the influence. Least of my worries. I could also get nailed for making a false report, obstructing justice and conspiring to conceal a crime.

You might think I had lofty motives. You might think, hey, he's doing just what a TV detective would do, holding out on the cops, protecting his client, keeping the information to himself so he can solve the case on his own.

You would be wrong.

I had lied to the cops because I was chickenshit and I didn't want anything to do with it anymore.

If you can't understand that, you've probably never been shot. You probably watch TV shows where private detectives get shot every week. You probably saw the remake of *Scarface*, where Al Pacino gets shot six hundred times and he's still standing and it takes a shotgun blast to finish him off. You're probably used to seeing Arnold Schwarzenegger and Sylvester Stallone shoot a couple of hundred people a picture as if there was nothing to it.

There's something to it.

If each one of those two hundred people was a real person, with a name, a life, a job, a family, then you wouldn't cheer so loud when Arnie or Sly wipes 'em out. But you *can* cheer, because they're *not* real people, and they're made to look reprehensible. And the funny thing is, the way they're made to look reprehensible, the thing that convinces us that they *are* reprehensible, and in many case the *only* thing that indicates that they *are* reprehensible is the fact that Arnie shoots 'em.

A confusion of cause and effect. But, what the hey, it's only film and it's only make-believe.

And the real killings, the real shootings, the ones you see on the TV news, well, they're fictionalized too, made palatable by association. It's possible to watch and listen to accounts of these shootings without flinching, because the line is so blurred between fiction and reality that it's impossible to see the victims as real people, any more than it is the ones Rambo shoots. So it's possible to have a Zodiac Killer or a Son of Sam and it is possible to discuss him without rising an eyebrow or turning a hair or stomach.

Very impersonal.

Very unreal.

Hard to relate to.

And so there's really nothing I can say that can make you understand the difference that getting shot made in my life.

30

word, and I had trouble already.
. . . it . . . d at me, looked at the officer, rolled
. . . . . k his head . . . to say, "What an

DEPARTMENT OF HORRENDOUS ANTICLIMAX.

I'm referring, of course, to my grand jury appearance. As you might recall, I had envisioned myself as feisty, argumentative, combative, challenging the prosecutor on points of law, raising issues of relevance and admissibility, winning the support and admiration of the grand jurors themselves and fighting the exasperated prosecutor to a standstill.

That was before I got shot.

Now I felt I should get points just for showing up.

Show up I did, nine-thirty sharp, just like it said on my subpoena. Actually, I got there at nine-fifteen, overcautious, overprotecting, let's not give anyone any reason to be mean to me.

I located the right room, where I was, of course, denied entrance by a court officer who instructed me to sit on a bench in the hall. I was not, as I say, looking for any trouble. I sat on a bench in the hall. I sat alone, it being nine-fifteen.

About nine twenty-five another man showed up—

fiftyish, plump, graying dark hair and a moustache. The court officer stopped him at the door and consigned him to the bench too. He sat down next to me, looked at my sling, then up at me.

I didn't want to talk about my sling, but I felt impelled to say something. "Witness?" I asked.

The court officer gave us a stern look. "No talking."

Amazing. One word, and I'm in trouble already.

The man looked at me, looked at the officer, rolled his eyes and shook his head as if to say, "What an asshole."

I wasn't about to express my agreement in any manner the court officer could pick up on. I contented myself with a slight smile.

About then a third man showed up, fortyish, faded suit and tie, and he was instructed not to talk and consigned to the bench too.

The three of us sat there on the bench not talking to each other until well after nine-thirty, when three other men showed up and stood in the hallway, gabbing and joking and laughing. The court officer didn't tell them not to talk to each other or instruct them to sit on the bench. From this I gathered either they weren't witnesses or else they *were* witnesses, but they also happened to be cops.

The latter proved to be true, because about ten minutes later the court officer came out, called one of them by name and ushered him into the room. That left the other two cops to stand and horse around and me and the other two guys to sit on the bench like dopes and feel like second-class citizens.

Having correctly pegged the wiseacres for cops, I was curious about the guys I was sitting on the bench with. They were obviously civilians like me, and from what I knew of the case, the only thing I could figure out they might possibly be were mail room employees who had overheard Melissa Ford threaten David Melrose, or the locksmith who had copied David Melrose's key. In either case, it was interesting, and it would only take a question or two to pin it down. But the court officer had told us not to talk. He wasn't always present, but the two cops were, and they were obviously buddy-buddy and part of the system, and would be bound to report any transgressions.

Wouldn't they?

Or would they? And if they did, what the hell difference could it make? What were they gonna do, keep us after court? I mean, you can't be in contempt of court if you're not *in* court, can you?

No, but it occurred to me there were other crimes. How about tampering with a witness? These guys were obviously witnesses. Would talking to them constitute tampering?

Hell no, I told myself.

But I kept quiet.

And felt like a schmuck.

The other cops went in, one by one. And when they came out, they didn't hang around, they left. So when the third cop went in, that left the three of us alone sitting on the bench.

I still said nothing.

I felt like shit.

But the other guys had no such restraints. As soon as the cops were gone, they started chattering away like school kids when the teacher leaves the room.

And it turned out I was absolutely right. The first guy with the moustache was the locksmith, and the second guy in the faded suit was a mail room employee.

Which was great. I could sit there without violating any rules and let the two of them drop it in my lap.

I'd just had time to think that when the door opened and the court officer came out.

"Hastings?" he said.

That figured. Today just wasn't my day. I got up, followed him into the grand jury room.

Small shock.

Things are often so different than you picture them. Thinking of the grand jury, I had imagined a high bench, like a judge's bench, only long, across the whole front of the courtroom, with perhaps Ls down the side walls, an immense lofty bench to accommodate all the grand jurors, forming a three-sided arena in which the witness would sit and the prosecutor would stand to do combat while the grand jurors peered down from on high.

Not quite.

The grand jurors sat in individual little desks that looked like the ones you sat in back in high school. There were two rows of them across the room in a slight semi-circle. The witness chair sat facing them within the arc.

The court officer led me up to the chair and one of the grand jurors, probably the foreman, got up from his little desk and administered the oath.

After I swore to tell the truth, the whole truth, and nothing but the truth, I sat down in the witness chair and he sat down at his little desk, and there I was, sitting facing them as if I were a schoolteacher (most likely a substitute) whose desk had just been stolen.

I looked over my class. They were, as Richard had

promised, absolutely ordinary people, well mixed in terms of age, sex, race, what have you. They were dressed in ordinary street clothes, a far cry from the regal justices I had once envisioned in flowing black robes.

There wasn't time to count them. The two rows were not entirely filled, but I had no way of knowing if there were exactly twenty-three desks, for the maximum number of grand jurors allowed, or possibly more, so that didn't help me much. On a guess, I'd say there were eighteen to twenty grand jurors, but that's as close as I could come.

I was working from a high degree of paranoia, but I would have to say the faces I saw did not seem hostile. They didn't seem friendly, either, just neutral and interested. Which, I guess, was exactly what they should be.

If this description seems sketchy, it's because I saw all this in about two seconds from the time I took the oath and sat down to the time a man who had been standing off to the side stepped in front of me, blocking my view and commanding my attention.

He was a young man, but when I say young, once again I'm using the yardstick of Sergeant Reynolds and the doctor. Was it just coincidence that since I got shot to me everyone looked young? Anyway, he did. His brown hair hadn't started to gray like mine. It was straight, short and neatly combed straight back. He had a plump face and a plump body, which his tailored suit seemed to accentuate rather than hide, as if he'd gone for the opposite of the lean and hungry look— the well-fed, prosperous look.

As if in keeping with his image, his expression was smug. He smiled and said, "Mr. Hastings, I'm

A. D. A. McNulty and I'd like you to answer some questions, please.''

With that he turned and walked away from me, back to the grand jurors and past them until he turned and stood behind the two semi-circular rows, so that in looking at him I would be facing them. Of course, that put *him* out of the picture—where he was standing the grand jurors couldn't see him at all. That struck me as a showy gesture—giving stage. "Never mind me," it seemed to say. "Look at him. This is gonna be good." I wondered if this was a pet tactic on his part, or if all prosecutors did it. At any rate, it sure changed the picture I had envisioned. I had imagined the two of us in the arena, slugging it out with the grand jurors looking on. But, no, it was as if I were in a shadow box, with a disembodied voice prompting me as to what I should say.

The first questions were easy: name, address, married or single, how many years have you lived in New York? Nervous as I was, I'm pretty sure I got most of those right.

While I was answering, I was studying the faces of the grand jurors, trying to judge their reactions. As far as I could tell, there were none.

Until the prosecutor asked my occupation. They perked up on the answer to that one. People always do. A private detective. Wow. You could feel a change in the room. Some jurors smiled, some glanced at each other. This, they told themselves, was going to be good.

It wasn't.

It was dull as dishwater. I promised you an anticlimax, and you got it.

"And in the course of your work," A. D. A. Mc-

Nulty asked, "were you ever employed by one Melissa Ford?"

"Yes, I was."

"Could you tell us when that was?"

"She first contacted me on the morning of Thursday, September 21st."

"She employed you at that time?"

"Yes, she did."

"And what did she employ you to do?"

"To investigate her boyfriend, David Melrose."

"You accepted this employment?"

"Yes, I did."

"You investigated David Melrose?"

"Yes, I did."

"In the course of your investigation, did you have occasion to put David Melrose under surveillance?"

"Yes, I did."

"And just when was that?"

"The evening of the following day."

"That would be Friday, September 22nd?"

"That's right."

"At what time?"

"Approximately five o'clock."

"Where did you being this surveillance?"

"I picked him up when he left his place of work."

"That would be the Breelstein Agency on Third Avenue?"

"Yes, sir."

"And what did he do?"

"He met Melissa Ford and took her out to dinner."

"You followed them?"

"Yes, I did."

"What did he do then?"

"He took her home."

"How?"

"In a cab."

"What time was that?"

"About eight-thirty."

"Did he go home with her?"

"No, he dropped her off."

"He kept the cab?"

"Yes, he did."

"You continued to follow him?"

"Yes, I did."

"Where did the cab go?"

"The cab went five blocks, and he got out and made a phone call."

"Do you know who he called?"

"No, I do not."

"What did he do then?"

"Got back in the cab and went down to an address on Grand Street."

"Do you know the address?"

"Not offhand. I could consult my notes."

"Please do."

I took out my notebook, looked up Charles Olsen's address, read it into the record.

"And what did he do there?" McNulty asked.

"Rang the bell and conferred on the sidewalk with a man who lived in the building."

"Did you know who that was?"

"Not at the time."

"Do you know now?"

"Yes, I do. Charles Olsen."

"Who is Charles Olsen?"

"A graphics artist employed by the Breelstein Agency."

"How long did David Melrose talk with this man?"

"Not long. Maybe five minutes."

"What did he do then?"

"Got back in the cab and went uptown."

"To where?"

"A building on East 89th Street."

"What did he do then?"

"Got out and rang the bell."

"Was he buzzed inside?"

"No. A woman came down and opened the door."

"A woman?"

"Yes, sir."

"An attractive woman?"

I'd had no problems with the questions so far. I had a problem with this one. And I was prepared for it. I'd already played the scene out in my mind. *That question is objected to as calling for a conclusion on the part of the witness.*

And here's the anticlimax I promised.

"Yes," I said.

"And David Melrose went inside with this woman?"

I have no idea where David Melrose went after he went inside.

"Yes."

"And how long was David Melrose inside with this woman?"

I have no knowledge of the fact David Melrose actually was inside with this woman. He could have gone anywhere after she let him in the door.

"Two hours."

"So he spent two hours in the apartment of this lady whom you have described as attractive?"

I have no specific knowledge as to that, and I object to your summarizing my testimony.

"Yes, sir."

"I see. And did you communicate this to your client, Melissa Ford?"

Objection to the characterization "this" as too broad in the context. I did communicate with my client.

"Yes, sir."

"You told her David Melrose had spent the evening in the apartment of another woman?"

Objected to as leading and suggestive, particularly with regard to the phrase "other woman." I reported to her only what I observed.

"Yes, sir."

"An attractive other woman?"

Objection to the characterization "attractive," objection to the characterization "other."

"Yes, sir."

"And what was Melissa Ford's reaction when you told her this?"

Objected to as calling for a conclusion on the part of the witness.

"She seemed surprised."

"Surprised? Was that her *only* reaction? Wouldn't you say she was outraged, angry, in fact, totally furious, Mr. Hastings? Wouldn't you have to say she seemed angry enough to want to kill?"

Objected to as argumentative, calling for a conclusion on the part of the witness, assuming facts not in evidence, and viciously leading and suggestive! And what's more, Melissa Ford couldn't have killed David Melrose—I should know because I shot the son of a bitch myself!

I took a breath.

"Yes, sir."

31

THE LOCKSMITH AND THE MAIL ROOM CLERK WERE THE ONLY WITNESSES LEFT, their examination was bound to be brief, and it occurred to me I could hang around outside and nab 'em when they left. They were obviously eager to talk, and I was sure I could pump 'em for all they had. Not that anything they had to say was likely to do me any good, but anything they had, I'd be welcome to it.

The mail room clerk was probably a washout, but what about the locksmith? Maybe there was something he'd observed, something in her manner, some insignificant fact that wouldn't mean anything to anybody else, but in some way would furnish a clue. Or, better than a clue, something she said that, taken in the right context, could definitely establish the fact that at the time she made the key she had no idea David Melrose was dead.

But wait a minute. She *did* know he was dead. Either way around, she knew that. Her story was she took the key from his dead body to copy because she was afraid the cops wouldn't believe her story that she found the door open. If I couldn't even remember that, you can imagine where my head was at. But, nonetheless, even so, there might have been something that she did, something that she said that was inconsistent with the actions of a killer. I had no idea what that might be, but of course, if I did, I wouldn't need to ask. And it wouldn't hurt me to stick around and find out.

But after my ignominious performance before the grand jury, I just wasn't up to it. No, I just slunk home with my tail between my legs.

Well, not exactly home. I wasn't up to going home either. Wasn't up to facing Alice. Letting her know how miserably I'd failed. What a wretched piece of man-flesh she'd married.

Man-flesh?

Good lord. There's a word. Talk about being depressed. I wonder what the feminists would make of that? Man-flesh. Dead meat, that's more like it. That's what I was feeling like. Dead meat.

No, I wasn't up to going home. I took the subway uptown to my office. I got off at Times Square and walked up Broadway, past the hookers and sleaze merchants. Past the weirdos, junkies and bums. All of them, I was sure, with more dignity than I could muster.

I went up to my office, unlocked the door. The sign on my door read STANLEY HASTINGS, PRIVATE DETECTIVE. Friends had given it to me as a joke, and I'd hung it up as a joke.

Some joke.

I went inside, collected the mail that had been slid through the slot in the door. Three bills. I wondered if Melissa Ford's five hundred bucks would cover them. That was a fair price—five hundred bucks to help convict her of murder. I'm sure some detectives would have charged a grand.

My answering machine was blinking. Three blinks meaning three calls. I wondered if I wanted to hear them. I figured I probably didn't.

I slumped down in my desk chair, rubbed my head. With my good arm, of course. That was something. The whole time I'd testified, the prosecutor had never asked me about my arm. Of course not. If he knew about it, as he surely did, he would never bring it up in a million years. Never let that implication get put in the grand jurors' minds. That I'd gotten shot investigating the murder. Because, even with the statement I'd given Sergeant Reynolds, the cops had to figure that was a possibility.

That was the killer. That was the cruncher. Because I knew it was a damn sight more than just a possibility.

And I wasn't gonna do a damn thing about it. Hadn't done a damn thing about it. Had just stood quiet and helped to indict an innocent woman.

Pardon me if the cup of my ignominy runneth over, but, oh, Jesus Christ.

The blinking light on my answering machine was starting to give me a headache. And I never get headaches. I stared at it, fascinated. Blip, blip, blip. Are you really capable of causing me pain?

Blip, blip, blip. I couldn't take my eyes off it. It was hypnotizing me. Blip, blip, blip. It's a message. It's a code. Morse code. Blip, blip, blip. It's the letter S. The beginning of an S.O.S. A cry for help. A distress signal, that I'm sitting here refusing to heed.

Either that or the fucking office wanting to know

why I wasn't answering my beeper. I may be bummed out, but let's get things in perspective.

I sighed, reached over, pressed the button on the answering machine.

Beep.

"Stanley, this is Wendy. You're not answering your beeper. Please call the office."

Right again. Wendy/Janet. Or Wendy, actually, since she'd identified herself. The girl was inaccurate, but surely I could trust her on the subject of her own name.

Beep.

"Stanley . . . If you're there, pick up."

Shit.

Alice.

"Look, Stanley, I know you don't feel like talking. And I know it probably didn't go well. But if you're there, pick up the phone . . . Okay, you're not there. But if you get there, call me. Okay? . . . Call me . . . Love you . . . Bye."

Oh, shit.

Nothing could depress me more than that.

Wrong again.

Beep.

"Mr. Hastings, this is Melvin Poindexter. Please call my office at your earliest convenience."

32

I DIDN'T CALL MELVIN POINDEXTER AT MY EARLIEST CONVENIENCE. I didn't call Melvin Poindexter at all. Not only that, I got the hell out of the office before the son of a bitch could call me.

Now, I know that's silly. I didn't have to answer the phone, I have an answering machine. But I was afraid Alice might call again. And if she did, I couldn't bear the thought of her saying, "Stanley, please pick up the phone," and me sitting there not doing it. So I got the hell out.

I did call Rosenberg and Stone. I called 'em from a pay phone on the street corner.

Wendy/Janet answered on the first ring. "Rosenberg and Stone."

"It's Stanley."

"Stanley. I've been beeping you all morning. Where are you?"

"Didn't Richard tell you? I was in court."

"Richard didn't say a thing about it. In fact, he's been asking for you too."

"But he knew all about it. He . . ."

"What?"

I realized from *my* point of view Richard knew all about it. I'd discussed the whole thing with him, shown him my subpoena. But only in terms of how it related to me. Not the fact it was this morning and that I wouldn't be working.

"I guess he didn't know it was today," I said. "What does he want?"

"Something about some pictures. Whether you got them or not."

Shit. The Raheem Webb shots. The last thing I wanted to deal with now.

"Oh. Anything else?"

"That's all Richard wants. But a man's been calling all morning asking me to beep you. He seemed pretty upset that you didn't call back."

"Oh?"

"Yeah, I have it here. Let's see. Mr. Poindexter. You want the number?"

"No, I have it."

"You better call him. The guy's pretty upset."

"Okay. Anything else?"

"Yeah. A Sergeant MacAullif called, wants you to call him back. That was just a little while ago. I told him you weren't answering the beeper but if you called in I'd tell you."

"Okay. Thanks."

"So, what's the story? You on the beeper now?"

"Yeah. Why, you got a case?"

"Not any more. I couldn't reach you, so I gave 'em all out."

"Right."

"Don't worry. I'll give you the next one that comes in."

"Great. Make my day."

"What?"

"Fine. Thanks."

"So what's the story on the pictures?"

"Pictures?"

"The pictures Richard wanted. Did you get 'em?"

Oh, Jesus, the Raheem Webb pictures. That seemed so long ago. That was before I got shot.

There are events in your life that change things, things that happen that, once they do, your life is never the same again. They can be catastrophic, like losing a leg, or pleasant, like having a kid, or perfectly mundane, like getting a job. But once they happen, it's impossible to envision life as if they hadn't happened.

Needless to say, I have never lost a leg, but if I had, I would be dealing with life on that basis and it would be hard for me to relate to life in which I *hadn't* lost a leg. I have had a child, and it's hard for me to envision a life in which I hadn't. And I got a job, my private detective work. I've only had it a few years, but it seems as if I've always been one, as if I couldn't envision what life would be like if I weren't.

And now my life had changed again. By an event which would have to fall into the catastrophic category. Oh, don't get me wrong—it wasn't catastrophic in any physical sense—physically I was fine.

But I *had* been shot.

And from now on, my life would fall into two categories—before I was shot, and after I was shot.

From now on, it would be hard to envision what life would be like if I hadn't been shot.

And that was what I was dealing with here. Because

I hadn't talked to Richard Rosenberg since Friday morning. And, I suddenly realized, Richard Rosenberg didn't know I'd been shot. Richard Rosenberg, Wendy/Janet, et al., were treating me as if this were just another ordinary day. Well, fine, why shouldn't they? They didn't know my life had changed. And even if they did, what the hell, *their* life hadn't changed. Just another ordinary day. Richard agitating, Wendy/Janet beeping, life goes on.

Well, what the hell, I can deal with that. Give me an assignment and I'll go do it. Just what I need, simple busywork. All I'm really up to right at the moment. Suit me just fine.

Only life has a way of sticking the knife in, twisting it, turning, gouging a bit.

Richard Rosenberg wanted to know if I had the pictures of Raheem Webb.

Yeah, I had 'em. And they were gorgeous, exactly what he would want.

And I couldn't give them to him.

33

RICHARD LEANED BACK IN HIS DESK CHAIR, sighed and shook his head. "Jesus Christ."

"I know," I said. "It's a mess."

I'd come in to the office to tell Richard about the Raheem Webb pictures. I'd been saved from having to do so by my sling. When I walked in with that on, Richard naturally wanted to know what had happened.

I told him. I told him everything. The whole shmear. I held nothing back. After all, he was a lawyer. Anything I told him was confidential. Maybe he'd have some good advice.

Besides, there weren't too many people I could talk to anymore.

"Why didn't you call me before?" Richard said.

"Before what?"

"Before you went to the grand jury. Before you talked to the cops."

"I didn't know what you'd tell me to do."

"Of course not. That's why you needed the advice."

"All right. I figured you'd tell me what *not* to do."

"Like what?"

"Like what to tell the cops."

"Exactly," Richard said. "You're now on the hook for making a false report. You lied to the cops in an official investigation. They've got it in writing. You signed it."

"You wouldn't have advised me to do that?"

"What, are you nuts?"

"That's the point, Richard. I would have done it anyway. Would you have wanted me to do it with your knowledge?"

"I wouldn't have *let* you do it."

"How were you gonna stop me?"

"By talking some sense into your head. There're ways to do things. Legal ways. You wanna withhold things from the police, that's entirely possible. But you don't have to out-and-out lie. You could have had me present when you made your statement, and I could have advised you what to say."

"Wouldn't that just make the cops suspicious?"

"You think they're not suspicious now? You tell some fairy tale no third-grader would believe. Whaddya think the cops are gonna do? Thank you very much and go act on it? All you've done is double your troubles. The cops were investigating a simple shooting. Now they're investigating a *suspicious* shooting, and they're investigating you."

"I know."

Richard sighed, tipped his chair forward. "Well, what's done is done. Let's take it from there. Which actually makes life easier. You've already committed the crime. Now we just have to figure out how to get you off.''

''I haven't committed a crime.''

''Of course not. You're innocent until proven guilty. And so far, no one's charged you with anything. They haven't even connected you with the murder.''

''You think they haven't made the connection?''

''Oh, sure, they've made the *connection*. You were a grand jury witness, for Christ's sake. These two sergeants, Thurman and, uh . . .''

''MacAullif?''

''No, the other one. The one who questioned you.''

''Reynolds.''

''Right. They've undoubtedly talked. And Thurman knows you were messing around in this. And they can put two and two together. No, I mean they haven't thought to charge you with the murder.''

I stared at him. ''What?''

He shrugged. ''It's the next logical step. You were messing around in this thing, you were bird-dogging the guy. Working for his girlfriend. Then he gets killed and you keep messing around and get shot. It isn't a far cry for the cops to start thinking maybe you killed the guy, either alone or as the girlfriend's accomplice.''

My mouth dropped open. ''Are you shitting me?''

''Not at all.''

''The cops have an open-and-shut case against this woman.''

''Sure, but what if you were in it too? You kill the guy, you call the broad, say things got out of control, he's dead. She comes rushing over and you arrange an elaborate coverup.''

I stared at him incredulously. ''Richard. Why the

hell would she do that? Put herself on the spot? If I killed the guy, she'd just smile sweetly and let me take the rap.''

''Yeah, but maybe you had something on her.''

''What?''

''You were digging around, getting dirt. Maybe you got some dirt on her. You call her, tell her, help me out or I'm gonna blow the whistle.''

''Richard—''

He held up his hands. ''I know it's farfetched. I'm just telling you, once you start lying to the cops, it starts 'em thinking. Who knows how far their imagination can go?''

The phone rang.

Richard picked it up. ''Yes?'' He listened a moment, then covered the mouthpiece, cocked his head at me. ''A Mr. Poindexter on the line wants to talk to you.''

''Jesus. I'm not here.''

''Wendy/Janet told him you were.''

''Great. I'm in conference with my lawyer, I'll call him right back.''

Richard relayed that message, hung up the phone. ''How long you gonna keep ducking him?''

''As my lawyer, how long would you recommend?''

''I don't know. How often does hell freeze over?'' Richard spread his fingers wide, put his hands on the desk. ''All right,'' he said. ''Here's the situation. From now on, you are talking to no one. And I mean no one. A cop asks you about this case, you say, 'Call my lawyer.' This Poindexter calls you at home, you say, 'Call my lawyer.' Someone asks you the time of day, you say, 'Call my lawyer.' ''

''Fine by me. And what do we do then?''

He shrugged. "Depends what they want. This is the kind of case, you gotta play it one day at a time."

"Richard, I can't pay you."

"Who asked you?"

I sighed. "Thanks."

"Forget it. Now, have you got those pictures?"

Shit.

I told Richard the situation. To say he was pissed off would be a gross understatement. The man was practically speechless. In fact, when I finished talking, it actually took him several seconds before he could think of a single thing to say. "Moron" was the first word that he latched onto. "Unbelievable, incredible moron. You're not a social worker. You're not a do-gooder. You are a private investigator working in my employ. You are assigned certain simple tasks which you are expected to do. That is all that you are required to do, all that you are expected to do, all that you are *supposed* to do. I thought that we had discussed this case. You told me when you handed in the fact sheet that you had certain reservations. And what did I tell you at the time?"

"I know what you told me at the time."

"And then you go and do this."

"What was I supposed to do, just let the kid get beat up again?"

"You don't know he got beat up."

"Yes, I do, and so do you. Come on, Richard, cut the shit. You wanna sue anyway, go ahead and sue anyway. I can't stop you. I'm just telling you how it is."

Richard sighed. "Let's see the pictures."

I opened my briefcase, took out the packet, handed it to him.

Richard pulled the pictures out, leafed through them one by one. He stopped, looked at one, shook his head. "A dream come true."

The phone rang.

Richard scooped it up, listened a moment, covered the mouthpiece again. "You're a popular guy. Now Sergeant MacAullif wants to talk to you."

"Shit."

"What's the message?"

"I'll call him back."

Richard relayed that, hung up the phone. He picked up the photos, leafed through the rest of them. He sighed, put them on his desk.

"What you gonna do, Richard?"

What he looked like he was gonna do was jump over the desk and bite my head off. Instead, he waved his hand. "All right, all right. I'm rejecting the case."

"It's the right thing to do."

Richard grimaced. "Thank you, Wilford Brimley."

The phone rang again.

Richard snatched it up. "Yes?" he barked impatiently. He listened for a moment, shook his head, opened his mouth and rolled his eyes. He covered the mouthpiece, cocked his head at me. "Unbelievable," he said. "Now I have a Sergeant Reynolds on one line and a Sergeant Thurman on another."

I stood up.

"That's enough for me. I'm getting the hell out of here before these guys figure out I'm not calling back and start showing up."

Richard nodded. "Probably a wise idea."

I looked at him. "Oh yeah? You're a lawyer and you tell me that? I thought flight was an indication of guilt."

"It is," Richard said. He shrugged. "But what the hell. You're guilty."

34

I WENT OUT ON A CASE. Wendy gave it to me on my way out. Wendy and Janet were real sympathetic and real solicitous, what with me being shot, and Wendy was real happy to have something for me.

Don't get me wrong about Wendy and Janet. They're perfectly nice girls. Totally inept at their chosen profession, but otherwise fine girls.

I shouldn't call them girls. They're in their twenties. I'm a sexist pig. The feminists are gonna get me. And the cops are gonna get me. And Poindexter's gonna get me. And the grand jury's gonna get me—they'll listen to all the testimony, and instead of indicting Melissa Ford, they'll indict me. Just like Richard predicted. And then the IRS will get me for tax evasion. Even though I pay my taxes. They'll come up with some new tax I never even heard of and they'll nail me for that. And then they'll throw me in jail and my cell mate will turn out to be the Black Death. But he won't kill me, he'll *get* killed, and then they'll peg me for it.

Yeah, a simple mindless case was just what I needed, and I was duly grateful to accept a signup out in Queens. I got out of the office ahead of the posse and took the subway home to get my car.

Well, not home again, I still hadn't called Alice, but into my neighborhood. I got my car and I drove out to Queens to see Felix Cortez, who had slipped in his bathtub and broken his wrist.

Yeah, that was about my speed. That was about the sort of case I could handle.

And I couldn't even handle *that.* Boy, when things go wrong, they just go wrong. When I asked Felix Cortez how he fell, he told me he slipped on a bar of soap.

Wonderful. Who the hell did that make liable?

Ordinarily, that wouldn't bother me. Because Richard has explained the situation, not that particular one, but the general idea, usually with regard to ice and snow. Say a guy slips on icy pavement. When I go to shoot it, the ice isn't there but the pavement is cracked. Those cracks didn't trip him, but I shoot 'em anyway, because the cracked pavement is a contributing factor.

In this case, even though the guy slipped on a bar of soap, the unsafe tub floor was a contributing factor and I would have to shoot that.

Oh yeah? Tell me about it. It's a horseshit case, Richard. Are you really gonna sue someone for that?

I felt like telling Felix Cortez I was sorry he didn't have a case, but if he was stupid enough to slip on a bar of soap, it was his own damn fault.

I restrained myself with a great effort. Richard would flip out. It was bad enough I'd just talked him out of the Raheem Webb case. If I screwed up this one for him, I would advance rapidly to the top of Richard's all-time shit list, not a prime position to be in with one's pro bono lawyer when facing a slew of felony counts.

Self-preservation is the first law of nature. I kept my mouth shut, signed up Felix Cortez, and dutifully photographed the offending bathroom fixture.

But I wasn't happy about it. No surprise there. I was pissed off at life in general and this case in particular. And having to do this nothing case, this stupid, pointless, trivial case—but one which Richard might well win, for Christ's sake—well, that just seemed like the ultimate humiliation. So this is what it's come to. This is what I've been reduced to. A spineless, sniveling worm, incapable of standing up for anything he believes in, dutifully following other people's orders in a world that made no sense.

Not, I admit, the brightest of philosophies. But the point is, on top of everything else, I had all of that going on in my head when I left Felix Cortez's to go out and get my car.

The thing is, I am generally cautious. I have a keen sense of danger—not surprising in a paranoiac. And I've certainly been on this job long enough to have learned to be wary. And I have to believe if this had been Harlem or the South Bronx or someplace like that, my preoccupations notwithstanding, I'd have been looking out.

But this was Queens, which always seems safer, perhaps unrealistically so, but it does. And it wasn't some deserted residential street either. Felix Cortez happened to live over a grocery store on a perfectly decent, heavily populated, commercial block on Northern Boulevard, which is a major two-way street. My car was actually at a meter, for Christ's sake. And who expects trouble just walking down the street and getting into their car at a meter? Anyway, I sure wasn't. I just walked up to my car and stuck my key in the lock.

Which is when he grabbed me. Suddenly, without warning, from behind. He grabbed my upper arms in vicelike grips. My briefcase, which I'd tucked under my good right arm, fell to the street, bouncing off my foot. My key ring slipped out of my hand and my keys clattered against the side of the car, dangling from the door key in the lock.

My shock was so great I almost wet my pants.

Good god, this can't be happening. Good god.

The man spun me around, grabbed my shoulders, slammed me up against the car so hard my teeth clicked and my eyes teared.

I blinked them, looked up into the face of my attacker.

It was MacAullif.

35

"WHAT THE FUCK DO YOU THINK YOU'RE DOING?"

The speaker was not me. I hadn't recovered my faculties enough to be able to talk. No, it was MacAullif who said that.

When I blinked at him stupidly, too overwhelmed to answer, he slammed me up against the car again.

The spectacle of a beefy bruiser like MacAullif manhandling some poor guy with his arm in a sling was too much for two young jock types passing by. They actually stepped out in the street to break it up. MacAullif let go of me with one hand, the other being quite sufficient to hold me still, reached in his pocket and flipped out his badge.

"I'm a cop," he growled. "Fuck off."

They did. So much for the rights of ordinary citizens. A police officer can abuse any defenseless cripple he wants.

Their intervention had at least given me time to catch my breath. "MacAullif," I said.

He shoved me against the car again. "Shut up! Do

you hear me? Just shut up! I'll tell you when to talk. Right now you better listen.

"You don't return my phone calls. You don't *take* my phone calls. You have some ditsy bitch say you'll call back, but you don't. Not surprising, the way things worked out."

"MacAullif—"

He slammed me against the car again. "Slow learner? Keep your mouth shut. You said enough already, believe me." He paused, exhaled. "So, you tell me in the hospital you're too doped up to talk. I don't buy that, but I give you the benefit of the doubt. I even pull strings for you. Make a call downtown, get 'em to give you a break. Give 'em my personal assurance you'll show up and make a statement the next day." MacAullif's eyes blazed. "My personal assurance, fuckface!"

"I made a statement," I said. I shouldn't have. It got me slammed up against the car again.

"You sure did. I'll say you did. I read your statement this morning, asshole. Who the hell do you think you are?"

I took that for a rhetorical question. I was also getting tired of being slammed up against the side of my car. I said nothing.

"Don't you wanna know *why* I read your statement? A statement in a case that ain't got jack shit to do with me? Well, I have to tell you, I didn't ask for it. I didn't go checkin' up on you. I didn't call Sergeant Reynolds up and say, 'By the way, could I read this guy's statement just on the off chance he turns out to be some incredible asshole?' "

"So, why do you think he brought it to me, aside from the fact I vouched for you in the first place? Well,

Sergeant Reynolds is a diligent cop. Not the most experienced cop in the world, not the most seasoned investigator, but a perfectly intelligent cop. And he's a farm boy—the man knows horseshit when he sees it.''

"MacAullif—''

"Shut the fuck up. So, you make your statement yesterday. It don't mean nothin' to Reynolds, 'cept he knows it's shit, but he's not gonna bother me on my day off, 'cause I don't take 'em often and he knows I'll hit the roof. Embarrassed to bring it to me, really. 'Excuse me, sergeant, but why did you vouch for this flaming asshole?' Besides, he's got no reason to think it's that important.

"Except, I told him you're a grand jury witness. One of the reasons for leaving you alone, letting you go home and recuperate. So when you sing funny, he pulls the file. First thing this morning. He pulls the file and he reads about Melissa Ford, and like any good cop, he puts two and two together and he makes six.

"So, now he doesn't come back on me, he goes to Sergeant Thurman, the officer in charge of the case, and he says, 'Hey man, I think you got a problem with this one.' Well, that would work with nine officers out of ten, but Sergeant Thurman's a moron, he don't wanna hear shit, he's got his murderer and he don't care if you got shot just so long as you didn't get shot so bad you can't testify. But Sergeant Reynolds is a persistent son of a bitch, he won't quit till he has the dope, so he gets outta Sergeant Thurman, yeah, you been messin' around in the case, you been comin' around askin' questions about drug paraphernalia. Well, it don't take a genius to link drugs and Harlem, so now Sergeant Reynolds is *real* interested, only Sergeant Thurman *ain't* a genius and he still won't tumble.

"Now Sergeant Reynolds wants to talk to me bad, only I'm not in the office, I'm out on a case and he can't reach me. By then you're singing to the grand jury so he couldn't reach you, and he's not sure he wants to anyway till he's got some more dope, so while he's waiting for me, he calls Melvin C. Poindexter to see if you were investigating this murder for Melissa Ford."

"Shit."

"Right. Well, that gives Melvin C. Poindexter a severe case of indigestion. He says absolutely not, no go, no way, you are poison, you got smallpox, you're the kiss of death, he wants nothing to do with you, nothing you've done should reflect on his client in any way, and the whole nine yards. So Reynolds pins it down that you were absolutely not working for Melissa Ford or Melvin C. Poindexter when you were shot."

MacAullif made a face. "Well, Reynolds shouldn't have spilled that. If Poindexter didn't know that, there was no reason to hand it to him. But, like I said, Reynolds is young, the eager beaver type, wants to get a rise out of him.

"Well, he gets one. Poindexter flips out. Does an abrupt about face. Now he wants to hear all about it. Figures he hit the jackpot. You can bet your ass he'll be lookin' for you."

"He already is."

"No shit. So what's the upshot? I get back from a perfectly routine homicide investigation with a perp in tow. Husband/wife thing, guy croaked her, gonna sing, all I gotta do is the paper work and process it, chalk one up on the plus side of the ledger, and how many days do you get a piece of cake like that?

"But, no. Suddenly I got a fuckin' three-ring circus on my hands. I got Reynolds all over me for stickin' up for you. I got Sergeant Thurman up my ass, wantin' to know what the fuck Reynolds is doin' messin' around in his investigation—as if that were *my* fault, for Christ's sake—fuckin' Reynolds had to go and mention me, that guy has really got to watch his mouth. And then I got Melvin C. Poindexter, whom I never met, talked to, or even fuckin' *heard of,* for Christ's sake, and he's suddenly my fault, cause Sergeant Thurman's flippin' out and wants to know if I'm the jerk who sicced the asshole onto him."

MacAullif paused, took a breath. He was very red in the face. "You understand all that? You followin' all that? If not, I'm not surprised, cause I've been tryin' to sort it out all fuckin' day. Anyway, the upshot is, you're suddenly Public Fuckup Number One. Sergeant Reynolds wants you bad. This Poindexter lawyer wants you bad, and I want you bad. The only one who doesn't want you bad is Sergeant Thurman, and that's just 'cause he's too fuckin' dumb."

"He called me too."

"Oh yeah? Well, that ain't 'cause he gives a shit. He's just callin' to tell you as far as he's concerned the case is closed, and if you go back on, add to, or in any way change what you told the grand jury, he'll rip your fuckin' lungs out. Now that may not sound like too cordial a message, but it's a valentine compared to what you'll get from everybody else. To say that Sergeant Reynolds is pissed would be a small understatement. Cops don't like it when you lie to them. When you lie in a signed statement, they like it even less. Particularly when it fucks up an investigation. In this case, it fucks up *two* investigations. You're on Sergeant Reynolds' shit list. You're on Sergeant Thurman's shit list. Right now you're Melvin Poindexter's pretty boy, but that's cause he don't know no better. He thinks you're gonna help him out. As soon as he hears your version of how you got shot, you're gonna be on the top of his shit list too.

"At any rate, you're on the top of *everybody's* Most Wanted list. The whole fuckin' world's tryin' to find you."

"How'd you find me first?"

"How do you think? I called Rosenberg and Stone to tell 'em to beep you. They tell me you're there. I say, put him on, and they tell me you're talkin' to your lawyer and you'll call back. Well, I'm not stupid. The minute you don't take the call I know you're duckin' me, and I don't wait for no call back, I go over there. Probably just missed you. The girls say they'll beep you, I tell 'em if they do I'll rip their tits off, just tell me where you went. And if they tell anybody else, I'll haul 'em in on obstruction. Now I'm damn sure neither one of them knows what that means, but they get the idea."

MacAullif paused, possibly for breath. He inhaled and exhaled. "So, I'm here and you're here and there's nobody else here. With so many people after you, that's a situation that's not gonna last."

"So?"

"So we gotta talk."

36

"You gotta get back on the horse that threw you."

"What?"

MacAullif and I were sitting in a small coffee shop down the street. I always seem to sit in coffee shops when I talk to MacAullif. MacAullif lives on coffee. The thing is, he seems to hate it. Treats it like it was a chore. Anyway, he took a sip, grimaced like his mother'd just given him castor oil.

"Look," he said. "I know what you're goin' through. I been a cop a long time. I never been shot myself, but I seen enough cops who got shot. Rookies in particular. And it's just like with you."

"Whaddya mean?"

"You know what they do when a cop gets shot? Well, it depends how bad it is, of course. But say the guy's O.K., he can go back to work. They take him off the street a while. Give him a desk job. Ease him back into it." MacAullif shook his head. "Never believed in that. For my money, that's fucked up."

"Why?"

"Gotta get back on the horse that threw you. Know where that comes from? Bronco bustin'. Cowboys. Cowboy's tryin' to break a horse that's too wild, it bucks him off. Busts him up some. What do they do, say, 'Oh shit, take it easy, try some of these tamer horses, break a few of those and work your way up to this bronc?' Hell, no. They get right back on. Soon as they're able. Sometimes *before* they're able. A guy with two cracked ribs and a busted arm'll be climbin' up on the same fuckin' horse.

" 'Cause the cowboys know. The *longer* you take, the more you put it off, the harder it is to get back on. It's the fear, you know? And it ain't the fear of the horse. It's the fear of the fear. It fucks up your head. You start thinkin', am I afraid of this horse? Am I afraid to get back on? Maybe you're not, but you're afraid you *will* be afraid. See what I mean? The fear of the fear. It grows on itself, feeds on itself, gets worse and worse.

"No, you gotta get back on the horse that threw you. Right away. Soon as you can. Before it's too late. 'Cause if you wait too long, it builds up. The fear. And you reach a point where you can never get back on that horse again."

"You ever gonna get back to present-day New York?"

MacAullif glared at me from over the top of his coffee cup. "You got a wise mouth for someone in your position." He took a sip, grimaced. "I'm talkin' present-day New York. You too dumb to see the connection? I gotta spell it out for you?"

"No. Go on talking about horses."

MacAullif took a breath. "Jesus Christ. You sure

have the balls when it comes to talkin' to me. Me, the one guy you shouldn't be talkin' that way to.''

"Sorry. I just get tired of being used as a punching bag.''

MacAullif put up his hands. "Oh. My fault, of course. Like you did nothin' to bring this on. You'll pardon me, but just who's punchin' who? As I recall, I'm the guy who got dumped on, lied to, fucked over and made to look like a fool. And here I am, instead of chewing you out, sittin' here tellin' you I know how you feel.''

"Talkin' about horses.''

"*Fuck* the horses!'' MacAullif banged the table so hard coffee jumped out of his cup. He rubbed his head. "Jesus Christ, you know why you don't wanna hear about horses? It's not 'cause you don't understand or you think it's stupid. It's cause you *do* understand and it hits too close to home.''

I said nothing, sipped my coffee. MacAullif was right. About the coffee, anyway. It was pretty bad.

"Look,'' MacAullif said. "You got shot and now you're scared. That's normal. That's a typical reaction. If you weren't scared, there'd be something wrong with you. You'd have to be a fuckin moron.'' MacAullif took a sip of coffee, set it down, leaned in. "So, you take the fact that you're scared as a given, and you deal with it, see? You say, hey, I got a problem, I gotta deal with it, and you do. I'm not sayin' that's not hard, I'm just sayin' you gotta. 'Cause the only alternative is to say, I'm scared, I can't do nothin', I'm too scared. And if you do that, it builds on itself like the fuckin' cowboy and then you can't get back on the fuckin' horse.

"So, here's you. This guy shoots you, you say fuck

it, I can't take it anymore, I'm scared, he shot me, I'm scared he'll shoot me again, I don't want him to shoot me again, I'm scared, I can't deal with it, I'm bailin' out. So when the cops say 'Who shot you?,' you tell some stupid lie. And when I say stupid lie, I mean *stupid* lie. I mean, Jesus Christ, 'I don't remember, my mind's a blank?' ''

"You don't believe in traumatic amnesia?"

"Sure I believe in traumatic amnesia. I've seen cases of it. When I see it, I believe it. In your case, I'd sooner believe in the fuckin' Tooth Fairy."

MacAullif glared at me, took a sip of coffee, glared at it. "Jesus," he said. I didn't know if he was referring to me or the coffee. Probably both.

"Look," MacAullif said. "Believe it or not, I didn't get to be a sergeant by bein' a dumb cop. I look at you, I see how scared you are and the fact you lied to the cops, and I put all that together and there's only one thing that makes sense."

He waited, made me ask. I knew it was a tactic on his part, but I couldn't help myself.

"What's that?" I said.

"You know who shot you. You know it perfectly well. That's why you're so scared, and that's why you lied. It's the one thing that makes sense. If you didn't know who shot you, there'd be no reason for you to lie to the cops."

I said nothing. I sat quiet, hardly breathed.

"You waitin' for more?" MacAullif said. "That's it. That's all there is. That's the story. You know who shot you and you're afraid of him, so you lied to the cops. Perfectly simple and straightforward. And perfectly understandable. But it ain't gonna work."

That was where I was supposed to say, "Why not?"

But hell could freeze over before I'd do that. Saying "why not" would be tantamount to admitting what MacAullif had said was true. Instead, I took a sip of coffee. An unpleasant alternative. The lesser of two evils.

"You wanna know why it ain't gonna work?" MacAullif said. "I'll tell you why not. Because it's too fucking stupid. Looking for potholes to register. Give me a break."

"Happens all the time."

"Sure it does," MacAullif said. "That's why it would make a perfectly legit story. But you can't carry it through." He shook his head. "You're such a moron. You can't even lie straight. You wanna lie to someone, at least be consistent. Say something like, 'I was out looking for potholes and I saw this big rubble-filled lot and it occurred to me, Jesus, here's a place a guy could really fall down in,' and I'm walkin' around the lot lookin' at the defect and suddenly I hear a loud noise like a shot and the next thing I know I wake up in the hospital." MacAullif shrugged. "See, that's a lie, but it's simple, straightforward. It's one lie and you carry it through. As it happens, it wouldn't work, since the evidence indicates you were shot in the building, but at least it would be a step in the right direction.

"Conversely, you say, 'I was callin' on this kid and I walked out of his building and that's the last thing I remember till I woke up in the hospital.' See, that's a lie too, but it's also simple and straightforward.

"But you, no, you start in on one lie and right in the middle you switch to the other one. You throw in potholes *and* amnesia. What a fucking moron. Now, Reynolds didn't go into it, 'cause it wasn't important at the time, but whaddya wanna bet the next time he talks to you, he asks you for a list of the potholes you were gonna register? Whaddya gonna tell him, that you hadn't found any yet?''

That's *exactly* what I was gonna tell him. Hearing MacAullif ridicule the idea didn't exactly make my day.

"No," MacAullif said. "Here's the problem. Your story's so transparent I can see right through it. The pothole thing is bullshit. You made that up to cover the time you were working on something that had to do with Melissa Ford. The amnesia thing is also bullshit. You made that up because while the pothole thing gave you a good excuse for walkin' around Harlem, you couldn't figure any way to stretch it into a reason for being in that abandoned building. And you *were* in that abandoned building—the evidence is quite clear.''

MacAullif drained his coffee cup, grimaced. "God, this is terrible," he said. He waved his arm for the waitress to fill it up again. She did, and he dumped in milk and sugar, stirred it around.

"What makes you so transparent," MacAullif said, "is the fact you're not a good liar to begin with. You're not inventive, you always stick pretty close to the truth. Now the pothole thing, it's not true, you weren't out registering them. But you've photographed enough potholes in Harlem, so to you that seemed close enough to be true.

"The amnesia thing is something else. You say you don't know anything from the time you're walking down the street till you wake up in the hospital. That, of course, is bullshit, but there's a little bit of truth in it. I would imagine you don't remember anything from the time you got shot till you woke up in the hospital. And that's interesting, 'cause of where you got found.''

MacAullif held up one finger. "Everything indicates that you were shot inside that building. Yet you were found in the empty lot. That leaves only two theories. Either you managed to crawl there before you passed out, or someone dragged you there. The way I see it, everything points to the fact that someone dragged you there."

I frowned. "Why?"

"Like I said, 'cause you're not that good a liar. 'Cause you made up the I-can't-remember-anything-my-mind's-a-blank story. And the way I figure, if you made it up, it must be partly true. I figure the part that's true is you can't remember anything since you were shot, which means you didn't crawl out of the building."

"Interesting," I said.

MacAullif shook his head. "You are a major pain in the ass. Anyway, the way I see it, someone dragged you out of the building. Ten to one it's the shooter. Why? Because I can't imagine anyone else was there. And if that's true, it's interesting. Very interesting. 'Cause if you stay in that building, odds are no one finds you and you die.

"But the shooter didn't want you to die. The shooter wanted you alive."

"Why?"

"How the hell should I know? I'm makin' this all up from interpreting a pack of lies. But some people don't like murder on their records. Or maybe the shooter doesn't want to kill you, he just wants to send a message. You dyin' in an abandoned building where no one finds you is a very poor message."

I frowned. "I see."

"But you alive, and knowin' damn well you got shot for messin' around in whatever you were messin' around in, would be a very nice reminder to the parties involved to butt out."

I frowned again, said nothing.

"If that were true, you would develop a very bad case of lockjaw, and become strangely unhelpful on the subject of your bein' shot. And there would suddenly be a corresponding lack of interest on the part of the other parties involved."

MacAullif held up his hand. "Now, where the shooter fucked up here is in not knowin' you weren't workin' for the parties involved. As a result, this Poindexter, instead of bein' warned off by the shooting, just becomes all the more interested. But the shooter would have to be a psychic to anticipate that."

MacAullif put his hands on the table. "So you're in a mess. A big fucking mess. You got the shooter pulling you one way, Poindexter pullin' you another way, Reynolds pullin' you another way and Thurman pullin' you another way." He shrugged his shoulders. "Now, me? Me, I'm just neutral. I got no stake in this. I'm just the guy who got fucked over. But of all those people right now I'm probably the only one with the slightest chance of helpin' you out. So whaddya say? How's about we drop all the horseshit and talk turkey here?"

I took a breath. "Richard Rosenberg has agreed to act as my attorney in this matter. He has instructed me to say absolutely nothing about this case outside of his presence."

MacAullif's face hardened. "Well, that's one way to go. It's always advisable to get the advice of a reputable attorney.'' (MacAullif's rendering of the word ''reputable'' was one I was sure Richard would take exception to, if not find actionable.) ''If that's the route you wanna go, that's fine, there's nothin' I can say.''

MacAullif shrugged, took a sip of coffee, once again looked as if it had just poisoned him. He frowned, put the cup down, put his hands on the table again. ''Only one problem with it.''

''What's that?''

''You gotta live with yourself.''

37

ALICE WAS CRYING. And I could tell she'd been crying off and on all day long. No surprise there. Bad enough to have your husband get shot. Then to find he's dug a hole for himself he can't possibly get out of. That he's some incredible chickenshit asshole. Yeah, I could see how that wouldn't really make Alice's day.

"So what are you going to do?" Alice said. It was not the first time she'd asked the question.

"I don't know," I said. It was not the first time I'd given that response.

It was one Alice found somewhat less than adequate. "That's no answer. You may feel that way, but that's not true. You have to do something. You *are* doing something. Just doing nothing's doing something, don't you see?"

"Yeah, I do."

"So, you see, you have to do something."

I took a breath. "Alice, look. You're the one who said this had to end. You're the one who wanted me out of it."

"I know that. So what?"

"So that's what I did. I'm out of it."

Alice stopped crying. Her face got hard. "So now you're blaming me?"

"No, of course not."

"Yes, you are. You're saying I made you do it."

"That's not what I'm saying."

"What *are* you saying?"

"I'm just saying, isn't that what you wanted?"

"What?"

"For me to be out of it."

Alice's eyes widened in exasperation. "Of course I want you out of it. But take a look. Do you think you're out of it now? All you've done is make things worse."

"Alice—"

"No, really, do you call this being out of it?"

"No, but—"

"I didn't say I wanted you to lie to the police. Did I say that?"

"No, but—"

"All I said was you got shot for nothing. All I said was you were working for an ungrateful woman and there was no reason for you to work for her anymore."

"You said more than that."

"No, I didn't."

"Well, you *meant* more than that."

"No, I didn't. And if I did, all I meant was for you to leave it alone. Stop pushing, stop prying, stop investigating. That's all."

I sighed. "Right."

"We went over all this last night. Don't you remember?"

I remembered. It was one of the reasons I hadn't wanted to come home.

"And I told you the grand jury would make you feel worse, and the grand jury made you feel worse. And now everybody in the world is after you, and it's like you took your problems and blew them up a hundred times, and what the hell are you going to do now?"

If that sounds like where you came in, you're lucky. As I said, we had reached this juncture many times.

"Alice, I'm doing everything I can. I've put myself in the hands of an attorney."

"Richard."

"He's an excellent lawyer."

"A negligence lawyer."

"That's not his only field of expertise."

"Well, you're trusting him with your life."

"Let's not be melodramatic."

The phone rang. Alice picked it up. "Yes . . . I'm sorry, he's not in right now, can I take a message? . . . Yes, I'll tell him." She hung up the phone.

"Which one was that?"

"New one. Officer Andrews calling for Sergeant Reynolds."

"The night shift."

"What if they stop calling and come and get you?"

"Then I'll call Richard."

"I don't think he can help you."

"That's my problem."

"And ours. What the hell do we do if you go to jail?"

I reached for her but she pulled away. "No, I'm angry, damn it. You didn't tell me what you were gonna do. You just went and lied to the cops. You took a risk you had no right to take."

"Maybe."

"No maybe about it. You're now in a position where you could go to jail. You say you put yourself in the hands of an attorney. Yeah, you have. That's what criminals do. And if the attorney is good enough, they don't go to jail."

"Alice, what do you *want* me to do?"

"I don't know."

Instant replay, with roles reversed. Only Alice *does* know. It's just I keep resisting her pitch.

She makes it anyway. "Look, I know you don't want to hear it, but I'm going to say it anyway. Go to the cops. Take Richard, if you have to. No, that's not fair. Take Richard, he'll be fine, he'll be good at it. Take Richard, go to the cops and have Richard make a deal. The deal is that you want to change your statement. Or amend your statement. Or augment your statement. Whatever the hell it is lawyers say so they don't have to out-and-out admit that you lied. And then tell the cops everything you know. Everything. And then you're out of it. Then you're off the hook. Then you can forget about it."

"Until the cops go after the son of a bitch and he comes looking for me."

"Why would he do that?"

"What, are you nuts? You think I just make a statement and that's it, they lock the guy up? I gotta identify him. And they gotta make a case against him. And how can they do that, when I didn't even see him shoot me? I mean, if he was stupid enough to keep the gun, maybe. Yeah, maybe then, they'd bust him and they'd get the gun and they'd have a case. But as things stand, no matter what I say, this guy's gonna walk."

"If what you say is true, they haven't got enough to pick him up at all."

"What, are you kidding? Of course, they'll pick him up. They'll pick him up and question him just to confirm my story. Or, disprove it. Anyway, to check up on it. You think I'll make a statement and they'll say, 'Aw, gee, that's not enough to convict, let's just let this go?' No, they'll pick him up all right."

"What if they do?"

"Alice, the guy shot me just for following him. What do you think he'll do to me for having him arrested?"

Her face twisted. "I know, but . . ."

"But what?"

"But you have to do something."

I sighed. "Yeah."

"So what are you going to do?"

38

I SUBLIMATED.

At least, that's how I like to think of it. That's how I like to put it. The other way would be to say I ran away. Which, of course, is what I did. But it's hard to live with that. And I had to live with myself, as MacAullif had said. So "sublimated" seemed a somewhat better word to use.

At any rate, that's just what I did. I took a situation that I couldn't deal with, and threw myself into a much less extreme situation that I *could* deal with, and occupied myself with that. I still wasn't up to facing the Black Death, but I was up to handling Raheem Webb's pusher. Heavy irony there—can't deal with the big boys who traffic in drugs and carry guns, just the small-time neighborhood pusher with his gang of street kids. But at that point, any victory was better than none.

And so I sublimated.

I took a day off work, something I should have done anyhow. I mean, with my entire fate in the balance, did I really need eighty bucks so bad that I should spend the day racing around, jumping to the tune of the beeper, driving all over hell and back trying to get time and mileage on the sheet? Given the state of my finances, the answer was probably yes, but even so, I wasn't up to it. I called Richard, told him to have Wendy/Janet take me off the roster for one day. One day, for Christ's sake, what the hell. It would give me time to get my thoughts together, get my head together, do the things I wanted to do.

Sublimate.

At any rate, I got up and told Alice that's what I was gonna do. I took Tommie and dropped him off at the East Side Day School and drove back into our neighborhood and double-parked the car for the alternate side parking, leaving a sign in the window, of course, in case the person I was parked next to wanted to get out. Then I went up and told Alice where the car was, so she could move it back at ten-thirty in case I wasn't home. Then I went into the bedroom to check myself out.

My arm, I mean.

It really wasn't bad. I take it out of the sling, it hangs down at my side. It hurts, yeah, but I can move it. I don't intend to move it, not much anyhow, but that's good to see.

I looked through my dresser drawers and found an old pair of shorts, cut-off jeans, actually, not the designer kind you buy precut, but an old pair the knees had worn out on and I'd cut off myself. Then I dug out an old T-shirt, red, slightly tattered, originally extra-large, but now shrunk to fit me fine. I pulled that on. Sneakers, no problem. I always wear sneakers when I'm not in my suit. I took my shoes off, put on white cotton socks and my sneaks.

Next, the hall closet. I expected this to be difficult. It was. The object I sought was not there. I finally found it in the back of Tommie's closet, underneath the Voltron castle and other long since unused toys.

My basketball.

As expected, it needed air. Also as expected, Tommie's bicycle pump would have doubled quite nicely to pump it up, except I couldn't find the needle. No surprise there. A basketball needle is one of those things no one has. It is the most infuriating piece of equipment ever invented. One small twenty-five-cent piece of metal without which you cannot play the game.

Alice was no help on the subject, but surprised me by expressing no surprise that I was looking for it. All she said was, "Good idea."

I went out, walked up and down Broadway and eventually located a sporting goods store. The needle was seventy-nine cents. I found that encouraging somehow. Like I didn't have to feel that I'd been thwarted for a quarter. I brought it home and pumped up the ball until it tested out to my satisfaction—when held overhead and dropped, it bounced between waist and chest high.

I took the ball and went down to Riverside Park. I don't have to tell you it had been a long time. I tried to think back, couldn't remember if it had been before Tommie when I used to go down to Riverside Park and shoot around. Not on the weekends or late in the day—by then the courts were always jammed—but weekdays in the morning and early afternoon, I found I could always get on. In fact, in cooler weather, I was often the only one there.

It was that way now. I went into the park at 108th,

walked down the hill and looked over the stone fence to discover the courts next to the highway were empty. Not a soul. Being paranoid, that usually gives me pause. You don't want to get caught alone down there. And you usually have to stumble over a couple of homeless living under the steps to get down. Not a great place for a guy with his arm in a sling. But today I didn't mind at all. The deserted court seemed a warm and friendly place compared to some of the other choices I had.

I bounced the ball a couple of times, started down the steps.

The thing I hate most about the public courts in New York is that they have no nets. I shoot for the net. I like to hear the ball go swish. See, if you bank it off the backboard, the ball comes back. But if you shoot for the hoop, the ball goes through clean, and with no net to stop it, it just keeps going. Your best shots are the ones you have to chase.

The least of my worries.

I bounced the ball, walked out onto the court. My left arm was still in the sling, but, what the hell. I shoot one-handed anyway. The left hand is just for guidance, to steady the ball. And even where my arm is in the sling, I can get my hand on the ball for that one split second in between the dribble and the shot, the transition move I need to be able to score.

I started out slow. A few easy layups. A lazy, jogging pace. It's been years, but it's like riding a bicycle, you don't forget. Layups are no problem.

Jump shots are harder. Much harder. Try shooting one-handed jump shots some time, I mean with your arm down at your side. It's too awkward. Layups, yeah. Set shots, yeah. Jump shots, no way.

I put the ball down, took my arm out of my sling. Too early. Way too early. The arm hung down. And hurt. Well, not the arm itself, but hanging it down hurt the shoulder. I was off painkillers by now, so it hurt pretty bad.

A voice inside my head said, you deserve to hurt.

I bent down, picked up the ball in my right hand. I gritted my teeth, raised my left arm, put my hand on the ball. I took a deep breath, blew it out again, the way the coach taught us to do to relax before each foul shot.

This wasn't a foul shot. I dribbled once to my left, stopped, pivoted, went up for the shot.

The ball clanged off the front of the rim.

A miss.

But a shot. A controlled shot. Not an awkward one-handed fling. My left shoulder hurt like crazy, but it had done the job. Fair enough. The doctor had said you could do anything you were able to do.

I went after the rebound, my left arm flopping at my side. I got the ball, dribbled back to the top of the key. Faked right, went left, went up. Clanged the rim again.

Got the rebound and did it again.

And again.

And again.

Until the shots started dropping through.

I must have shot for forty-five minutes to an hour. Then I hung it up, literally, hung my arm back in the sling. I put the ball under my other arm and walked out of the park.

My car was still double-parked. I went to the pay phone on the corner, called Alice, told her never mind the car, I'm going for a ride.

"Oh yeah?" she said. "Well, two cops called."

"Who?"

"Thurman and Reynolds. Wanted to know when you're gonna call back."

"Tell them something noncommittal, like go fuck themselves."

"Great. Where are you going to be?"

"If you don't know, you don't have to lie."

"Yeah, but—"

"Don't worry. I'll be around."

I hung up, called Sheila Webb, made sure Raheem was home. I got in the car and drove up there.

The pusher wasn't in evidence. Or the neighborhood kids. Too early for them, I guess. I parked in front of the building, went inside.

Sheila Webb was surprised by my appearance. So was Raheem, when she finally got him out of the bedroom. He looked at me, said, "Hey, man, what's with you?"

"I don't always dress like a cop. Today's my day off."

"So what you want with me?"

I smiled at him. "Come on, Raheem. Let's you and me take a ride."

He frowned. "What for?"

Sheila said, "Raheem. Go with the man." She didn't know what was up, but after our talk the other day, I was O.K. in her book. The boy needed a father figure. If I wanted to play Big Brother, that was all right with her.

He came. He looked at me real funny, but he came.

Outside, he looked up and down the street a lot, like he didn't want his friends to see him leaving with the crazy honky. But there was no one around. We got in the car and drove off.

For a while we rode in silence. Then Raheem began to fidget, then to glance around. He looked in the back seat, saw the basketball.

"Basketball?" he said.

"Yeah."

We drove across 145th to Broadway, headed downtown. We'd passed 125th before he said, "Where we goin'?"

I glanced over at him. "You and I are gonna play a little one-on-one."

Up to that point, I'd felt perfectly good about what I was doing. Then it suddenly hit me. Jesus Christ, some fucking liberal. What a racist schmuck. The kid's tall and black, so you automatically assume he can play basketball. For all you know, the kid's never played ball in his life.

Not to worry. Raheem thought a minute, pursed his lips and cocked his head.

"Straight up or take it back?"

39

He killed me.

He beat me fifteen to six, but it wasn't really even as close as that. I hit a couple of set shots late in the game he probably could have blocked if he was really trying.

The problem was the kid could jump. He was half a head shorter than me, but he could outjump me all day long. And in one-on-one, rebounding is the key. Particularly when you're playing straight up, which is what Raheem had asked me, and what, given the choice, he opted to play. For those of you who don't play basketball, in a half-court game, which one-on-one is, you are, of course, both shooting at the same basket, so if you get the other guy's rebound, the question is can you go right back up with it and score—straight up—or do you have to first clear the ball out behind the foul line before you can shoot—take it back. As I said, Raheem chose straight up, and as soon as we started playing I knew why. The kid could outjump me no sweat, which meant if I missed a shot all he had to do was grab the rebound, go back up and stick it in. Which he did with amazing regularity. By the time he was finished, I was exhausted, humiliated and my arm hurt like crazy.

"Run it back," I said.

Raheem, who was dribbling and twirling the ball near the basket, looked over at me. "Huh?"

I jerked my thumb. "Run it back."

He crinkled up his nose, squinted at me as if to say, are you sure? Which wasn't a stupid question. I was breathing pretty hard after chasing him all over the court the first game, and I hadn't put up much of a fight.

"Your ball," I said.

He shrugged, dribbled out beyond the foul line and tossed me the ball. That's a courtesy check. To make sure I'm ready before he starts. We do it after every basket. I threw the ball back to him, signaling the start of the game.

The first game, as I said, I'd been tired, I hadn't played well and I'd forgotten the fundamentals. That's partly because he was a kid. A ten-year-old kid and shorter than me. And awkward to boot. I hadn't expected much. Particularly in the way of shooting. But it doesn't matter how awkward you are—if you can touch the rim, you can drop the ball in. Raheem's jumping ability had caught me flat-footed—literally. That wouldn't happen again.

Back to the fundamentals. A shorter man can keep a taller man from getting the rebound by boxing out. And a taller man is anyone who can jump higher than you. So I had to consider Raheem Webb a taller man and act accordingly. When the shot went up, I had to box him out. The idea is simple—you play the man instead of the ball. The first game when he'd shot I'd been going for the rebound. No more. Now I'd go right for him.

So when Raheem dribbled in and shot, that's exactly what I did. I went to him, wheeled around, boxed him out. The rebound was mine.

Except he made the shot.

One nothing.

I took the ball, flipped it back out to him. We were playing winner's outs, of course. He tossed me the ball for the check and I flipped it back. He took it, dribbled at the top of the key. I hung back—if he wanted to shoot from there he was welcome to. He didn't. He turned, keeping the ball away from me, and dribbled into the lane, keeping his back to the basket. I stayed between him and the hoop, my good arm up, letting him dribble the ball. If he made a hook shot, I couldn't stop him, but hook shots weren't really his thing either. He'd have to turn to shoot.

He did and I was in his face. He faked left, went right, went up. I couldn't block him, but I bothered his shot. The second it was off, I wheeled around, boxed him out, blocked him away from the board.

The shot, an awkward two-hander, hit the rim, bounced off the backboard, hit the rim again and dropped through.

Two zip.

Third time's the charm. Raheem came dribbling in, backing his way to the basket, and I kept in front of him, forcing him out. He turned, stopped the dribble. Faked up. Once, twice, three times. Then shot a two-handed set shot that glanced off the backboard and caromed right in.

No fair. He wasn't supposed to make that kind of

shot, not even from six feet out. In my book a two-hand set shot has no right to go in.

Three zip.

Raheem dribbled in again, bouncing the ball lazier now, with the careless arrogance of one who is winning easily. I stuck to my game plan, just stayed on him, waited for the shot. When he went up, a two-hand jump shot, awkward as can be, I had already boxed him away from the basket before the damn thing hit the rim. It caromed off the other side, bounced away out of bounds.

My ball.

I trotted across the court, picked up the ball, bounced it in to Raheem to check. He bounced it back to me.

I dribbled slowly down to the top of the key. Raheem, as usual, held back in the lane waiting for me to make my move. I dribbled up to the foul line, slowly, easy, no need to rush it, and straight off the dribble went up for the shot.

Swish. At least if there'd been a net it would have gone swish. As it was, it hit nothing. Just sailed through the circle of steel.

Three, one.

Raheem chased down the ball, tossed it back to me. I threw it to him for the check, got it back and immediately began dribbling in. Again slow and lazy. I dribbled past the top of the key to the foul line and went up for the shot. Same thing. The ball hit nothing, smooth as silk.

Three, two.

This time when Raheem checked the ball, he came out further before he threw it back. I knew he'd play me tighter now, get a hand in my face, try to make me miss.

He was standing just short of the foul line, waiting for me to get there, go up for my shot.

I didn't. Instead, I fired it up from the top of the key.

Swish.

He turned around and gave me a look, then went trotting after the ball.

Three, three.

Tie game.

And suddenly it's the battle of the century. Never mind that it's a middle-aged man with a bad arm against a ten-year-old kid with a bandaged head. This is war.

I don't know how to describe what happened next. Suffice it to say that I played over my head, shocked the hell out of a gawky kid who couldn't quite believe it was happening, and actually made a game of it.

Most of it was a blur. I was playing through pain and on my second wind, having passed exhaustion somewhere back in the first game. But under the circumstances I was playing well, and the long and short of it is we got to fourteen, thirteen his, he missed a layup, I got the rebound, dribbled to the foul line, let fly a jumper, and swish!

Fourteen all.

Game point.

And my ball.

I remember what happened next as clear as day.

He's cautious giving it to me. He doesn't want to get too close, let me throw a fake before I have to dribble. On the other hand, I had shot from there before. Maybe I'm just the type of fool to risk the whole game on a twenty-five footer.

Maybe, but not today.

I fake right but go left. Put my whole body into it, lean, actually, step forward on my left foot.

But that's a fake too. As the ball leaves my hand, I'm dribbling right. Not the best fake in the world, but effective. He's half a step behind. Hustling to make up lost ground.

Which is when I reverse again. Suddenly cut back to the left across the top of the key. He sees me do it, but he can't turn in time. I dribble and I'm flashing sideways across the foul line. A good move, but I'm headed away from the basket not toward it, he's already recovering, and before I could stop and shoot it, he'll be on me blocking the shot.

But I don't stop. In full stride I raise the ball, twist just my hand, and, without even turning my head, let it fly.

It is a shot that used to drive my high school coach bananas. Because no right-handed person can shoot running parallel to the basket to the left. The other way, yes, you'd be shooting across your body in a natural motion. But going left across the foul line you can't shoot with your right. Particularly without turning your head. It's simply a shot you are not supposed to take.

I used to take one almost every game. And the coach could never say anything because the damn thing usually went in.

It went in now. I saw it with my peripheral vision. It went straight in. No backboard, no rim, no nothing. Just a perfect arching, spinning shot. The soft touch, as the coach used to say.

The soft touch.

Fifteen, fourteen.

Game.

I let out a deep sigh, clenched my fists. A victory gesture. That's when the exhaustion hit. I bent over, breathing deeply, my hands on my knees.

Raheem said, "You gotta win by two."

My head stayed down a few more seconds, then came slowly up. By two? No one said anything like that. Any rule like that has to be spelled out before the game. Or at least before it occurs. At fourteen, fourteen, he could have said, "You gotta win by two." It wouldn't have been kosher, but we could have had a discussion and I might have actually agreed. Which would have been a large concession on my part, since I had the ball. But no, the kid waits till I plunk it in and then says, "You gotta win by two."

I was pissed. Really pissed. I had to tell myself, you're dealing with a ten-year-old kid. But even that didn't cut it. I wanted this victory and I'd fought for it hard. If that sounds stupid to you, then you've never played the game.

And I needed a victory right now. So what if it's only a ten-year-old kid? Somehow, some way I needed to win. I felt I deserved to win.

And, in that instant, I could see it being taken away. I could hear myself explaining to Alice, "Well, I beat him fifteen to fourteen, but he said, 'You gotta win by two,' and—" It just wasn't fair.

"Fine," I said. "Win by two."

And I walked up to the top of the key.

Which made Raheem realize he hadn't retrieved the ball. Slightly embarrassing, if he'd *really* been thinking you had to win by two. Obviously, he hadn't, the thought had just occurred to him.

He said nothing, chased down the ball, dribbled it back. He came up close, tossed me the ball. I tossed it back to him to check. He held the ball, but he was looking in my eyes. I knew that look. He was telling me I wasn't going to score.

He flipped me the ball. I didn't set him up with any fakes this time. When the ball was coming, I was going. I caught it in mid-stride, went around him to the right, down the side of the key half a step ahead and put up a half-layup, half-hook from just outside the side of the lane. It hit backboard, rim, backboard, rim.

And dropped off the side.

Where Raheem promptly stuffed it back up.

Fifteen all.

And immediately drove down the lane.

Sixteen, fifteen.

I don't know how to explain how badly I wanted to win. All I can say is, I was on that kid like glue. The fact he got the next shot off at all is some small miracle. I boxed him out, got the board, went back up and stuck it in, even with his hand in my face.

Sixteen all.

This time I foxed him again. A twenty-five-footer the second my fingers touched the ball. But I wasn't going for the rim. The second I shot, I was around him, going for the hoop. My shot hit all backboard, off to the side. It caromed down to me for a layup. The only legal self-pass in the game.

Seventeen, sixteen.

In your face, Raheem.

Next shot I faked the same thing. The second my hands touched the ball. Faked the shot-pass and the sprint for the hoop. And he went for it. Backed off a step.

Which is when I pulled back and let fly.

The twenty-five-footer I mentioned before. The shot I was disparaging as the desperate gamble of a total asshole.

I can still see the ball. Arcing through the air. Spinning. Spinning with the soft touch. Curling out and down and through.

Game.

No pretense this time, no hanging my head and leaning on my knees. I sat down. Sat down right where I was standing. Sank down on the asphalt and sat.

I sensed, not saw, Raheem come stand in front of me. I opened my eyes, but didn't raise my head. Saw the shoes, the two black legs.

And then the voice. "Two out of three?"

I didn't bother to answer, just waved him away.

Two out of three my ass.

He was quiet in the car going back. Just sat there in the front seat next to me, never said a word. He hadn't argued much about the game I wouldn't play. Even a ten-year-old kid could see that wasn't gonna go.

So far he hadn't commented on my win, hadn't said, "Good game," or anything like that. In fact, he had said nothing since the question, "Two out of three?" I wondered if he was sulking 'cause I wouldn't play the third game. Or maybe 'cause I'd beaten him in the second. That had to be a bit of a shock. Lose to a short white guy who can't jump. With his arm in a sling, no less. Well, not during the game, of course, but my arm was sure back in the sling now. My shoulder hurt like hell, but I didn't care. For the first time since I got shot, I actually felt good.

I don't know how to explain how important it was for me to beat Raheem. I mean, this was not the battle of the century here, just a gimpy old man versus a ten-year-old kid. But it really mattered to me. I think part of it was, I wanted to help the kid, and I realized somehow I'd never really have his respect unless I won. Because if I lost, I'd still be a fool in his eyes. One more person he could get around.

But that was just part of it. And a small part. Because, deep down inside, basically, I just needed to win.

Just for me.

I pulled up in front of Raheem's door. The pusher and two of the kids were standing in the street. As Raheem got out of the car, the guy's eyes narrowed and he took a step toward him.

I was out of my car in a flash, sling and all. I came barreling around the front of the car, planted myself between him and Raheem.

I poked my finger in his face. "You stay away from the kid," I said. "You don't go near the kid. You make a move on this kid, you're history. Just let me hear you give him any trouble, I'm runnin' you in."

For a second I thought he was gonna tear me apart. But, my basketball clothes not withstanding, odds were the guy still figured me for a cop. And you don't kill a cop with your bare hands in broad daylight with witnesses. Bad for business.

He just glared at me, shook his head slightly, as if in disbelief, then turned and walked away.

I turned to find Raheem standing watching him go. His mouth was actually open. He watched him go the whole length of the street, till the guy turned the corner out of sight. And even then he kept looking.

I put my hand on his shoulder. "Come on, Raheem Let's go."

He looked up at me then. I *was* taller than him, even though you wouldn't know it on a basketball court. He looked up at me with awestruck eyes, with the respect I'd been trying to win from him in the game.

He looked up at me and he said, "Man, you brave."

That killed me.

40

THE NICE THING ABOUT TAKING THE DAY OFF WAS it meant I didn't have to wear my beeper. So I had no idea whether the shit was hitting the fan.

Of course, it was.

I called Alice from a pay phone on Broadway. "Hi. Anybody call?"

"Very funny," Alice said. "Stanley, I can't take this anymore."

"Just put on the answering machine."

"I know, but I kept thinking it might be you."

"Then you'd hear my voice and pick up."

"I know. I just can't bear to record these calls either. To have them on tape and have to hear them back."

"Don't save them. Just rewind each time. Let 'em record over each other."

"Stanley, don't give me practical. I'm beyond practical. The phone's been ringing all day."

"All right. Who?"

"Mostly the cops. Thurman and Reynolds. Mostly Reynolds. And that other one that called last night.

And this Poindexter—he's the worst. He keeps trying to sound calm and polite, but you can tell he's really upset. And then Wendy/Janet who keeps calling to say all these same people are calling them.''

"Richard call?"

"No. Why should he?"

"I don't know. Just wondered."

"No. Not him and not MacAullif. No one you could call a friend. I'm really hassled, I'm starting to lose it. The mother of one of Tommie's friends called to try to set up a play date, I almost took her head off.''

"I'm sorry."

A pause. "I know you are. So what you gonna do?"

"Just hang in there. I'll be right home."

I drove home, parked the car, walked up West End Avenue to my building.

There was a guy with a briefcase in the lobby sitting by the elevator. As I walked up, Jerry caught my eye and almost imperceptibly shook his head.

The man stood up. "Stanley Hastings?"

I hated to let Jerry down by not heeding his warning, but I was in enough trouble already. Whatever it was, I wasn't running from it.

"Why?" I said.

He reached in his jacket pocket, took out a paper, thrust it in my hands. "Subpoena. Don't blame me, I'm just doing my job. I understand you do this yourself, so you know the drill. The details are all in there. Sorry about this and all that, but you know how it is.''

The guy smiled at me as if we were old buddies, picked up his briefcase and walked out.

"I tried to warn you," Jerry said.

"You did fine, and I got the signal," I told him. "I just can't duck this."

I looked at the subpoena in the elevator going up. As expected, it was from Poindexter. I was hereby ordered to appear as a witness for the defense in the case of the People of the State of New York versus Melissa Ford.

Alice was on the kitchen phone when I walked in. I heard her say, "I told you, I have no idea when he'll get home, I'll tell him when he gets in."

I heard the sound of the phone being hung up. It was not a gentle sound.

Alice came barreling out of the kitchen, met me in the foyer. "The cops again. They're not giving up."

"Neither is Poindexter," I said. "He subpoenaed me in the lobby. I gotta testify for the defense."

"What?"

I handed her the subpoena, headed for the kitchen.

She trailed after me, torn between reading the damn thing and keeping up. "He subpoenaed you?" She said. "Can he do that?"

"Evidently. He's done it. I gotta call Richard."

I grabbed the receiver off the wall, called Rosenberg and Stone. It was a bitch getting through. Wendy/Janet wanted to take me to task for all the phone calls they'd been getting. But finally I got Richard on the line.

"Yeah?" he said. "What's up?"

"The cops are on my ass. They haven't caught up with me yet, but it's just a matter of time. And Melvin Poindexter's slapped a subpoena on me."

"Oh?"

"Now I'm a witness for the prosecution *and* the defense."

"Shit."

"Do I gotta go?"

"Of course you gotta go. It's a subpoena."

"Do I have to answer questions?"

"Yes and no."

"What does that mean?"

"I'll be there as your lawyer. I'll advise you which questions you should answer."

"Yeah? Which ones are those?"

"None of them."

"Can you do that?"

"Watch me."

I took a breath. "Richard. You're a lawyer. You understand this stuff. But I don't know shit. Just what the hell are my rights here?"

"Don't get so worked up. We got time on this. When's the court date?"

"October 30th."

"What's that, three weeks from Monday? That is soon. So they indicted her for murder, huh?"

"Yeah. The grand jury worked fast."

"Well, I'm sure your testimony was very persuasive."

"Fuck you. So how do I deal with this?"

"Don't worry. We'll get together tomorrow, we'll go over the whole thing. Can you come in tomorrow afternoon?"

"I don't see why not."

"You workin' tomorrow?"

"I planned to. Now I don't know."

The phone beeped. We have call waiting, one of the great modern inconveniences. I said, "Hang on, I got a call," clicked the button down. "Yeah?"

"Hastings?" came the voice.

"Yeah?"

"This is Sergeant Reynolds. I been tryin' to get you for two days."

"I'm on another line, I'll get back to you," I said, and clicked the button down again. "Richard?"

"Yeah?"

"I got Sergeant Reynolds on the other line. What should I tell him?"

"Just what I told you. Your attorney's advised you to make no statement outside his presence. He wants to talk to you, take a number, wait in line."

"That's gonna piss him off."

"No shit. You wanna talk to him just to keep him happy?"

"No way."

"No shit. So just give him the message."

"What can he do to me?"

"Theoretically, nothing. In practical terms he can pick you up and run you in."

"What do I do then?"

"What do you think? You're not talking, you wanna call your lawyer."

The phone beeped again. It shouldn't have done that. With a call waiting, it can't ring.

"Hang on," I said. "Another call." I clicked it down, said, "Yeah?"

"Hastings, this is Sergeant Reynolds. I'm not waiting for you to call me back, I need to talk to you now."

"Then hold the phone," I told him, clicked the button down. "Richard?"

"Yeah?"

"Reynolds again. Pissed off, demanding satisfaction."

"Then give him the spiel."

"What spiel?"

"On the advice of counsel, you're not talking. I'm

your lawyer, if he wants to talk to you, he can call me.''

"Fine," I said. I clicked the button down, relayed that message.

Reynolds was understandably pissed. ''You're making a big mistake,'' he growled.

"On advice of counsel, I have no comment," I said, and clicked the button again. ''Richard?''

''Yeah.''

''What time tomorrow?''

''I don't know. How's two o'clock?''

''If I'm not in jail by then, fine.''

41

I WASN'T IN JAIL. No cops came and picked me up.
In fact, after that, things were pretty quiet. I did get
one more call from Sergeant Thurman, but it wasn't
bad. He wasn't at all unhappy that I had no comment
and referred him to my attorney. He realized if I was
doing that to him, I was doing it to Reynolds too,
which suited him just fine. As far as anything connected to my shooting was concerned, he didn't give
a damn. He was perfectly happy if it would just go
away. He had his killer, he didn't need me messing up
his case, and if I wasn't talking it was score one for
the good guys. The grand jury had indicted Melissa
Ford, she'd been arraigned for murder, and was out
on bail. As far as he was concerned, that wrapped up
the case until trial, and he wanted nothing more to do
with it. If I could manage to fall off the end of the
earth in the next few days, that would be just fine with
him. So things more or less calmed down.

I didn't.

I was wound up tighter than a spring, jumping every

time the phone rang. Snapping at Alice. Being short with Tommie too. I *did* work the next morning, at Alice's suggestion. It was a relief just to get me out of the house.

I dropped Tommie off at the East Side Day School, called in and managed to ram the concept through Wendy/Janet's head—I had a two o'clock appointment with Richard, but I was working this morning, I could take anything that would be finished before then.

The result was a ten o'clock in the Eastchester section of the Bronx in a project that turned out to be a cut above most, as far as its cleanliness and my paranoia level. Of course, my mind was so full of other things, it was hard to be nervous about your usual, garden variety junkie. I still watched my back passing stairwells, but not like I really expected anyone to be there. And no one was.

The client, James Clay, who had fallen in one of those stairwells and broken his left arm, was pleasant and agreeable about pointing it out. And the stairwell actually had a handrail missing, the screw holes of which were gonna show up great in the roll of film I shot. All things considered, the signup was a piece of cake.

So was the one I did at noon in the Fordham section of the Bronx, signing up a woman who had been hit by a car. It was a hit-and-run which made it easy on details—no driver's license, registrations, or names and addresses of defendants to fill in. And no accident photos, just injury shots. A gleaming white leg cast, two full-figure shots, two closeups and call it a day. I got out of there with time to spare to get downtown by two o'clock.

Only I got beeped. That figured. Count on Wendy/

Janet to throw an assignment at me I wouldn't have time to do.

But when I called in, it turned out I was wrong. Wendy/Janet was innocent. She'd just beeped me to tell me Richard was tied up and couldn't make the meeting and to ask if I wanted more work if it came in. I said, sure, what the hell. She didn't have anything yet, but promised to beep me when she did.

I hung up the phone feeling betrayed. Shit, Richard, can't you understand what I'm going through? I mean, I could see it from his point of view. The trial was three weeks off, what difference could it possibly make if we met today? Practically none. But in terms of my peace of mind . . .

I wished to hell Wendy/Janet had had a job. I had nothing pending, so Richard canceling had left me high and dry in the Bronx. With nothing to occupy my mind. Or what was left of it.

I drove back down through Harlem, stopped at Raheem's. I had no idea if he was in—I didn't call, I just took the chance. He wasn't hanging out in the street, so I went in and rang the bell. Sheila Webb was surprised to see me, but said, yes, Raheem was home. I told her I'd come to take him out.

We didn't play basketball this time. In the first place I was in my suit, and in the second place I didn't have a ball. And I wasn't really up to another game like the last one. No, I just took him to the store for an ice cream sundae. Just like a big brother. Or a social worker.

The pusher wasn't in evidence, so I didn't have to pull my macho act, shine in the kid's eyes. That was good. I wasn't up to the thought of him looking up to me as a hero.

I found an actual soda fountain a few blocks down. I took Raheem in and ordered us hot fudge sundaes. If the counterman was surprised to see me, he didn't let on. He served me just like anybody else.

Raheem and I ate our sundaes in silence. When he finished, he just sat there, staring down at the dish.

"He bother you?" I said.

Raheem said nothing, didn't look up. After a few moments he shook his head no.

"If he bothers you again, just let me know." I felt bad saying it—as if I could really do any good. But I felt I had to.

I signaled the counterman, held out a ten dollar bill. He took it, rang it up, brought back the change. I left a buck on the counter, pocketed the rest. Then looked over at Raheem.

He hadn't moved. He was still sitting there, looking at his dish.

He didn't move now.

"Name's King," he said.

"What?"

"Name's King. Don' know what else. Jus' King. Only name I know."

I didn't have to ask him who he was talking about.

"Come on," I said. "Let's go."

Raheem was quiet walking home. When we got to his door, he went inside without a word. I got in my car and drove off.

Feelin' good.

A breakthrough. A small victory, but mine own. It's amazing how much better something feels when you really need it. I actually felt like I had accomplished something.

I drove downtown. No one beeped me by the time

I hit my neighborhood, so I parked the car. I wasn't cruising around Manhattan all day for my health. If no one wanted me, hell, I was going home.

Someone wanted me. He was standing on the sidewalk, right outside my building.

Poindexter.

42

"I ASSUME YOU GOT MY SUBPOENA."

"You can assume anything you like."

Poindexter smiled. "All right, then. I *know* you got my subpoena. I have the process server's affidavit."

"Good for you."

I started into the building. Poindexter moved in front of me, put up his hand.

"We really need to talk."

"My attorney is Richard Rosenberg. He's making all statements for me."

Poindexter nodded. "Understandable. Statements, sure. I wouldn't want you to make a statement. I'm suggesting a little talk off the record."

"My attorney talks off the record too."

Poindexter frowned, then nodded. "I'd like to talk to your attorney. Let's go see him."

"He's in court."

Poindexter frowned again. "This isn't getting us anywhere."

"No shit."

"Look," Poindexter said. "My client's been indicted for murder. I have the responsibility of preparing her defense. And you have information that may be critical to that defense."

"I told you that last week."

"Yes, you did."

"You didn't want to hear it."

"Things have changed."

"The information is the same."

"Yes, but you got shot."

"So what?"

"Don't be silly. Getting shot gives you credibility. Before, you were pissing in the wind. You had nothing. Just a wild theory. Getting shot is a hell of a confirmation."

"Glad you like it. Maybe I can get knifed tomorrow and make your day."

Poindexter looked at me. "What are you holding out for, money? You still pissed off that you got fired? If that's your tack, you're wasting your time. She couldn't hire you now. It would be like buying your testimony. It would ruin your credibility with the jury."

"You mean I'd have to get shot again to be believed?"

His face darkened. "I'm glad you think it's so funny. There's a woman on trial for murder. And maybe, just maybe, she didn't do it. And you're going to let her hang. For what? Out of petty spite? 'You fired me, so you can take the fall?' That's a hell of an attitude. Hardly understandable. But if that's your game, that's your game."

Poindexter drew himself up, stuck out his chest. Or more precisely his stomach, which preceeded it by a good deal. "If you don't wanna talk now, you have that right. But don't think that's the end of it. You got your subpoena, and you're going to court. When I get you on the stand, you're gonna talk. And if we haven't talked first, you're gonna be on the stand a long time. I'll be able to show you wouldn't talk to me, and I'll be able to get you declared a hostile witness. Which means I can ask leading questions. Which means I can delve. We'll talk then, and we'll talk all day long."

He paused, took a breath, then lowered his voice, as if conspiratorially. "And if you win, and if you beat me at the game—which I don't think is possible, but say you do—then what do you win? The satisfaction of seeing an innocent woman found guilty of murder." Poindexter shook his head. "Boy, that's gotta be some satisfaction. That's gotta be some feather in your cap."

He paused, shook his head again.

"You must be awfully proud of yourself."

43

I WOULDN'T WANT YOU TO THINK IT WAS POINDEX-
TER THAT WORE ME DOWN. As far as I was concerned, that smug son of a bitch could talk himself
blue in the face and it wouldn't cut no ice with
me.

And it wasn't MacAullif telling me I'd have to live
with myself, either, though that certainly was true.

No, in the end I think what really got to me was
Raheem Webb telling me I was brave.

That was the ultimate irony. That was the killer. The
thing was, Raheem Webb was the one positive thing I
managed to do, the one thing in my life right now that
I could be proud of and feel good about.

Only I couldn't. His thinking me brave had soured
that. And the thing was, there was nothing I could do
about it. What could I do, tell him, no, I'm not brave,
I'm a chickenshit? Tell him the only reason I'm with
him now is 'cause I'm running away from something
else? Well, not the only reason—I'm a softhearted

schmuck and I was trying to help the kid, but you know what I mean.

It wore me down. It ate away at me.

And it balanced in the great scale of things.

On one side, the fear of the Black Death. And of the white hospital room. And of the ether and the void. The loss of wife and kid. The loss *to* wife and kid. And the pain. Fear of the pain. Fear of the hurt. Fear of the horse—fuck you, MacAullif.

Fear of the fear.

Jesus.

Fear of the fear.

And on the other side, the guilt, the shame. Having to face Alice. Having to face Tommie. Varying degrees there. Tommie too young to know, too young to understand. Having bounced back from the initial fear, now a big man on campus with his father being shot. Alice old enough to know, to know all too well, and to be there. Loving, supporting, understanding. Understanding all too well. What I lacked, why I couldn't. But not complaining, not reproaching. Just encouraging. Helping. Loving. Being there. And knowing, as MacAullif had said, that I had to live with it. And she had to live with me. And we had to live with it together. Our burden.

And then Raheem.

Raheem, who had no fucking idea what was really going on at all. Who looked at me now with something just short of adulation. No, kid, no. I can take anything, almost anything, but you thinking of me as brave.

As I say, it wore me down. I suffered all weekend

the torments of the damned. Sunday night I nearly slept a wink.

Monday morning I was waiting for Richard when he showed up at his office.

"I wanna make a deal."

44

THE CAST WAS ASSEMBLED.

Present in the interrogation room were me, Richard, Sergeant Reynolds, Sergeant MacAullif, and the stenographer. We were there only after considerable discussion which had hammered out the arrangements. One aspect of this discussion had naturally been concerned with the persons present. Or rather, who they would be.

Sergeant Thurman and A. D. A. McNulty were not present. Their inclusion had been considered and rejected. Though it was agreed that they would probably need to become involved at a later time.

Also not present was Melvin C. Poindexter, though, in his case, his inclusion had never even been considered.

As to our respective parts, I was there to recite, and the stenographer was there to take it down. Sergeant MacAullif was there as an interested observer. Sergeant Reynolds was nominally in charge. but everyone knew it was Richard's show.

"Now," Richard said. "Let's make sure we have the ground rules clear. My client is going to make a statement. The stenographer is going to take it down. When my client is finished, the stenographer is going to leave to type up that statement for my client to sign. Any questions you might wish to ask will be off the record, and not part of my client's statement. Even then, I will use my discretion in advising him whether to answer them."

Richard looked around the table in case anyone wished to protest.

Sergeant Reynolds didn't. He'd taken a big enough beating during the prior negotiation. You could tell he was smoldering, but he wasn't about to make a fuss.

"Let's just get on with it," he said irritably.

"Fine," Richard said. "And in return for this *voluntary* statement, supplying you with additional facts which may be of aid to you in your investigation, you have agreed that no action will be taken against my client for any failure on his part to supply you with this information during any prior interrogation."

Reynolds seethed, said nothing.

"Please say 'yes' for the record," Richard said, nodding at the stenographer.

"Yes," Reynolds hissed.

"Nor will any attempt be made to take action against my client for finding any prior statement inconsistent, inaccurate, insufficient, or even false."

Reynolds took a breath. "Right."

"My client is under no obligation to be here," Richard said. "And I might advise him to get up and leave at any time. He is here because he wishes to do his civic duty and aid the police in their investigation.

273

His intentions are commendable, and should not lay him open to censure.''

"He's a saint," Reynolds said. "May we proceed?"

"If all that is agreed to, we may."

"You got it," Reynolds said. "Now, let's hear it."

I told the story, told it all. Starting with what I told the grand jury about following David Melrose for Melissa Ford. I told of following David Melrose to SoHo, and seeing him pick up something from Charles Olsen.

I moved on to the work I did after I was fired, pulling Olsen's record, finding out he had a history of drugs. And then checking with the art director and the mail room and finding out David Melrose had no business reason to be seeing Charles Olsen.

I told of tailing Charles Olsen to the house in Harlem, and seeing him deliver the package to Alan Harrison. And subsequently tailing Harrison to the same house, seeing him pick up another package and leave with the Black Death.

I could see Sergeant Reynolds starting to squirm. Not surprising. He doesn't give a damn about this, he wants to hear about the shot. All right, sergeant, here goes.

I'd gone over this carefully with Richard, so I knew exactly how to start. "It was Friday, September 29th," I said. "Late afternoon, say four, four-thirty. I spotted the man I call the Black Death coming out of the building where he lived carrying a paper bag."

I heard a sharp intake of breath. It was Sergeant Reynolds. His eyes narrowed, murderously.

I ignored him, went on. I told of following the Black

274

Death down the street to the empty lot, following him into the abandoned building and getting shot.

"End of statement," Richard said. "Just type that up and my client will sign it."

Sergeant Reynolds was on his feet. "Wait a minute, wait a minute!" he said.

Richard looked at him in surprise. "Sergeant, remember the ground rules."

"Ground rules, my ass! You told me this guy was gonna augment his statement."

"That's just what he's done."

"The hell he has. Augment, my ass! Suddenly you got a drug ring, a motive, and he *saw* the shooter!"

"Tut, tut," Richard said. "He never saw him shoot."

"You think I give a fuck?" Reynolds roared. "You think that's not enough to make a case? Jesus Christ! You tell me this guy's gonna come in here and add a few details. A few small things that he forgot to mention."

Richard came to his feet, finger pointing, eyes flashing. His nasal bark cut through the room like a whiplash. "Hold it right there, sergeant! You call me a liar and you've bought yourself a lawsuit. There are witnesses here. You wanna tell me what I said, then don't you misquote me. Did I ever use the word 'forgot'? Did I say these were things he had 'forgotten' to mention? No, I told you my client had *remembered* some things he had neglected to tell you. Well, he *does* remember them. If you don't like it, that's tough shit, but you haven't got a leg to stand on, so back the hell off."

Richard wheeled on the stenographer. "You takin' this down?"

He shook his head. "No, sir. Per agreement, I stopped when he stopped."

"Too bad," Richard said. "I probably could have had a cause of action just from your notes." He wheeled back on Reynolds. "Now let's cut out the bellyaching about who didn't say what when. We got some new information to deal with. I suggest you accept it as given, take a good hard look at it, and figure out just what the hell you're gonna do."

45

IT WASN'T THAT EASY. Sergeant Reynolds was fit to be tied. In spite of our agreement, he just wouldn't let go. He kept coming back to my original statement. Pointing out the inconsistencies. He kept demanding to know how Richard could reconcile my current statement with that. Richard pointed out that it was perfectly consistent for a person who had amnesia to gradually recall more and more details. Without, of course, actually stating that I *had* had amnesia, or admitting that I hadn't. Sergeant Reynolds had a few choice comments to say about that. Fortunately, none of them were being taken down. At any rate, it was a while before the smoke cleared and we could begin discussing it rationally.

When we did, the first order of business was who should be told. Sergeant Thurman was voted out. At least at the present time. Reynolds and MacAullif kicked it around a bit, but they both agreed Thurman would neither appreciate nor credit my story in its present form. It would be, to Sergeant Thurman's point of view, not hard evidence, and insufficient to influence his investigation. However, if it panned out, if something more than my unsubstantiated statement should turn up, if what I said should be corroborated in any way, at that point he would need to be informed.

I must say that through all this, neither MacAullif nor Reynolds said anything that could be considered disparaging of a fellow officer. Nonetheless, both made it quite clear that in Sergeant Thurman's case, the later he could be informed the better.

In A. D. A. McNulty's case, it was decided he would have to be told that a matter had come up which might create a problem with the case. But it should be soft-pedaled, down-played, and he should be spared as many details as possible. Just alerted to the fact the cops were investigating, and if anything came up, he would be the first to know.

In short, what was decided was that what I had just told the police should be treated as matters bearing on the investigation of my shooting, rather than matters bearing on the investigation of David Melrose. Undoubtedly, a wise decision.

With that squared away, Reynolds finally got to where he wanted to be. Which was the question of what to do next. My statement had left him with a very big problem. Now he knew who the shooter was. But he didn't have a damn thing on him.

Reynolds and MacAullif worked on it together. It was Reynolds's case, of course, but MacAullif had a vested interest, and he kept his hand in. Here's what they found out.

First off, Charles Olsen had a history of drug arrests. MacAullif already knew that, but it was an eye-opener for Sergeant Reynolds. Yeah, I'd mentioned it in my statement, but that hadn't really thrilled him. It was a little different when he saw the rap sheet in black and white.

What really got him was that Alan Harrison had one too. Just one, and just possession, and nearly ten years old. But it all tied in. My stock, which had been sub-zero with Reynolds, actually began to rise.

The only one they had no info on was the shooter. That was not surprising. You can't just go to the computer and ask for the rap sheet on the Black Death. Even with the guy's address, that's not gonna fly. No, the only way to do it would be for me to I.D. him to the cops, and then for them to investigate and find out who he was.

But no one really wanted to do that. If these guys were trafficking, they'd be on the alert. The hint of any investigation would tip 'em off. If that happened, they could clean up their act and sit tight, and the cops could try to bust 'em till doomsday and it would do no good.

Worse, we would have shot our wad. In terms of the shooting, at least. There was only a slim chance to make that stick. If we went for it, it was one time, over and out. In terms of the shooting, there was one prayer, and one prayer only. That the Black Death was stupid enough to keep the gun. If so, a tipoff would be fatal.

No shit.

The problem was, practically anything would be fatal.

But that's why we chose to go the way we chose to go.

46

MacAullif didn't like it. Funny, since he was the one who'd pushed me into it. But when push came to shove, he was the one with the cold feet.

I know he was only warning me. But it was almost as if he were trying to talk me out of it.

"You understand how it's gonna go?" he said.

I nodded. "Yeah."

We were sitting (where else?) in a small coffee shop, downtown, near One Police Plaza. We'd just come from a skull session with Reynolds, where we'd all agreed on what I was gonna do.

"I'm not sure you do," MacAullif said. "I wanna be sure you understand the consequences here."

"I understand the consequences."

"I'm not sure you do. To nail this guy, you gotta make the I.D. You gotta meet him face to face. Then it's out in the open, you and him, the whole thing."

"I know."

"And even if you do, the odds of makin' him as the shooter are slim. If he's got the gun on him, we're home free. If he doesn't, we can hold him long enough to get a warrant on his apartment. If the gun's there, same thing.

"But if it ain't . . ." MacAullif shrugged. "Then we're talkin' drugs. If we're lucky, we nail him with quantity. But that's an iffy thing. We nail him movin' a kilo, that's the best bet, yeah. And if we're lucky, there'll be more in his place. But even so, the minute you're not talkin' murder, it's a whole new ballgame. Drug peddlers are cash-heavy by definition. Even with a good word to the judge, he'll still have to set bail. The guy will make it. Twenty-four hours after you finger him, he'll be back on the street."

"I know that too."

"Just so's you know."

"I know, I know. Christ, MacAullif. It's not enough that I'm doing this, you want me to be upset about it too?"

"I want you to use all due caution. If this guy walks, we can't give you twenty-four-hour police protection, you know. Not on something like this. The commissioner would have our ass."

"How about a police cruiser drives through my neighborhood once or twice a day?"

"It's not funny."

It wasn't, and I was only joking so I wouldn't have to hear my teeth rattle. I didn't need MacAullif's voice of doom.

I knew I was doing something I didn't want to do.

47

It went down in the early afternoon.

That surprised me. Somehow, I'd expected it to happen at night.

I was staked out with a cop in an unmarked car across the street and a few houses down from the Black Death's. That fact did not cheer me. If this was the cop's idea of inconspicuous, it didn't bode well for the rest of the venture. We were getting cold stares from everyone who came down the street.

The cop with me was Officer Andrews, the one who'd tried to call me for Sergeant Reynolds. He didn't say much, but seemed a nice enough sort for someone who thought I was a total asshole.

We were sitting in the front seat, not saying much of anything and looking like cops, when the Black Death came out the door. He was dressed, as usual, all in black, and was carrying a paper bag about the size of a kilo.

Officer Andrews reached under the dashboard, pulled out the mike from the radio, and phoned it in, a good move just in case there was anyone left in the neighborhood who hadn't yet made us for cops.

The Black Death didn't. He was walking down the street away from us the other way. Andrews started the car and pulled out. The theory, as he'd explained it, was we'd follow him in the car so if he hailed a cab or car service we'd be on his tail. On the other hand, if he took the subway or went into a building, we'd hop out and follow on foot. That would leave the car standing in the middle of the street, but I guess when you're a cop that's no worry. At any rate, we tagged along behind.

I kept my head down in case the guy looked back. That way, if he did, he wouldn't spot me, and all he'd have to wonder about was why a tan Ford was driving down the street behind him at five miles an hour.

But he didn't look back. He just walked down Lenox Avenue to 145th and went into the subway. Andrews parked the car at a hydrant and we went in too.

Which was tricky as hell. It was broad daylight. Which doesn't mean anything in a subway station, but what the hell. In my *mind,* it was broad daylight. And if this guy saw me, the show was over. And where the hell do you hide on a subway platform?

We hung out on the steps till he went through the turnstile, then bought tokens and hung out by the booth. We couldn't see him—he'd walked slightly down the platform out of view—and the idea was to wait until the train came, barrel through the turnstile and get on last. Not the best of all possible moves, but the only real option we had.

Suddenly he came walking back up the platform. I ducked back behind the side of the booth. My heart was in my mouth. I couldn't be sure he'd seen me, but I couldn't be sure he hadn't either.

I looked up at Andrews, who was still standing his ground. After all, the Black Death didn't know him.

"Take it easy," he said. "The guy didn't react."

"You sure?"

"Hey, I'm a cop."

That did not exactly inspire me with confidence. But I kept the thought to myself.

The train came. When it did, the Black Death was once again out of sight. So we took a two count from the time the doors opened and went through the turnstile. It's a good thing we didn't take a three count, 'cause we wouldn't have got on. As it was, the conductor nearly closed the door on us.

I looked quickly up and down the car, but he wasn't there. Thank god. The car was over half full, and most of the riders were black, but none of them were him.

Andrews pushed me into a seat. "Stay here and keep out of trouble," he said.

He went to the front of the car, slid the door open, stepped out onto the platform between the two cars.

He was back moments later, sat down next to me.

"He's in the next car sitting down," he said. "I'm gonna stand up near the door. You stay here. When I move, you move. Go out the last door of the car. It will put you farther from him."

"What if he comes my way down the platform?"

"There's no way to figure that. Some stations the exit's uptown, some downtown. If he comes your way, you beat it out the exit ahead of him, fade into some doorway on the street. I'll be right along to give you your cue."

The train slowed down for a station.

"Better start now," I said.

He got up, went to the door.

He was there a long time. 125th. 96th. 72nd.

42nd Street was the move. Andrews signaled me, I stepped out the rear door of the car, glanced down the platform, and, sure enough, the son of a bitch was coming at me.

I turned quickly, tried to blend into the crowd, headed up the platform ahead of him according to plan.

Only 42nd Street isn't your simple, ordinary station. You don't just go up the stairs out the exit to the street. As I said before, Times Squares is where about half a zillion lines converge. There are dozens of tunnels, tracks, walkways, stairs and exits.

For instance, just ahead of me is a staircase to the 41st Street exit, an alternative to walking up the platform to the 42nd Street exit. Only it doesn't just go to 41st Street. It also offers two separate tunnels, one to the shuttle to Grand Central and one to the BMT. The staircase itself is a choice, and if you take it, you're hit with an even wider choice and the problem escalates geometrically.

So, what the hell am I supposed to do, guess where this guy might go and then go there? Sorry, Andrews, but your scenario just won't play.

I stepped behind a column and turned, facing the downtown local track as if I'd gotten off the express to transfer to the other train. I peered around the column, trying to catch sight of the Black Death. There were a lot of people on the platform and I couldn't spot him. But that also meant he'd have trouble spotting me.

Unless he'd spotted me already.

That thought made me jerk my head, turn and look

behind my back. No assassin's hand was there. I did a slow curl around the column on the track side, looking down the platform.

And almost bumped into him. He'd just come around a woman the size of a small house who'd been blocking him from view.

I ducked back behind the column again. I couldn't tell if he'd spotted me. I didn't really want to look to see if he had.

But not looking was worse. I peered around the column. And there was the back of his head going up the 41st Street stairs.

Andrews grabbed me by the arm. I was so wound up by then I nearly jumped a foot.

''What the hell was that move?'' he said.

''I had to get around him. You think he spotted me?''

''Half the people in the station spotted you. Him I don't know. Come on.''

We sprinted up the stairs in time to see him take the tunnel to the BMT. It's a long winding tunnel, lots of bends and angles, so we could follow pretty close. He came out of the tunnel, took the ramp to the downtown BMT. Stopped at the bottom.

Small problem.

It's a long, straight ramp, totally exposed, no cover. And much too long to get down after a train pulled in. And if he didn't move, we couldn't.

I knew the subway better than Andrews. I should, I photographed enough of it. I grabbed him by the arm.

''Come on,'' I said.

Besides the ramp, there's a staircase at the north end of the platform. If you go down it, you come up underneath the ramp. Which is what we did. We came down the stairs and walked under the ramp to the point where it got too low to stand. Perfect. We were on the platform, totally hidden, about one car length away.

A train pulled in. He got on and so did we and off we went.

Same drill. I sat, Andrews stood. We rumbled downtown.

14th Street he still hadn't got off. It seemed too much to hope for, but somehow it just had to be.

Sure enough, he got off at Canal.

This time, there was no problem. We were in the last car in the train, so there was no way he could turn toward us. Plus there wasn't any other line.

We got off, followed him up the platform to the street. He walked up Broadway to Grand, across Grand to a building I knew well. He rang the bell, and minutes later Charles Olsen came down and opened the door.

I was praying it wouldn't be a drop-off. If he gave Olsen the bag and split, it would be ten times messier, ten times harder to prove.

My prayer was answered. It wasn't just a drop. The two of them went inside, closed the door.

Andrews was already on the horn, calling it in.

It seemed an eternity before the cops got there, but it was probably more like ten minutes. Here I must admit, the cops really were prepared. They'd already drawn up search warrants for Charles Olsen, Alan Harrison, and the Black Death's apartments, and ever since Andrews had phoned in from Harlem that we were on the move, they had had a judge standing by ready to issue them when we gave the word, our say-so being necessary for probable cause.

At any rate, I stood there on the corner with my life

flashing before my eyes, hoping like hell he wouldn't leave before the cops got there. Before I knew it, three unmarked cars pulled up on the corner and six cops got out. A fourth car arrived a minute later with Sergeants Reynolds and MacAullif.

"Still there?" Reynolds said.

Andrews nodded. "He's there."

"And it's the guy?" he asked me.

"It's him."

"All right, let's move."

Move they did. The locked downstairs door, which would have baffled me, was half a minute's work for one of the cops with a set of keys. I didn't know what apartment, but fortunately it was on the mailbox inside the door. "Loft 3," it said. The cops went up the stairs, Reynolds and MacAullif in the lead. I had to be there of course, to make the I.D., but not at first. Only after it went down.

The cops stopped on the third floor. There was no chance for confusion, no wondering was the ground floor one or the loft up the first flight, making this loft two or three. There was a number 3 right on the door.

I watched the scene from down the hall. The cops fanned out on either side of the door, drew their guns. Reynolds stepped up and knocked on the door. Then stepped carefully away to one side. That was the scary thing. That was what got me. Not the drawn guns. Not the threat to them. No, the realization that Reynolds was prepared for them to start shooting through the door.

That didn't happen. Instead, there came the sound of a peephole sliding open, and a voice said, "Who is it?"

Reynolds held out his badge in front of the hole. "Police. Open up."

If they didn't, I wondered if he'd kick it down. It was a solid-looking door, and I wondered if he could. And if he tried, I wondered if that's when the bullets would come flying through. But no, there came the click of the lock and the door swung open.

The cops surged through, guns drawn. In less time than it takes to tell it, Andrews and I were alone in the hall.

Showtime.

My big moment. To walk in, meet the shooter face to face. To say in his presence, "That's the man."

I didn't want to do it. Needless to say. But I had Andrews with me, which helped. No chance of me turning and walking quietly down the stairs. Not that that would have been an option. Not that that would have even helped.

From the moment I set this thing rolling, there was no turning back. There was only one outcome, only one choice.

No choice.

Showtime.

You're on.

I took a breath, walked through the door.

It was a huge, one-room, floor-through loft. High ceiling. Exposed pipes. Floodlights dangling from them. Spotlights. All switched on. Illuminating an incredible scene.

In the middle of the side wall were two huge canvases, each maybe twelve by twenty feet, side by side. It was on these that the floodlights were aimed. They were each only half finished, but enough to show they both were part of the same scene. And only a small part at that. Each panel clearly depicted portions of the same child's face.

Standing in front of them were the eight cops and the three suspects. Yes, three, Alan Harrison was there too. The cops no longer had their guns out, unnecessary now, since they had the suspects handcuffed. Two cops flanked each man, held him by the arms. Charles Olsen. Alan Harrison. And the Black Death.

I can't say they looked too tough, caught there in the glare of their spotlights. They looked intimidated. Helpless. Confused.

And the Black Death. The mighty Black Death. He no longer looked large and threatening. If anything, he looked soft and flabby now.

I walked into the room.

MacAullif and Reynolds turned to meet me. They had been standing in front of Alan Harrison, blocking his view, and when they turned, he saw me for the first time.

He started, blinked, his mouth dropped open, and he said, so help me God, "Jesus Christ. I tell you. I swear. I didn't *see* any damn accident!"

48

IT DIDN'T HIT ME THEN. I suppose it should have, but there was so much happening, so much to sort out. Not that I was doing the sorting. I just stood there as if in a daze, while the cops pieced it all together.

The Black Death was Lionel Wilkens, an artist of some renown, with several New York exhibitions, mostly in SoHo, to his credit. His work, I gathered, had already won widespread critical acclaim, if not great financial success. On the basis of his reputation, he had been commissioned to render a mural for Martin Luther King Day. The mural, intended for outdoor display, was gigantic, so much so that it could only be broken down and done in sections, which would ultimately be pieced together to form the finished work. It was also too large for a single artist to paint. For that reason, Lionel had enlisted the aid of Charles Olsen and Alan Harrison, two fellow artists who happened to admire his work, to help him in the execution. Each man was entrusted with two sections of the mural to paint in accordance with Lionel's design. The theme, of course, was brotherhood, and the scene depicted children of racially mixed backgrounds playing in harmony.

Lionel, of course, was in charge of the whole operation, including mixing the paint. Since the sections of the mural naturally had to match, it was crucial that the same mixture be used for each one. For that reason, bags of powdered paint, mixed by Lionel for the project, were often picked up and distributed to the various parties involved.

David Melrose, who knew Charles Olsen from work, and who had done favors for him in the past, had been assisting in the distribution. Whether this was out of the goodness of his heart, or out of a desire to curry favor with what he considered to be the artistic in-crowd, was not entirely clear, but in view of the fact that David was deceased and not there to defend himself, the artists tended toward a more charitable interpretation of his actions.

His demise had also left them without a messenger, requiring them to carry on the distribution themselves.

By the way, if you think the cops took their word for any of this, you are mistaken. All three were taken downtown and officially questioned. And Charles Olsen's loft, Alan Harrison's apartment and Lionel Wilkens's were duly searched. The searches turned up nothing but bags of paint and four other sections of the mural.

The interrogations turned up even less.

Charles Olsen admitted to having once had a problem with drugs, but insisted that he had been clean for years.

Alan Harrison, while in college (my god, was he *that* young—or am I just that old?) had indeed been busted at a pot party along with half a dozen other students, but, as he said with a shrug, in those days, who wasn't?

Lionel Wilkens had no police record whatsoever. He *did* have a letter of commendation from Mayor Dinkins, praising him for both his artistic talent and humanitarian work.

In response to the question of what he was doing in that abandoned building on the day in question, Lionel stated that he had gone in one door and out another, a short cut he often took that allowed him to get from 146th Street to 145th without going all the way around the block.

In response to a question suggested by me and asked by Sergeant Reynolds, Charles Olsen stated that what David Melrose had picked up from him on the Friday evening prior to his death was a sketch suggesting an alteration of one unfinished corner of the mural for the purpose of saving time and labor, to be delivered to Lionel Wilkens the next time David picked up paint. Since Lionel had never received it, and Charles Olsen had been forced to draw him another sketch of the alteration (which, by the way, Lionel had graciously approved—by all rights the man was a saint, when anyone tries to change my work, I go bananas), it was suggested that if the police were to search the personal effects of David Melrose, they would probably find the original sketch.

Whether the cops actually looked or not, I don't know. All I know is by that point Sergeant Reynolds had lost a good deal of enthusiasm for the whole affair, and within the next half hour all three men were gone, having been released without charge after cheerfully

signing waivers relinquishing their rights to sue for
false arrest.

That left me alone with Sergeant Reynolds and Sergeant MacAullif and in a slightly unenviable position.
I had attempted to extricate myself from trouble and
exonerate myself from the charge of making a false
report. As a result, I was now guilty of making *two*
false reports. Although, as MacAullif was kind enough
to point out, in the latter case I was actually innocent.
To be guilty of making a false report, you must make
it *knowing* it to be false. Since everything I told the
police about Charles Olsen, Alan Harrison and the
Black Death I believed to be true, there was no way
they could hold me liable.

I found that small consolation.

The whole thing was just too much for me. To have
gone through the fear, the anxiety. And then to have
conquered my fear, at least to the degree of doing what
had to be done. And then to have the whole thing blow
up in my face.

I felt like I'd stepped into a fantasy world, a parallel
universe, where nothing was quite what it seemed to
be, where anything might change at any time.

That's why my head was spinning. Why I was in a
daze.

Why I hadn't gotten it yet.

When Reynolds and MacAullif finally let me go, I
stumbled out of the office and walked down the hallway as if in a dream.

And bumped smack into Sergeant Thurman.

I hadn't even seen him. And Thurman's hard to miss.
But it took me a few seconds to even recognize him.

He stood there, blocking my way. He was grinning
from ear to ear.

"Hi, hotshot," he said. "Heard about it."

I was sure he had. By now I was sure everyone had heard about it.

"Oh," I said.

That was not the response he wanted.

"Well," he said. "Heard about it?"

That time I caught the inflection. A question, not a statement.

"What?" I said.

"You mean you haven't heard?"

"Heard what?"

"She confessed."

"What?"

"Melissa Ford. She confessed. She killed him."

I blinked. "What did you say?"

"She killed David Melrose. Bang, over, finished. Hey, don't look so surprised. Didn't you know she killed him?"

"I—"

"Of course you did. Everyone knew that. Easiest case I ever had."

My mind was reeling. I took a breath. "You're telling me she confessed to the murder?"

"Of course she did. I knew she would. That type always does. She killed him. Did it for love. He betrayed her with another woman. If she couldn't have him, no one could. You ought to hear her." He chuckled. "She's so *happy* now she's confessed. They always are. Those mousy types. They love it. The tragic heroine. As if they were born to play the part. It's like they can't make it as lovers, but as killers who *did it* for love—that they can handle."

He banged me on the shoulder like we were old pals. Thank god it was my good one.

"So this one's all wrapped up. We may not even need your testimony anymore. But if we do, don't worry, we'll be in touch."

He grinned the happy grin of the blissfully ignorant, and walked off down the hall.

That's when it hit me. About a year too late. Hell, you probably knew it all along.

Melissa Ford had killed David Melrose.

David Melrose had not been killed for being involved in any drug ring.

And I had not been shot for investigating his death.

That didn't leave much else.

49

I FOUND RAHEEM SITTING ON THE HOOD OF A PARKED CAR. Head down, arms folded in his lap, legs swinging slightly.

"King shot me," I said.

He didn't react. Didn't look up. Just sat there, eyes to the ground.

The scar on his forehead had faded, seemed paler now, not nearly so garish. If it healed right, he was going to be a good-looking kid.

"You don't have to tell me, Raheem," I said. "I know. King shot me.

"But that's not all."

He didn't look up then, didn't say, "What?" I hadn't expected him to.

"You're the one who pulled me out. You got me out of there. You're the one who called the cops, too. Told 'em you heard a shot.

"The cops came, but they didn't go inside. So they didn't find me and they went away.

"So you had to call them again.

"But you didn't want to tell them where I was—that I was in the building. That would be admitting that you knew too much, saying that the body was in there. It was one thing to say you heard a shot. Another thing to say you found a body. In a place no one would go. Like admitting you knew the whole scene.

"So you dragged me out of there. Into the empty lot. And called the cops to report a body there. No explanations needed, even on the phone. Body in an empty lot. Easy enough for any fool cop to check out."

He still said nothing. I could see his eyes were fixed quite determinedly on the ground.

"It's all right, Raheem," I said. "You don't have to tell what you saw. You're not a witness. You don't have to testify. You don't have to talk to the cops, anyone." I paused. "Even me.

"I know why you're scared, Raheem. Because you followed him that day. I left here and you saw him follow me. So you tagged along. You saw me go into the building. You saw him go in too. And then you heard the shot.

"You know who shot me. That's why you're scared. You figure that makes you a witness. Someone's gonna make you stand up to him, force you to say he did it. You know he shot me, and that's why you're afraid."

I smiled slightly. "And that's why you think me brave.

"Well, no one's gonna do that, Raheem. No one's even gonna know. Particularly not him. You don't have to face him, Raheem. Believe me, you never have to deal with him again."

I paused, looked down the street. It would be just my luck to have King walk up right then. But there was no one in sight.

I looked back at Raheem. ''I'm glad you think I'm brave. I wish I were. But I wanna tell you something. Going into the building. Pulling me out. Calling the cops. That was really brave. You're the brave one, Raheem. You.''

He still said nothing, but his eye glistened, as if a tear were trying to form.

That was more than I could take. I patted him on the shoulder, walked away.

The whole time Raheem hadn't said a word. But then I hadn't expected him to. And I didn't really need him to.

He didn't have to tell me the shooter was King.

Nothing propinks like propinquity.

50

IT WASN'T EASY.

First, there was the little-boy-who-cried-wolf factor. Had you thought of that? Well, trust me on it, my stock with Reynolds was not high. The I-know-who-shot-me routine was not gonna be a particularly easy sell.

Worse, it required Richard and the whole shmear again, to make sure my rights were protected, to make sure nothing in my third statement would make me criminally liable for anything I might have said in my second or my first. And, believe it or not, Reynolds was not so free with the concessions this time. After the pasting Richard had given him the time before, I think Reynolds actually enjoyed getting a bit of his own back. But in the end they got it done and I told the tale.

Without Raheem, of course. Oh yes, he was in it, he had to be. I just mean without some of the details. Like him following King, hearing the shot, phoning the cops, pulling me out. Little things like that.

Now, I wasn't really holding out on the cops. I didn't *know* any of that. Raheem hadn't confirmed it. It was all stuff I'd surmised. Nothing I could testify to in court. Surely I had every right to leave it out.

But it did leave a few gaps in the story. Not great with Sergeant Reynolds not in a particularly receptive mood to begin with and not inclined to be convinced. And when you came right down to it, by leaving out the Raheem Webb part of the story, all I really had left to support the theory that King had shot me was the fact the Black Death hadn't.

To say I took a pounding on that one would be a gross understatement. This time Richard had not been able to get away with the my-client-will-make-a-statement-no-questions-asked routine, and when it was his turn to bat, Reynolds tore me apart. I stuck to my guns and when the smoke cleared, when Reynolds had finished displaying an aptitude for sarcasm not likely to be surpassed in the twentieth century, he was finally forced to consider the basic concept. And what made my simple-minded premise convincing was the fact that it *was* so simple. Basically, King had to have shot me because no one else did.

If all that sounds confused, you gotta understand what I was going through just then. I mean in my own head. See, King being the one who shot me turned everything upside down. Ever since I'd been shot, I'd been scared to death to confront the shooter. To meet him face to face. Well, I'd confronted him all right. Actually taunted him, told him to fuck off. Stood right up to him without turning a hair and laid it on the line. So what if I didn't *know* he was the shooter, the fact is he *was*. Did that *really* make a difference?

Yeah, it did. Of course it did. It's no act of courage

to go in the lion's cage if you don't know the lion's there. Ignorance may be bliss, but it's not guts. Case closed.

And what about standing up to the Black Death? He *wasn't* the shooter, but I *thought* he was. Didn't standing up to him make me brave?

Not quite. It was a little better than the other scenario, but not much. It's no act of courage to go in the lion's cage with a *kitten,* just because you *think* it's a lion.

No, I would have to say the danger had to be both real and perceived as such.

Anyhow, I had all that going on in my head while Reynolds was questioning me. So it's not surprising if my answers seemed a little off base. I finally had to say to myself, schmuck, stop your head. This guy didn't shoot you to test your moral character. He's a low-life scum who needs to be put away, now how the hell are you gonna do that?

I talked it over with Reynolds and MacAullif, once they were ready to listen, once Reynolds was done bashing me. I must say the general consensus was our chances weren't good. We had not one shred of evidence, not even my testimony, since I actually hadn't seen a thing.

It was suggested that I talk to him wearing a wire, but King didn't strike me as the talkative sort. As I could recall, in all the times I'd seen him, "motherfucker" and "nigger" were the only things I'd heard him say. Illuminating, perhaps, but rather skimpy in terms of an admission.

In the end, Reynolds finally agreed to my plan. Which, believe me, wasn't much. In fact, it was the type of plan, after which, in the old movies, one character would inevitably say, "That's so crazy it just might work!"

In this case, frankly, there wasn't much chance of it working. Still, it had basically two things going for it. One, if it didn't work, there was virtually nothing lost. And, two, we really didn't have anything else.

And for me, it had a third thing going for it. It solved my moral dilemma. About facing the shooter knowing it was him, I mean. Not that I wanted to do that, you understand. I just didn't want *not* to do that.

At any rate, as I said, it was a rather stupid plan. Basically, it had only one real hope for success. Which, even given odds, I'm sure neither MacAullif nor Reynolds would have bet on.

That was that King was stupider than I was.

51

KING WAS OUT IN THE STREET WITH THREE OF HIS MULES when I came walking up. Raheem wasn't with him. I'd called his mother, told her to keep him home. As I neared the building I saw his face in the upstairs window. And hers. I hadn't told her why, but they knew something was going down.

I hoped it wasn't me.

Okay, champ, you're on. It's the lion's cage, and it's the real lion this time, and what's more, you know it. Screw your courage to the sticking point. Whatever the hell that means. Schmuck, you want a literal translation? You got the gist. Let's do it.

I walked up to King. He was leaning against the parked car. When he saw me, he shoved off from it, stepped out in the street. The three kids gave way, moved off, formed a loose semi-circle behind him.

I walked up, stopped, stuck my finger in his face.

"You're through," I said. "You're finished around here. Don't come around here no more. I see your face again, you're goin' down." I jerked my thumb.

"These guys too. They stick with you, they're history. But that's no matter, 'cause you won't be here. Last time I'm lettin' you walk."

I patted my jacket pocket. "I got the goods on you now. You call me on it, we'll let the court decide. That's up to you. Me, I just want you out of here."

I turned, walked off down the street. I didn't look back. Don't look back, someone might be gaining on you. She's got everything she needs, she's an artist, she don't look back. Well, good for her. Toughest job I ever did in my life.

When I turned onto 146th my palms began to sweat. That was something—it meant they hadn't been sweating up till now. I walked on down the street, still not looking back, and suddenly there it was.

The empty lot.

The rubble-filled lot where my body had been found. I'd missed that scene, thank you very much, lost it somewhere in the ether, so the last time I'd seen the lot was when I'd walked across it to the building beyond. The building with the fake wall, where the Black Death did his disappearing act. Nothing special in that now—like most illusions, nothing to it once you know the trick.

I turned, walked into the lot. I experienced the feeling of revulsion, a rush of fear. I kept going, didn't look back. Crossed the lot, reached the illusion wall.

I stopped, just for a moment.

Jesus Christ, could I really do it?

And to what end? There was nothing special about this place to make King follow me here. The scene of the shooting, yes. But beyond that. There were no secrets that I might discover that King might wish to hide.

I tried to get inside the man's mind. If he were following me now, if he's back there where I am not looking—thank you Bob Dylan and Satchel Paige—what the hell does he think I'm up to? Why the hell does he think I'm here? No rational answer. No rational motive. The way I see it, it can only be a trap. Is that how you see it, King? No way for you to guess the answer—aside from a trap, I mean. No, King, it's my own personal demons I'm wrestling with here.

I took a breath, walked around the illusion wall and into the door.

First room. Two doors.

Straight ahead, the road not taken. At least not by me. Taken by Lionel Wilkens, a.k.a. the Black Death, into the next room and out, the short cut to 145th Street.

Not for me. I turned right into the next room.

A wise man would have had a flashlight. A wise man wouldn't have been there. If I were a wise man. No, that's *rich* man. No matter, you aren't that either.

My heart is beating a mile a minute, whatever the hell that means. My throat is dry. I *know* what that means. Good thing no more dialogue is required. Nothing required but staying on my feet, not passing out, not peeing in my pants.

Was that a footstep?

Not imagining things, not running like hell.

I passed on into the next room. Into the valley of the shadow of death.

Low expectations. A high-risk, low-yield situation. King would not be carrying. Not with three mules with beepers to keep him clean—that was the whole point. So King would have no drugs.

By rights, he would have a gun. You don't shoot

someone with your bare hands. A weapon figured. But not likely the one he'd used before. If not, what were we talking here? Illegal possession of a firearm. Big deal, even with the TV ads about the one-year mandatory. Wanna make book on what percentage serve it? No, just having it is no big deal. Using it's the key.

Attempted murder, that's the charge.

Let's keep it that way.

I'm not facing him anyway. I'm just walking, not looking back.

Next room.

This is it. The room with three doors. Christ, what did I do? I checked out the one over there. And there was nothing, so I tried the one over there and what did I find? I don't remember, I didn't check it out because there was a sound and I came back here and—

This is the room. What the hell does it matter what I did, this is the damn room.

This is where it went down.

My blood is somewhere on this floor.

I took a breath and walked in. Waves of nausea engulfed me. My head was spinning, and suddenly I was swimming in the ether again. A drowning man going down for the third time.

this is the way the world ends fear is the way we die in spite of the tennis qua qua qua windy boy and a bit and the black spit of the Black Death

I shook my head to clear it. Get a grip on yourself. You're here. You did it. And nothing happened.

Nothing.

There came a sudden flash and a roar like thunder.

Again.

Christ.

Again.

But no dull thud. Instead, another sound, the shrill whine of metal caroming off concrete.

Suddenly lights were clicking on. Flashlights, by people more prepared than I.

I blinked through the ether into the flickering light.

And there was King, struggling in the grip of two muscle-bound cops.

52

THERE ISN'T MUCH MORE TO TELL.

The cops hauled King off to jail, and though it did
not cheer me that he knew my face and now had every
reason in the world to wish me ill, I had Sergeant
Reynolds's solemn assurance that this was one case
that would not be plea-bargained down, one defendant
who wasn't gonna walk.

I had every reason to believe him. The gun King
had in his possession turned out to be the same one
he used to shoot me, reducing it from a long-shot bet
to even odds whether he was stupider than I was.
Thanks to that, the cops now had him dead to rights
on *two* charges of attempted murder. They also had
him on illegal possession of a firearm, aggravated assault, assault with deadly weapon, assault with intent
to kill, hell, maybe even armand assante for all I know.
At any rate, there were a lot of counts, and Reynolds
promised me none of them were gonna go away.

On top of that, Reynolds's men had routed the three
mules—something I would not have approved had I

known of it, but I didn't and they did—and of course they were all carrying, so the cops were now putting pressure on them and their parents to have them all roll over on King, which it seemed likely they would. That added to the man's woes to the tune of at least three counts of possession, possession with intent to sell, conspiracy to distribute narcotics, plus generally being an undesirable person. Even with crowded courts, turn-'em-loose judges and a criminally lenient parole system, the man was not gonna be around for a while.

And where was Raheem in all this? Absolutely nowhere, I'm happy to say. Raheem wasn't involved. Oh, not that he stayed in the window like a good boy, just 'cause his mama said. The kid is no saint. He followed King, as you would expect, and saw the whole thing go down. The cops picked him up along with the other three, but they didn't hold him. He had no beeper and no drugs. Just an innocent bystander like others, attracted to the scene.

How he'll turn out, I don't know. I can't play social worker forever. And hell, by next year the kid will be my height and he'll cream me on the court no matter what I do. It was important that I beat him at basketball, you know. Things might have turned out different if I hadn't. For him and for me.

So maybe he'll go straight, maybe he won't, there's not much I can do about that. But at least he'll have better odds. 'Cause King won't be in the way.

As to Melissa Ford, she has yet to stand trial. Just confessing to the crime doesn't get you out of that. Of course, if she changed her plea that would be something else, but there's no chance of that. Poindexter stepped in right away, disclaiming the confession, arguing that she was emotionally distraught and was not of sound mind when she made it and it shouldn't be allowed in evidence and the whole bit. How it will all turn out I have no idea—thank god, I have absolutely nothing to do with the case. Aside from being a potential witness, I mean. But my best guess is she'll probably eventually be convicted of something, do soft time at some fashionable detention center that poses as a jail, get out, go on talk shows, sell her story for a TV movie and become famous as the woman who did it for love.

And as for me, well, I got through it. That's the best I can say. But somehow that's saying a lot. Because there were times, many times, when it didn't look like I would.

It's not like I'm tougher now, or stronger now, or suddenly transformed into some macho figure that I'm not. But I still have the knowledge that I did it. And that counts for something. It counts a lot.

Like I said, there are things that happen and your life is never quite the same.

I think about it a lot in quiet moments, late at night when Tommie and Alice are asleep, or sitting in my office on slow days after riffling through the mail, or even driving to a signup in my car. The word "shot" will flash on me, and I'll think back.

And sometimes it's chilling. Sometimes I see the darkened room, the blinding flash, the ether, the void. Sometimes that's the shot I see.

But sometimes not.

Sometimes I see the twenty-five footer, that sweet game-winner, spinning in the afternoon sun, arcing gently with the soft touch and dropping cleanly through the rim.